AFTER THE DARKNESS

After The Darkness

JUSTIN RICHMAN

After The Darkness
November, 2024
First Printing, 2024

ISBN-979-8-9850601-6-4

Edited by Tim Major
Cover Design by Thea Magerand
www.ikaruna.eu/

Also By Justin Richman

<u>The Defenders Saga:</u>

1. **The Silver Hood**
2. **Deathwish**

<u>The Agency of Supernatural Events:</u>

1. **The Doctor**

Follow Justin on social media and sign up for his newsletter at www.justinrichman.com to stay up to date on what Justin's working on.

For Mom & Dad -

Thank you for teaching me the importance of hard work, resilience, and compassion. I'm so grateful for the love and sacrifices you've given me. And look—turns out daydreaming does pay off!

| 1 |

Izzy's green eyes fluttered open, feeling the pulsating grip of an unbearable headache. She reached for the back of her head, feeling for the source of the pain. Her hand brushed through her auburn hair, stopping over a lump. She flinched in pain when she touched it.

The incessant barking only intensified her headache.

Izzy sat up sharply. "Shadow!"

Shadow never left Izzy's side. He was a loyal and majestic Weimaraner dog, a seventy-pound hunter by nature, with striking gray fur and piercing blue eyes, and he was Izzy's ultimate companion.

"She's awake," a man said.

Izzy's vision came into focus. She caught sight of Shadow, beyond the large animal cage that confined her. He was tied to a metal table.

A man stood up from a chair beside the dog. He was tall, with a broad, muscular build. His salt-and-pepper hair was cropped short and swept back, matching his rugged beard.

Another man stepped into the room.

Shadow started to growl.

"Shut up, you mutt!" he said, and kicked the dog in the side.

Shadow collapsed onto his belly and let out a brief whimper.

The man who walked into the room then approached Izzy's cage.

Izzy recognized him. How could she not? His hulking figure and jet-black hair was immediately familiar. He was a part of a local scavenger group, the Reavers, and went by the name of Hawk. If he had a *real* name, Izzy didn't know what it was. It had been lost in the annals of their post-apocalyptic world.

Hawk had a fresh scar on his cheek. A thought crossed Izzy's mind—possibly a fight within his own group? He certainly wouldn't have gotten it from one of the *Drifters*. He'd be dead before that would ever happen. He wouldn't survive an encounter with those creatures.

As Hawk approached Izzy's cage, his heavy boots thudded against the concrete floor. A cruel smile twisted his lips as he gazed at her.

Izzy backed up against the wall of the cage. The cold bars against her bare shoulders added to the shiver running up her spine. She wished she had worn something less revealing.

Her green tank top hugged her athletic physique—it was her favorite to wear when hunting for supplies. It had stains of dirt and mud. Even with the tank top beginning to fray and the multiple holes in it, she still wore it almost all the time. Her rugged, muted, earth-toned cargo pants allowed her to stuff as much as she could into its pockets. On her feet she wore vintage Chuck Taylor Converse sneakers, once black and white, but now worn and encrusted with dirt.

Despite the unfavorable conditions, Izzy still managed to incorporate a hint of her personal style into her post-apocalyptic attire. A few bracelets were wrapped around her wrist, but the necklace was her most important piece. A thick black string wrapped around her neck, tied at the bottom to a silver ring.

"You've made a big mistake," Hawk growled, his voice echoing off the empty white concrete walls of his hideout. Rusted and worn out tables littered the musty cafeteria. He slowly backed away and turned to grab Izzy's backpack off the table behind him, then walked around to the other side of the table to face her. "You know what happens when you steal from us?"

She met his gaze, her heart pounding in her chest. Her survival instincts screamed at her to run—but to where? She was trapped inside this cage. She could possibly kick the door free, but what good would that do? Hawk and his minion were in the room with her. She wouldn't be able to crawl out of the cage before they got to her.

"I didn't steal anything from you," she said, her voice steady despite the knot of fear in her stomach.

Hawk gave a faint chuckle, then tossed her backpack onto the table. He unzipped the bag and began rummaging through her supplies.

"Hawk, I—" she started to say.

"Shut up!" he yelled. He continued to reach inside and toss item after item onto the table. He then lifted her backpack and dumped the remaining items out, scattering them all over. "All of this stuff is now mine," he said. "You see, we found you sneaking around our territory. We have rules about that."

"You can't just claim everything as your own," Izzy said.

With a burst of anger, Hawk forcefully brought his fist down upon the table, creating a resounding thud that echoed through the room.

"Did I ask you to speak?" Hawk said, before taking a deep breath, seemingly trying to calm himself down. "*Now*, as I was saying. We have rules. *You* break these rules, *you* need to be taught a lesson."

He glanced at the man with the salt-and-pepper hair by the door, and nodded. The man reached for his holstered gun and took a step towards the dog lying on the ground.

"Shadow! No! Stop!" Izzy pleaded.

Hawk brought his gaze to her. "I told you, there are rules."

"But I didn't steal anything!"

"You did. You took supplies from my territory."

"Your territory?" Izzy rolled her eyes. "You can't just claim everything as yours."

Hawk shrugged. "I believe I can. You entered *my* territory, filled up your bag with supplies without my knowledge, and then tried to leave. That's what I call stealing."

"Dammit, Hawk. You're upset because I found supplies two blocks away from here? And you want to claim everything within a giant radius of this building is yours? You can't do that."

Hawk smiled. "I believe I just did. Say goodbye to your dog."

"Stop! Please don't hurt Shadow!"

Hawk snickered. "Shadow?" He shook his head and said, "What a stupid dog's name." He turned to face the man holding the gun. "Do it."

"No!" Izzy yelled.

Suddenly, a bone-chilling howl echoed throughout the hideout, and Shadow immediately jerked his head around. The atmosphere in the room shifted. Hawk and his goon exchanged looks at one another. Gone were the smug smiles and their empowering sense of being in control. They all knew what that sound meant—chaos, destruction, death.

"Go check on that," Hawk said.

The salt-and-pepper haired man stared at Hawk wide-eyed. He didn't move.

Hawk took a step towards him. "*I said*, go check on that."

With a nervous nod, the man cautiously stepped out of the room with his gun raised, and disappeared into the darkness.

"You need to let me go," Izzy whispered.

"Shut up," Hawk said.

"Hawk, please."

"I said, shut—"

Multiple gun shots rang out in the hallway, distracting Hawk. The distant sound of someone screaming in pain pierced the silence. The chilling scream filled Izzy with a profound sense of terror. She gripped the cage's doors and pulled on them. She had to get out of this cage—*now*.

In a single swift motion, Hawk reached behind him and retrieved a concealed handgun that had been nestled in his waistband. He aimed at the doorway.

"Hawk—" Izzy said again.

He shushed her and moved towards the entrance, slowly peeking out into the hallway, aiming his gun in all directions. Hawk then disappeared, leaving Izzy behind. Her heart was pounding like a war drum in her chest. Another howl echoed through the otherwise silent building again, louder this time. Closer. The screams of dying men and sporadic gunfire punctuating the eerie silence. Izzy knew this was her chance to escape.

Shadow barked ferociously at the empty doorway. He knew what was coming. The two of them had seen enough to know what came next.

Death.

Izzy had to get free.

With her adrenaline surging, she swung her legs and kicked at the cage door with all the force she could muster. It shook violently under the impact, but held fast. She kicked again, harder, this time bending the metal hinges. She kicked again. And again. The cage rattled and the door pushed outward with each forceful kick. With a final kick, the hinges snapped, and the door flew open. She was free.

She crawled out from inside the cage and climbed to her feet. Shadow's tail wagged furiously as he started to bark in excitement.

Izzy made her way over and knelt down beside him. He began licking her face.

Izzy smiled. "Okay, buddy," she said, trying to hold him back slightly. "Let's get you free."

She had no time to untie the knot holding her companion to the table. She stood up and began rummaging through all the items Hawk had dumped out of her backpack. Not finding what she had wanted, she grabbed the bag and unzipped one of the smaller pockets in the front. She reached inside and pulled out a pocketknife. With one swift motion, she flicked the blade outward and knelt down to Shadow.

As quickly as she could, she worked on the knot with her knife, slicing back and forth, fraying the rope a little more each time.

The hallway continued to echo with the sounds of gunshots, adding to the growing chaos. Shrill screams were consumed by the chilling howls coming from the Drifters. Death was approaching, and Izzy needed to move fast.

With one more pass-through with the knife, she cut through the rope and freed Shadow. He immediately threw his front paws up onto her shoulders and licked her face.

"Shadow, down," she scolded. To her relief, he obeyed instantly, and looked up at her with attentive eyes. It was crucial for Shadow to be well-trained in this perilous environment. A single misstep, or even a moment of excitement, could be a matter of life or death for both of them.

The sounds of the Drifters grew louder.

Izzy's eyes were fixed on the doorway, her hope for freedom within reach. However, she had to postpone her escape for now. The menacing sounds of the Drifters were not far away.

Izzy glanced around the room and noticed a door on the far side.

"This way," she commanded Shadow.

The two of them hurried towards the door. Izzy opened it to find a small closet, possibly somewhere used to store food. It would have to do. They had no choice—they had to hide.

They stepped inside and Izzy slowly closed the door, careful not to make a noise. She bent down and placed her soft hand on his snout, quietly shushing him.

Izzy laid flat on her stomach and peeked through the sliver of space between the floor and the door. Two creatures suddenly glided into the room. She quietly backed away from the opening and snuggled next to her dog.

A high-pitched screeching sounded inside the room.

Izzy shuddered and held onto Shadow tightly. Her heart thumped loud and hard in her chest, making her terrified the Drifters could hear it.

A faint light came from under the door. Izzy became accustomed to the otherwise dark room she found herself in. She glanced at Shadow—his eyes were wide, his ears stood stiff, attuned to every sight and sound. Could he hear her heart beating? Her breathing? If he could hear her, could the creatures?

A low, guttural growl came from beyond the door, making Izzy's blood run cold. It was followed by the sound of the Drifter's tentacles slapping across the tiled floor. The closet door rattled slightly as a shadow passed by, causing Izzy to hold her breath.

Izzy felt Shadow's body twitch next to her, ready to spring into action. She held onto him tightly, and placed a calming hand on his head, hoping he'd understand her answer—no. They needed to remain still and quiet. One wrong move or sound and they'd be dead in seconds—or quite possibly worse: *infected.*

Seconds stretched into what seemed like minutes. Each one ticking by agonizingly slow. Izzy could feel the sweat trickling from her shoulders around her chest and onto the floor. Her heart continuing to pound against her ribcage.

A loud, and unexpected noise startled Izzy and made her jump, followed by a deafening silence. Had they been discovered?

She dared to peek through the tiny space under the door. To her horror, she saw that one of the creatures was hovering directly outside their hiding spot, its grayish figure illuminated in the dim light. Izzy immediately retreated back to a sitting position, covering her head with her hands.

Another gunshot went off. Someone then started yelling in the distance, and fired a few more times. The Drifters responded with loud screeches.

Izzy could hear them leave the room, but she was waiting for one more sound. A moment later, she heard it. The sound of death. Whoever had run off shooting at the Drifters hadn't got far. Screams of agony sounded from the distance, followed by silence.

Izzy held on tightly to Shadow, her fingers wrapped around his collar. He whimpered softly under his breath. Even he understood the gravity of the situation. Izzy knew better than to assume the coast was clear. She could still hear the faint howls of the creatures in the distance. She knew they were further away, but she wouldn't open that door until she was certain they were gone.

After what felt like an eternity, Izzy slowly turned the doorknob, wincing at the faint creaking sound it made. She cracked the door open just enough to peek outside.

Everything was still.

Silent.

Izzy pushed the door open wider, stepping out into the room. The cage in which she had been held captive was dented and unusable. The table Shadow had been tied to had been flipped over. Bullet casings littered the floor by the entrance.

She crossed the room and picked up her backpack. Her belongings were scattered across the floor, so she bent down and quickly started tossing everything into the bag, not wanting to linger any longer than she had to. Every second counted.

When she had finished, she zipped her backpack and tossed it over her shoulder. Then she and Shadow ventured towards the entrance and looked out into the hallway.

It was a gruesome sight. Bodies lay strewn about, some still clutching onto their weapons. The Drifters had left no survivors, as usual. Izzy tiptoed around the bodies, occasionally rummaging through their pockets for anything worth keeping. She grabbed two handguns, some ammo, a granola bar, and a small container of Advil.

Finally, Izzy reached the exit. The heavy metal door was already open, revealing the world outside. As she stepped outside, the sun was beginning to set, painting the sky with hues of orange and pink—a stark contrast to the horror she had just escaped. But she knew all too well how deceptive this beauty could be. After the sunset, the night would bring more danger.

Shadow gave a soft bark, nudging her leg. Izzy looked down at him, then back at the setting sun. They had to move. Their camp wasn't far, but they certainly didn't want to travel at night. With one last glance at the hideout, she set off towards their camp.

| **2** |

The sun was just setting as Izzy and Shadow made their way through the dense forest. They moved with stealthy precision, their senses attuned to every rustle, every twitch in the underbrush. The forest was alive with the sounds of the night—the hoot of an owl, the distant howl of a wolf, the whispering of trees blowing in the breeze.

The Drifters were nowhere in sight.

Their journey had been long, but they were finally nearing their destination—a small clearing emerged up ahead. Home. It was a welcoming sight. Nestled on a small mountain was their camp: a patchwork of cabins, tents, and makeshift shelters illuminated by the warm glow of several fires and lanterns.

Shadow, sensing their return home, perked up, his tail wagging in anticipation. Izzy couldn't help but smile at his excitement. Despite the hardships they had encountered from time to time, she was extremely grateful for his unwavering companionship. He wasn't just her pet—he was her partner, her family.

As the two of them approached the camp, the guards on duty spotted them. They lowered their weapons—one was holding a bolt-action rifle with a scope, the other an M4 Carbine. Relief washed over their faces.

"Welcome back, Izzy," Matt said, his voice cutting through the quiet night. "I was starting to worry."

Izzy tried holding back a smile. She had found herself drawn to him ever since their paths had crossed a few weeks ago.

Matt was thin, but toned—possibly an athlete in a previous life. He stood tall and confident, his rifle tilted down by his side. His hair was a wavy mess of dark curls. His brown eyes matched the mud-stained tee-shirt he wore.

"You were worried?" Izzy said.

"Of course," Matt said. "No one knew where you went. Someone said they saw you walk off earlier this afternoon, and—"

The other guard interrupted, clearing his throat. "Izzy, I need you to come with me."

Izzy turned her attention to him. He wore an old red Philadelphia Phillies baseball hat that he pulled down over his face, covering his eyes.

He continued, "Jason needs to talk with you." He stuck out his hand, gesturing for her to come with him.

Izzy nodded. As she followed the other guard, she couldn't help but glance back at Matt. He was still watching her, and gave her a slight nod and a smile.

Izzy turned away and continued up the hill to meet with the camp's leader, Jason. Izzy and Shadow entered the camp and were greeted with friendly smiles from people nearby. The campfires dotted around gave off a warm glow, illuminating the campground as the sun was setting.

As Izzy and Shadow made their way through the camp, a familiar figure darted out of one of the cabins. Sarah, a petite whirlwind of energy with a mane of flame-red hair, rushed towards them. Her freckled face lit up at the sight of her best friend, her brown eyes wide with relief and excitement.

"Where have you been, Izzy?" she asked, her voice filled with concern. She reached out to hug Izzy. Sarah was like that, always wearing her heart on her sleeve.

Izzy sighed, patting her friend's back gently. "I was out gathering supplies before Hawk captured me and took me hostage."

Sarah pulled away, her brows furrowed in annoyance. "What? He captured you?"

Izzy nodded and kept walking behind the guard. She whispered, "I think the Drifters may have taken out Hawk and his crew."

"How do you know?" Sarah asked.

"We were there when it happened," Izzy said.

"No one escapes those things! How did you get away?"

"I honestly thought we were goners. We hid in a closet. Luckily, one of Hawk's guys distracted the creatures, and we were able to get away."

Izzy acted like it was no big deal, but she knew what she had gone through. The terror she had felt. The fear of knowing any second could have been her last. She had been lucky to get out of there alive.

She swung her backpack around and unzipped it.

"Look what I was able to grab," Izzy said, pulling open the bag for Sarah to see inside.

"Weapons?" Sarah's eyes lit up. "That's great!"

Izzy dug down deep and until she found what she was searching for. She pulled out the small container of Advil and handed it to Sarah.

"For your migraines," she told her.

Sarah held onto the bottle with both hands. "Thank you so much!" She reached for Izzy and hugged her again.

"He's waiting for you," the guard grunted, nodding at the cabin in front of them.

Izzy and Sarah released their embrace.

"Can you watch Shadow for me while I go inside?" Izzy asked Sarah. "I shouldn't be long."

"Of course," Sarah said. She bent down and looked into Shadow's eyes. "We'll have a ton of fun outside, won't we?" She petted Shadow's head and back, and he licked her face.

Izzy headed inside the cabin. She was immediately hit by the smell of coffee. Books littered the bookshelves behind Jason's desk. The room was dimly lit with a few lanterns hanging on the wall and one stationed on his desk, which was piled high with maps and documents.

Jason stood by his desk, in deep conversation with another member of the camp. His hair was short and messy, graying on the side but still brown on top. A beard covered most of his face, giving him an intimidating appearance. His eyes were a piercing gray, always alert and assessing.

When he noticed Izzy standing by the door, he quickly ended his conversation and dismissed the other woman in the room with a curt nod.

"Izzy," he acknowledged, his voice stern.

Izzy prepared herself for the inevitable reprimand. As expected, Jason launched into a tirade.

"What were you thinking, going out on your own like that? We have rules for a reason, Izzy. We stick together. We work as a team."

Izzy's temper flared at his words. "A team? Really, Jason? When do you ever even let me go out? And when I go out, I'm always given a back seat. You know I can handle myself. I can lead."

Jason placed his hands on his desk and leaned forward. "Izzy, no one trusts you because of the way you behave. You act like a lone wolf, not a team player. It's disrespectful, and immature."

"Are you kidding me right now?" Izzy shot back. *Immature? Disrespectful?*

She reached into her backpack and dumped the two guns and the ammunition onto Jason's desk. He pulled his hands away, looking at the weapons and then back at Izzy.

"I'm more than capable," she said. "I even got medicine for Sarah's constant migraines."

Jason remained unfazed by Izzy's find. "It doesn't matter. You could have gotten yourself killed, or worse, infected. Then you would have opened us up to a world of danger." He took a deep breath and sighed, as if releasing a pressure valve. He rubbed his temple for a moment before speaking again. "From now on, you go out with a team, or not at all. Is that clear?"

"Yes," Izzy started to say. "But—"

Jason held up a hand, effectively silencing her. "Enough, Izzy! This discussion is over."

With that, Izzy stormed out of the cabin in frustration and resentment. She knew she had broken the rules to find Sarah medicine, but she also knew she was more than capable of handling herself. She just wished Jason could see that, too.

Sarah was playfully tossing a stick for Shadow to fetch. She looked up at her best friend as she made her way out of the cabin. "What happened?" she asked, her voice laced with concern.

Izzy's fingers curled into fists. "Jason has no faith in me—even after bringing him more weapons. Even after getting you medicine."

"Which I'm incredibly grateful for," Sarah said.

"At least someone appreciates me," Izzy said.

"You know I have your back. Whatever you need, I'm on your side. How many runs have you secretly made? How many times have you put yourself in danger to come back with supplies for us?"

"Exactly!" Izzy exclaimed. "Why does no one see that?"

Sarah put an arm around her friend as they made their way back to their shared cabin. "They will, don't worry. One day."

Izzy let out a giant sigh. "He thinks I can't handle myself."

Sarah's brow furrowed, her freckled face hardening into a scowl. "Given how much you do for me—for this camp—I don't understand why he can't see how capable you are." She shook her head in frustration. "You know what? Just ignore him. You're worth ten of him, anyway. Don't let it get to you. You and I both know you can handle yourself—especially after what you went through today."

Their cabin came into view, a modest structure made of roughly hewn logs. They made their way to the front door and stepped inside. Sarah placed a comforting hand on Izzy's shoulder.

"I believe in you, Izzy," she said. "You're stronger than they give you credit for. And sooner or later, they'll see that too."

It comforted Izzy to know that someone believed in her, even if it was only her best friend. There was a sense of comfort knowing she had Sarah by her side.

Once they had changed into clean clothing, they both settled into the familiar rhythm of their evening routine—endless conversation and gossip until they passed out from exhaustion.

| **3** |

Izzy awoke to the soft crackling of a fire and the distinct, comforting scent of mint tea leaves brewing. She blinked the sleep away from her eyes and propped herself up on one elbow, glancing at the fireplace. Sarah, already wide awake, was hunched over their small, makeshift stove, and the kettle whistling quietly on top of it.

"Morning," Izzy mumbled, rubbing her eyes.

"Good morning," Sarah replied. "I made us some tea."

Izzy patted Shadow's head, waking him up so she could move her legs. He slept on her bed every night, cuddled up with her. He stood and jumped onto the floor. Izzy swung her legs over the side of the bed and yawned. "I can see... or... smell."

Sarah giggled.

Izzy pushed a hand through her hair, her eyes still half closed. "Don't mind me. I'm clearly not awake yet." She stepped onto the wooden floor and moved over to the fireplace. Sarah poured a cup of tea, and Izzy reached out and accepted it, thanking her. The cup was warm against her hands. She brought it to her face, and the steam curled and danced, caressing and warming her skin.

"You think Jason is still upset about yesterday?" Sarah asked.

Izzy took a sip of tea. "Probably."

Sarah sighed. "Jason needs to learn he can't control everything and everyone. A little rebellion now and then is a good thing."

"Apparently he doesn't think so," Izzy replied.

"Well, then he—" Sarah said, before being interrupted by a knock at the door.

Shadow let out a quick bark.

Izzy and Sarah glanced at each other.

Izzy spoke first. "Who's that?"

"Probably Matt," Sarah said, winking at her.

Izzy rolled her eyes, but couldn't entirely hide her smile as she went to open the door. Sure enough, Matt stood there, looking a little uncomfortable.

"Hi," he said, scratching the back of his neck. "I… uhh… how are you?"

"Invite him in!" Sarah yelled from within the cabin.

Izzy spun to glare at her. She turned to face Matt again, and smiled. "I'm good. You want to come in? We have tea."

"I'd love to," Matt said, "but Jason's called a meeting. I wanted to come and let you know. Figured after yesterday, you probably wouldn't want to miss it or show up late."

"Yesterday?" Izzy asked. "How do you know what happened with me and Jason?"

He shrugged. "I mean, you sneak off on your own for most of the day. Then you come back and you're asked to meet with Jason. I can't imagine that went over well."

"Yeah, he wasn't too happy with me," she said.

"I'm sorry. I tried looking for you after my shift last night to talk with you, but I didn't see you. I didn't see Sarah either. I figured you guys were in your cabin, and I didn't want to bother you."

Izzy placed a hand on his arm. "That's sweet of you. We can talk more after this meeting. Save me a seat!"

Matt nodded. He peeked inside the cabin and waved goodbye to Sarah before saying goodbye to Izzy.

As Izzy shut the door and made her way back to her bed, Sarah started to sing, "Matt and Izzy, sitting in a tree. K-I-S-S—"

"Shut up!" Izzy said, throwing a pillow from her bed at Sarah.

Sarah started laughing. She had such an infectious laugh that it made Izzy start laughing too.

* * *

The early morning sunlight cast long shadows between the tents and cabins as Izzy and Sarah made their way through the camp. They walked towards the center of the campground where a group was gathered around a large fire pit. Benches and chairs were scattered all around the area. Jason stood in the center with his back to a large map pinned to a makeshift board.

Matt was already seated on a bench under a towering pine tree. Once Izzy locked eyes with him, he patted the empty space next to him. She made her way over and sat down next to him, while Sarah leaned against the tree, arms crossed over her chest.

Jason cleared his throat, drawing everyone's attention. His eyes scanned the group before he began speaking.

"Thank you all for joining me this morning," he said. "I'm looking forward to getting this started, as I have some good news for us all."

There were some mumbles in the crowd before he continued.

"I've been working very closely with our scouts," he continued. "They've found a facility that we believe was a base of operations for a drug cartel before the Drifters arrived."

A murmur ran through the group, but Jason lifted a hand to silence them. "I know you all have questions, and I'll get to them, I promise," he said. "Let me finish here and I promise this will all make sense."

Izzy didn't understand the purpose of this meeting. A facility owned by a drug cartel? What would Jason want to do with it? She continued to listen to hopefully have her questions answered.

"We can use this to our advantage," Jason said. "There could be supplies, medication and drugs still left there. We want the supplies and the medication. We can trade the drugs for supplies. I'm sure we have all come across gangs and scavengers out there that would gladly trade for drugs." He paused for a moment to let that sink in. Izzy thought back to a few times she had come across gangs that would have done exactly that.

Jason continued, "This would be a game changer. We could potentially gain so much!"

He then started assigning roles for the mission, calling out names and outlining tasks. One by one, Jason assigned roles and overlooked Izzy. As each name was called, Izzy felt a growing sense of frustration. Her skills were being overlooked and ignored again. She was an experienced scavenger and skilled navigator. She was also a pro when given a bow and arrow. But Jason seemed determined to sideline her.

Matt must have noticed Izzy's leg bouncing in place. He placed a hand on her knee, trying to calm her down.

"He'll call on you," he reassured her. "It's okay."

"No, he won't. He's probably still pissed about yesterday," Izzy said.

Finally, after what felt like an eternity, Jason called her name. "Izzy," he said, looking at her with a smirk. "You're the mule. You're in charge of carrying all the supplies and everything we bring back home."

Izzy was enraged. She was more than just muscle, more than just a mule. She thought about storming up to Jason and punching him. Maybe giving him a black eye would take that smirk off his face.

She felt the urge to stand up and let Jason have it, but she felt a hand on her arm. Matt was looking at her, shaking his head subtly.

"Don't," he whispered. "It's not worth it."

Izzy clenched her jaw, pulling her arm away from Matt's grip. She was ready to lash out at Jason. How could he give her such a lackluster assignment like that—a mule? Carrying the bags? Seriously? She was better than that. She was more valuable to the team than just *carrying bags.*

Jason finished his speech. "We all have a job to do here. This is important for all of us. Let's get started! The team leaves in one hour."

Everyone stood up and, moving in different directions.

"Izzy," Matt said. "I know you're frustrated. Don't let it get to you."

"Frustrated is an understatement," she said.

"I know what you're capable of. But Jason is in charge. We just have to go with it," Matt said.

Izzy stewed in her anger. She couldn't believe her skills were being wasted like this.

"Well," Matt began, a mischievous grin spreading across his face, "on the bright side, if we come across any stubborn donkeys on our expedition, we'll have the perfect person to deal with them."

Izzy's frown deepened. "And how's that?" she asked.

Matt gestured towards her with a dramatic flourish. "Because you, Izzy, are officially in charge of all *mule*-related issues. It's a position of great responsibility."

Izzy let out a quick snort of laughter, shaking her head at him. "You're ridiculous," she said. "You and your lame jokes." She gave him a friendly punch in the arm.

He rubbed the spot where she had hit him. "You laughed, didn't you?"

Izzy's tension faded away and felt a smile grow on her face. She rolled her eyes and shook her head at him. "Shut up."

She turned to see Sarah still leaning against the tree. Her arms were folded, but she was smiling at her. Izzy could imagine hearing Sarah's voice right now—singing to her.

"You too!" she yelled to Sarah.

Sarah let out a laugh and started to walk away. Izzy shook her head and turned back to face Matt.

"I'll see you in an hour," he said, standing up and offering a hand to her. She took it and he pulled her up.

"See you in an hour," she said.

| 4 |

As the morning sun shined through the windows of their cabin, Izzy methodically packed her gear. Her frustration from the meeting still lingered. Was she being punished? She assumed the answer was yes, but she was determined not to let her feelings affect her performance within the group.

Izzy reached into her trunk and took out some clothing to change into. She started with a pair of worn jeans and a black tee-shirt. She grabbed her Converse sneakers and put them on, then picked up her backpack and tossed it on the bed. Izzy rummaged through it, making sure she still had her main essentials—a first aid kit, a flashlight, a box of matches, rope, and some granola bars. She'd have to refill the water canister tucked into the pocket on the side of her bag before she left.

Sarah sat on her bed watching Izzy pack. "Not everyone thinks like Jason, you know," she said softly, attempting to soothe Izzy's simmering anger. "We all know what you're capable of."

Izzy paused in her packing, meeting Sarah's gaze. "It doesn't feel like it sometimes," she admitted.

"Trust me," Sarah said. "There are plenty who value what you bring to the group." She gave Izzy a slight smile. "You *and* Shadow."

"Thanks," Izzy said. "I appreciate it."

A few moments later, Izzy finished up preparing for her adventure. She slung her backpack over her shoulder, then made her way over to Sarah before leaving.

"Be careful, okay?" Sarah told her.

"I will," Izzy reassured her. "I always come back."

"Yeah, *you do*. But not everyone else does," Sarah said.

Izzy smiled and gave her a hug. "I'll be fine. I'll see you when I come back."

Izzy released Sarah and moved to the cabin door. She whistled briefly to attract Shadow's attention. He quickly stood up and trotted over to her, his tail wagging as he approached.

* * *

The rest of the group had already gathered at the camp entrance by the time Izzy and Shadow arrived. As they approached, the group welcomed her.

The first to speak was James, a seasoned scout. He would be the one leading the group to the facility. Given that he was also the person who had discovered it, having him guide them would be the key to their success. Next to him was Pete, a burly man with a kind smile and an uncanny knack for hunting. He was on one knee, organizing his gear. Audrey stood on the other side of James. She was one of the best scavengers of the group, adept at finding what others would normally overlook.

Rounding out the group was Matt, who stood with his bolt-action rifle resting on his shoulder. He reached down to pet Shadow, who stood between him and Izzy.

"Hi, boy," Matt said. Then he looked up at Izzy. "You got really lucky with him."

Izzy smiled and rubbed Shadow's head. "I know," she said. "He's a good dog."

"Everybody ready?" James asked, his voice loud and commanding.

Collectively, the group said yes.

Izzy picked up the two giant duffel bags by her feet and slung them over her shoulders, adding to the weight of her backpack.

They all walked away from the camp's entrance and into the woods.

The group was quiet. Usually, everyone was outgoing and talkative. Izzy couldn't help but think that some of these people had yet to experience one of the Drifters. Most of the survivors tended to stay local. Few ventured out across the fields and into the city limits. It became dangerous there. Not only were the Drifters lurking around, but murderous scavengers and gangs roamed the city streets.

An image of Hawk and the Reavers popped into her head. She wondered what had happened to them. She didn't remember seeing Hawk's remains among the dead.

"You look far away," Matt said, breaking her train of thought.

"Sorry. Just thinking," she replied.

"About what?" he asked.

She slowed down slightly, dropping back to walk with Matt. "You think they can handle everything?" Izzy asked, gesturing to James, Pete, and Audrey.

Matt looked at the three of them, then back at Izzy. "Jason wouldn't have asked them to go if he felt they weren't capable, right?"

"You're asking me?" Izzy said.

Matt shrugged. "More looking for confirmation." He nodded to himself and a smirk appeared on his face. "I can find out, though." He took a few quick steps forward to get close to the group. "Hey, any of you guys ever encounter those creatures before?"

"How subtle..." Izzy mumbled.

Audrey was the first to speak up. "I've never seen one of those Drifters up close. I hope I never do."

James nodded, his expression grim. "They're not something you want to cross paths with," he said. His tone hinting at experiences he didn't elaborate on.

"Why not?" Audrey asked.

James sighed. He stopped walking and turned to face Audrey, occasionally glancing at everyone else. "These things are like something out of a nightmare," James said. "They'll scare the shit out of you at first glance. They must be eight feet tall. Maybe nine."

Audrey's eyes opened wide. "I've never seen them before. They're really that tall?"

Pete nodded. "I remember the first time I saw one. It was from a distance, so I was safe… at least, I hoped I was. I was on top of a small roof, hunting a deer I found roaming the streets. Then I heard those *howls*." It seemed to send a chill up his spine, because he instantly gave a little shake. "Sorry, those things just freak me out. Anyway, I saw a lonesome deer trotting through the streets, but in the distance I noticed two scavengers trailing it. I knew if I wanted that deer, I'd have to take out those guys too. I decided to let it go, knowing I could track another one. But like I said, I heard a Drifter in the distance. I watched through the scope of my rifle as one of those creatures showed up in an instant. That slick, blackish-gray skin just seemed so otherworldly. It looked wet."

"Gross," Audrey said.

"I don't think they have legs either," Pete continued. "I remember it gliding across the street—like how a ghost would just float. It all happened in one swift motion."

"What did?" Matt asked.

"Its gruesome attack," Pete said. "In a flash, it was across the street and attacking the two men. One must have had a gun, because I heard shooting—which did very little to harm the creature. I watched as it's long tentacles just ripped apart the guy shooting at it."

"Oh my God," Audrey said.

"Oh no—God wouldn't create a beast like that," Pete said.

"What happened to the other guy?" Matt asked.

"He lost his head," Pete said.

"How?" Izzy asked.

"The Drifter's mouth dropped open. And I mean, this thing's mouth was huge. It lunged at the guy and just—" Pete clamped his teeth together.

Audrey covered her mouth with her hands.

"Yup," James said. "That sounds about right. Those creatures are not something you want to mess with." He turned and started walking again. Pete followed. Audrey stood motionless, her mouth still covered with her hands.

"You okay?" Izzy asked.

Audrey removed her hands. "Yeah, I'll be fine. It's just..." She trailed off, then caught herself. "Sorry. I've just always heard stories about the—you know—*monsters*. And after hearing Pete's story, I think I made the wrong choice about coming. I'm usually with large groups of people scavenging safe places. I don't want to be anywhere near those things. I don't want to die."

Izzy placed a hand on her shoulder, making Audrey flinch. "You'll be fine. There's a few heavy hitters here with us that should keep us well protected." Izzy glanced at Matt and smiled.

"Thanks, Izzy," Audrey said. She moved ahead to catch up to Pete and James.

"You have any experiences with the creatures?" Izzy asked Matt.

"Not exactly," Matt said. "I mean—yes and no. I've watched them from a distance, but I've had different experiences with the Drifters than Pete or James did."

"Like what?" Izzy asked.

"An infected," he said.

"I've heard Jason mention that before, but never really understood what it meant," Izzy said.

"Yeah. So, we don't see much of it. It's part of the reason why we want people in groups—to warn others in the event it does happen."

"When what happens?"

"They can infect humans. Use them against us."

"How?" Izzy asked.

"I'm not sure, to be honest. Back when we first started this campsite, we had a group go out and look for supplies one day. Four people went out, only one came back—James," Matt whispered, nodding at James up ahead. "James, myself, and Jason are the only *originals* left of this group. We had our fair share of death—this story being one of them. Anyway, James came back to camp and said the Drifters attacked everyone, and only he escaped. A few hours later, someone else entered our camp. Her name was Brittany. She was one of the people James said had died out there. Everyone, especially James, was surprised to see her. They welcomed her back, and everything seemed normal until she took out her gun and started shooting."

Izzy's mind was a jumbled mess of confusion. How did Brittany survive if James said she had died? Why did she open fire at everyone in the camp?

"Why?" was all Izzy could say.

"I don't know. James shot back and killed her. When she bled, her blood was a grayish color, not red. We assumed something must have happened to her."

"But you said she seemed fine when she got to camp," Izzy said.

"She was," Matt said. "I mean, we *thought* she was. She acted fine—she seemed normal. Then, suddenly, she completed changed into a murderous lunatic."

"That's awful," Izzy said. "How many people did she shoot? Did she kill them or just wound them?"

"She killed four. Wounded one." Matt pulled down his tee-shirt to reveal a scar on his shoulder.

"I'm so sorry," she said.

"It's okay. It wasn't that bad," he said.

"Oh, okay, mister tough guy. Getting shot isn't a big deal," she said, rolling her eyes.

Matt smiled. "I'm serious. I was fine in a few days."

Izzy reached out and touched his arm. "I'm glad you were okay."

"Alright, guys," James announced quietly, raising his hand to signal for them to stop. "We're approaching the fields. Time to pay attention." He scanned the open fields ahead. "We're going to be entering the city limits soon. Gangs and scavengers like to take advantage of wanderers. I don't need anything happening to anyone here. So stay alert everyone. Understood?"

Each member of the group nodded.

As they ventured out into the field, the tall grass provided some cover, but the lack of trees made them easy targets. Unfortunately, they had no choice but to cross and proceed forward.

As they made their way towards the city, the tall grass rustled around them, every sound magnified during their silent walk. Izzy glanced down at Shadow, who walked at her side. Matt was by her other side, his eyes constantly scanning in all directions.

As they neared the edge of the fields, a distant howl echoed through the air, freezing them in their tracks. James signaled for them to crouch down and huddle together.

Izzy whispered, "Shadow, down." He stopped and laid flat on his stomach.

She watched the horizon for any signs of movement. Matt used his scope to zoom in.

"What do you see?" James asked.

Matt continued scanning. "Nothing. Must be further away."

"But that means it's in the area, right?" Audrey asked, her voice shaking with fear.

"It sounded distant, but yes, it could be in the area," James said. "All the more reason to stay alert."

"What do you think?" Izzy asked Matt. "You think we have a chance of seeing one of those things?"

He lowered his weapon. "I don't know. But like James said, we need to stay alert. Don't worry," he raised his rifle again. "I'll protect you."

"I appreciate the offer, but I'm not sure that thing will protect us," she said.

"What do you mean?" Matt asked.

"When I was in Hawk's hideout yesterday, multiple people were shooting at the Drifter that was inside. It killed everyone and left like nothing had happened."

"How do you know it wasn't injured?" Matt asked.

Izzy considered this. She couldn't really know if it was injured or not. But the way it was able to move and kill everyone in Hawk's hideout made it seem like the thing was immune to bullets. Could the Drifter even be injured? Of all the stories she had heard, none had included any details about injuring one of the creatures. If they couldn't be injured, could they even be killed?

She hoped so.

Before Izzy could respond to Matt, James spoke up. "Let's move."

They made their way through the rest of the field and entered the city limits. They crossed the abandoned streets with extreme caution, finding cover behind vehicles and debris. The buildings with their dark windows loomed over them, providing cover to whoever, or whatever hid beyond them. The group moved silently, communicating with gestures and keeping their voices to a whisper.

"This way," James said, waving the group inside the skeleton of an old store. The first story's floor-to-ceiling windows had been smashed. Broken glass littered the building's interior.

Audrey grabbed a winter hat off a shelf and stuffed it in her backpack. She moved around the store, grabbing a few other items and putting them in her bag.

Pete held his handgun high, aiming in front of him with each step he took.

James continued to lead the group through the store and into a back room. He pushed open a door, which led to a storage area. The room was ransacked. Torn cardboard littered the floor. They exited the store out the back, stepping onto a cracked and uneven sidewalk.

As they were crossing an intersection, a rustling noise made them all freeze. James's hand shot up, signaling for them to stop.

"Hide," he said.

They all darted in different directions, looking for a place to hide. Izzy and Shadow ran with Matt back to the store they had just left. She watched as Pete and Audrey continued across the street and ducked behind a dumpster, and James slid underneath a car in the middle of the road.

A group of scavengers made their way down the street, slow and cautious. Izzy placed the duffel bags on the ground next to her as she watched them wander back and forth across the street, examining every nook and cranny.

They approached the vehicle under which James was hiding. Izzy saw him bring his gun up to his chest, watching the scavenger's movements.

"You think they're going to be a problem?" Izzy whispered to Matt. She noticed Matt's knuckles turn white where he gripped his weapon.

"I hope not," he said. "Definitely don't need a shootout in the middle of the streets with a Drifter nearby."

Two of the scavengers leaned inside the car's broken windows, but quickly retreated. The third waved them on, and they continued to move further down the street. Two buildings away, they found an open door and entered, disappearing into the darkness.

Izzy let out a sigh of relief.

"That was close," she whispered to Matt. "Are we good?"

"I think so," he whispered.

Pete peeked out from behind the dumpster, looking around to make sure the coast was clear. He stood up and gave a thumbs up. Izzy picked up the duffel bags, pushed opened the door of the store, and moved back onto the sidewalk with Shadow and Matt. James slid out from underneath the car.

"This way," James said. "We're almost there."

The group crept along the street, sticking close to the cold walls. When they turned the corner, James pointed ahead.

A three-story building loomed ahead, an imposing structure of concrete and metal. Its windows were boarded up from the inside, lacking any glass on the outside. A dangling sign hung above one third-story window, only displaying the remaining letters, T, R, and O. Whatever it used to say, Izzy didn't know.

They approached the front door and Pete pushed forward. The door barely moved. He pushed it again.

"Wouldn't make it that easy for us, huh?" Pete said. "Feels like something's blocking it from the inside."

"Maybe a window?" Audrey asked.

Pete took a step back and examined the front of the building. "Everything looks boarded up."

Matt walked up to one of the boarded-up areas and placed his hand against it. "Couldn't we just break in?"

"And alert any local gangs or Drifters with all the loud noise?" James said. "No thank you. Let's look for another way in."

"How'd you find out about this place anyway?" Matt asked.

"Jason traded information with one of the local camps," James explained. "They didn't have the resources, or people, to make the attempt here. We do. So, we go in, gather what we can, and they get a percentage."

"So, like a finder's fee," Matt said.

"Exactly," James said.

Izzy made her way down an alley next to the building.

"What about on the roof?" she asked.

The group followed her around the building and all looked up, like Izzy.

"What do you expect to find up there?" Pete asked.

Izzy shrugged. "Maybe a window I can get into? A vent?"

"Worth a shot," Pete said. "You okay with that, James?"

James looked at Izzy and then back towards the roof. He sighed. "I don't like us splitting up like this." He pursed his lips and took a deep breath. "Fine. But the bags stay here, and Matt goes up with you. He's got the scope on his gun. He can provide surveillance from above while Izzy finds a way inside."

Matt looked at Izzy. "Ready?" he asked.

Izzy nodded, and dropped the duffel bags at her feet. She kicked them over to James. She bent down to talk to Shadow.

"Stay here, okay? Audrey will keep you safe," she said.

"I'll watch him," Audrey said.

Matt made his way towards a pipe on the side of the building and began climbing. Once he had made it past the first floor, Izzy followed. She grabbed onto the pipe and begun to climb, using the screws and hinges for her footing. About halfway up, her footing slipped momentarily, threatening to make her lose her grip. A collective gasp came from below.

"You okay?" James asked.

Izzy quickly regained her grip and held on tight. She let out a sigh of relief. Her heart fluttered in her chest at the thought of falling.

"Yeah, I'm good," she said, and continued her ascent.

A moment later, Matt's hand was dangling over the side of the building, offering her some assistance in the final few feet. She reached up and took it. He pulled her up over the ledge and they both laid on the roof, staring up at the cloudy sky.

"Thank you," Izzy said.

"Anytime," Matt said. He stood up and swung his gun around, looking through the scope.

Izzy pushed herself up onto her elbows. "See anything?"

He looked in all directions before responding. "Seems clear to me. No one on the streets from what I can see." He walked over to the edge of the roof and gave a thumbs up to James.

Izzy climbed to her feet and found a vent on the far side of the roof. "What about that?"

Matt turned to look. "Yeah. Let's check it out."

The two of them walked over, then poked and prodded at the metal grate. Matt took his small tactical pack off his back and unzipped it, pulling out a screwdriver. He begun unscrewing the screws holding the metal grate. One by one, he dropped the screws onto the roof before pulling the grate free and setting it aside carefully. They stared into the dark, narrow passage beyond.

Izzy's stomach churned. The thought of crawling through a tight, enclosed space was slightly terrifying—especially not knowing where she was going. And to make matters even worse, she would be doing it alone.

Matt seemed to sense her fear and gave her an encouraging smile.

"Hey," he said softly, placing his hand against her back. "You've got this."

Izzy immediately looked back at the opening. "I know." His touch soothed her. She turned to face him. His presence suddenly eased her anxiety. She returned his smile, grateful for his support. She found herself staring at him for too long. She broke eye contact and focused back on the vent again. As much as she wanted to continue the moment, she had people waiting and counting on her.

"Here goes nothing," she said.

Izzy hoisted herself up into the vent and slid inside. She pulled out her flashlight. The metal was cold on her hands and knees. She switched on her flashlight, illuminating the darkness ahead, and crawled forward.

The silence within the vent was broken only by the sound of Izzy's own breathing and the faint clinging of her bracelets hitting the metal. Why had she even agreed to this idea? Why had she *come up* with this idea?

Izzy's anxiety started to resurface again. What would happen if she got stuck? Would anyone hear her? Could Matt come get her? What if this vent lead to a place she couldn't escape from?

Suddenly, the vent begin to shake beneath her. A cold wave of dread washed over her and she realized what was happening. The vent was loosening. She tried to scramble backwards, but it was too late—it gave way with a loud *snap,* plunging Izzy into the darkness below.

| 5 |

A cloud of dust and smoke billowed around Izzy, the stale air of the long-abandoned building having been stirred up by the sudden disturbance.

She laid there for a moment, her body aching from the impact, the taste of dust in her mouth. She slowly moved her limbs, relief washing over her as she realized she was mostly unharmed, save for a few minor cuts and bruises. The echo of her fall still seemed to reverberate through the building, leaving a soft ringing sound as everything settled.

From outside, she could hear muffled voices—her group trying to maintain their cover while simultaneously checking on her. Their worried whispers seeped through the walls.

"Izzy, are you okay?"

"What happened?"

Slowly, Izzy pulled herself out of the fallen vent and freed herself from the rubble. As she emerged from the dust and debris, she took in the extent of the damage from her fall. Her heart sank as she looked up at the gaping hole in the floor, then at the broken pieces of vent scattered all around. She realized she had fallen through the second floor above her. She couldn't believe she had suffered so few injuries from what had been a serious fall.

"I'm alright," she said, loud enough for the group outside to hear.

Izzy brushed herself off and made her way to the front door of the building. Multiple desks and bookcases were blocking the entrance. One by one, she began moving everything out of the way. The bookcases weren't too difficult, but the heavy desks proved a challenge. She dragged one of them aside far enough for James to be able to open the door. Then, Audrey started pushing her way through the small gap. Once inside, she helped Izzy drag the desk further away from the door, allowing James and the rest of the team to push from the other end, finally giving them enough room to squeeze inside.

As James, Pete, Audrey, Matt, and Shadow made their way into the building, their eyes widened at the sight of the destruction.

"Izzy, what the hell happened?" James asked, his voice echoing throughout the abandoned space.

Izzy quickly explained her fall, assuring them she was fine.

"Thank God you're okay!" Audrey said. She reached into her pocket, pulling out a small rag and handing it to Izzy. "Here, take this. You can wipe yourself off a little bit."

"Thanks," Izzy said, taking the rag.

James looked up at the broken floor above. "You're lucky to still be in one piece."

Izzy couldn't agree more. "I know." She brushed more dust off of her and put the rag in her pocket. "Now what?"

"We spread out," James said, scanning the interior of the building. "A lot of things look untouched. We could be sitting on a goldmine of supplies here."

The team agreed and split up to explore the contents of the building, moving swiftly along the dusty shelves, grabbing supplies and anything else they could find.

Shadow followed Izzy as she searched for anything useful. She held onto one of the duffel bags as she searched the first floor. She came to a pantry closet full of cereal boxes and snacks. Her eyes lit up. Her mouth suddenly began to salivate. They really had hit the jackpot with this place.

Izzy walked inside the closet and began filling her bag with the food. With every box of cereal she picked up, she imagined herself as a child, sitting at the kitchen table with a bowl of it. She could *taste* it. She wanted to open one of them up and start shoving handfuls of it into her mouth.

"What'd you find?" Matt asked as he walked up behind her. Izzy showed him a box of Lucky Charms. He was wide-eyed and a smile grew on his face. "I used to love this! My parents used to buy boxes and boxes of it for me. I remember I used to eat all the cereal first, pushing aside all the marshmallows. Then, when I had little to no cereal left, I'd eat giant spoonfuls of marshmallows. It was so good!"

Izzy laughed. "I used to do the same thing."

"Open a box," Matt said. "Let's have some."

Izzy unsealed the cardboard flap and opened the box, then ripped open the bag. The smell of sugar and marshmallows wafted up her nose, making her hunger even stronger. She grabbed a handful and shoveled it in her mouth.

"A little stale," she said. "But it's still good." She offered the box to Matt. He reached in and took a handful too, shoving the cereal and marshmallows in his mouth.

"Brings back so many memories," he said with his mouth full. "I don't care if it's a little stale. It's still so good."

Izzy noticed Shadow sitting calmly at her side, staring up at her, waiting patiently for his turn. She put a handful in her hand and brought it before his mouth. He scarfed it up in seconds and looked up for more.

"Don't be greedy, Shadow. This is for everyone—not just us," she told him.

She closed up the box and placed it inside the duffel bag.

"Hey..." Matt said. "About earlier..."

"What do you mean?" Izzy asked in confusion.

"When I was on the roof and heard the loud crash inside, I thought something had happened to you."

"I mean, something *did* happen to me. I fell two stories inside a vent." Izzy shrugged her shoulders. "No big deal, right? Kind of like your gunshot." She smirked.

Matt rolled his eyes and looked away, as if he were trying to avoid smiling. "Okay, okay. I get it. But, for the record—I was worried about you." He placed a hand on the back of her head. A small puff of dust fell from it to her shoulders.

"Sorry," Izzy said. "Kind of a little dirty."

Their conversation was cut short by a scream from the entrance of the building. They both turned in unison and hurried out of the closet. As they made their way towards the entrance, Izzy saw Pete lying on the ground. The three scavengers from the street had made their way inside the building. One of them, a tall man with shaggy brown hair, had an arm wrapped around Audrey, pressing a gun to her head. He looked like a member of a motorcycle gang with his faded black leather jacket and tattered jeans.

Everyone froze. Izzy could feel the tension in the air as they stared at the intruders. She locked eyes with Audrey, seeing her own fear reflected back at her.

Izzy heard a shallow growl coming from Shadow. She placed a hand on his head, trying to calm him down.

"Drop the weapon!" one of the scavengers yelled at Matt. This man seemed shorter than the other one—stockier and rough, with a patchy beard. He wore a camouflage jacket and a bandana. He was holding Pete's handgun and had it aimed at Matt.

Matt looked at Izzy before his gaze drifted to James and Audrey.

The scavenger with the shaggy hair who was holding Audrey hostage pressed his gun harder onto her head. "We said, drop it!"

Matt and James locked eyes. James nodded, quietly telling Matt to comply. Reluctantly, Matt placed his rifle at his feet.

The third scavenger rushed over to Matt and picked up his rifle. He wore a patched-up denim vest and ripped black jeans. Multiple tattoos snaked up one bare arm.

He made his way back to the entrance to rejoin with the rest of his group.

Pete started climbing back to his feet, looking like he was ready to attack.

"Stay down, dumbass!" the tattooed scavenger said, then swung the rifle at Pete's head, making him fall back to the ground.

"No!" Izzy yelled.

"Nobody else moves... nobody else gets hurt," the shaggy-haired scavenger said.

"What do you want?" James asked.

"Your stuff," the scavenger with the bandanna said. "Hand it over. All of it."

"And if we don't?" James asked.

The shaggy-haired scavenger holding Audrey hostage, pulled the hammer back on the handgun. "We kill you. See, the way I see it, we have the guns. And this one." He wrapped his arm tighter around Audrey. "So, do as we ask, and no one else gets hurt."

Izzy glanced at each of the scavengers in turn. After what she had just been through getting into this building, and seeing all the supplies inside, she hated having to lose to these assholes. If only one of those Drifters would just show up and murder these guys...

James slid one of the duffel bags over to the scavengers. Izzy looked at Matt, who had his hand extended towards her, asking for the other bag. Defeated, she took it off her shoulder and handed it to him. He then walked it over and placed it on the ground by the scavengers.

"Your packs too," the man with the bandana said.

James shook his head. "Come on, guys. We already gave you what you asked for."

The tattooed man aimed the rifle at James. "He said your packs too. Now hand them over."

James put his hands up in surrender. "Okay, okay. Packs too." He swung his own backpack off his bag and tossed it to the scavengers. Matt did the same. Izzy didn't want to part with hers. She kept it on her back, hoping the scavengers wouldn't notice.

"Hers too," the tattooed man said, aiming his rifle at Izzy.

Dammit, she thought.

She slowly pulled her arms out of the straps, then tossed it to the scavengers.

"Okay, you got what you wanted. Now let her go," James requested, his voice filled with frustration and anger.

The three scavengers exchanged glances. A smirk appeared on the shaggy-haired man's face. "I think we'll be keeping her for a little longer. We have a need for her still. We want to make sure you don't decide to follow us. Because if you do, we'll kill her."

James's nostrils flared, his lips curled into a snarl, but there was little he could do. The scavengers held all the power—the weapons, the supplies, and now Audrey's life hanging in the balance.

Izzy wished there was something she could do. Shadow continued to growl, but she held onto his collar, not wanting to make matters worse than they already were.

The scavengers picked up the duffel bags and backpacks, then turned to leave the building with their captive in tow.

Pete, bloodied but determined, slowly rose from the floor, his gaze fixed on the departing scavengers.

"Don't follow us or we'll kill her," the man with the tattoos said, then slipped out the front door to join the others. The sound of their footsteps faded as they walked down the street.

Pete climbed to his feet. His head was covered in blood.

"Pete, you okay?" Matt asked.

Pete put his hand to his head, wincing as he touched the wound. He brought his hand down and looked at the blood.

"I'll be fine," he said. Slowly, he made his way to the front door and peered outside, tracking the movements of the scavengers, his knuckles whitening as he clenched his fists. "I'm going to kill them all," he mumbled.

"Where are they going?" James asked.

Pete turned to look at James. "They're heading west."

Izzy's eyes widened with concern. She asked James, "What are we going to do now?"

A fierce determination ignited in James's eyes as he met Izzy's gaze. "We're going to go get Audrey back."

| **6** |

James inched cautiously towards the front door, replacing Pete as he moved out of the way. Pete began pacing like a caged animal, until his eyes flicked to Shadow.

"Izzy," he said. "Can your dog track things?"

"Track *things?*" Izzy asked. "Like animals?"

"Or humans," James said, peaking back inside the building.

Izzy looked at Shadow. "I mean, I never had him track humans before. We go hunting for smaller animals like rabbits or birds."

"And he could do that, right?" Pete asked.

Izzy nodded.

Pete continued pacing for a moment before he lost his balance and reached out for the table next to him to catch himself. Izzy rushed over to him, placing a hand under his arm for support.

"I'm fine," Pete said, trying to push Izzy off of him.

She reached out instinctively for her backpack. The realization that it was gone along with her first aid kit was a devastating setback. She wanted her stuff back. She needed it.

She fought back against Pete's defense and held onto him.

"Pete," James said, "Just sit down for a moment. We'll catch up to them, and we'll get Audrey back. But we need to make sure you're okay as well."

Pete pulled his arm away from Izzy. "I said, *I'm fine.*" He rolled his sleeves down and used one to dab the bloody wound on his head. He winced each time he pressed on it.

"Let me just look at it," James said.

Pete sighed and held still while James tried to determine the extent of the wound.

"May need stitches when we get back home," he said. "Can we just patch you up before we leave here? I don't need you collapsing on me from blood loss."

"I'll be fine," Pete said. He used his sleeve to dab at the wound again, then held his sleeve out. "Look, it's slowing down. I'm good. Let's just go." He brushed past James and made his way to the front door.

James looked at both Izzy and Matt, and shrugged his shoulders before he followed Pete outside.

Matt gestured his arm. "After you," he said to Izzy.

"Come on, Shadow," Izzy said, heading outside with Shadow by her side.

Immediately, Pete tried to command her dog.

"Shadow, find Audrey," he said. When Shadow only stared at him, he tried again. "Shadow, follow the people who just robbed us." He pointed in the direction the scavengers had gone. "That way. Go. Follow."

Shadow's eagerness was palpable, but Pete's frantic instructions seemed to only confuse him. He cocked his head to one side, clearly puzzled.

A ripple of giggles broke through the group, dispelling some of the tension.

"What's wrong with your dog?" Pete asked. "It's sitting there staring at me like I have three heads."

"You don't just tell a dog to *follow*," Matt said. "You have to guide him. Give him something to follow—a scent, maybe. Do you have something of Audrey's that Shadow can smell?"

"No," Pete said.

"Does anyone?" Matt asked.

Izzy was disappointed that they had hit another wall until she remembered the rag Audrey had given her earlier. She reached into her pocket and pulled it out, waving it in the air.

"I have something!" she exclaimed. She knelt beside Shadow, holding the rag to him. "Find Audrey. Follow the scent," she instructed gently.

Shadow sniffed the rag carefully, his tail wagging slightly as he picked up the scent.

"Did it work?" James asked.

Suddenly, Shadow perked up and set off down the street in the direction Audrey had been taken. His nose was to the ground, sniffing intently as he followed the faint trail. Izzy rose to her feet, a glimmer of hope reigniting within her.

"Looks like it," she said.

The group fell in behind Shadow, following him as he made his way down the street. Izzy wanted to get Audrey back, but she also wanted to prove to Jason that she was useful on missions. She had found a way inside the building and, without Shadow, they wouldn't have a means of finding Audrey.

Izzy hoped those scavengers wouldn't hurt Audrey. She didn't deserve that. Her mind was a whirlwind of worry for her, and anger towards the scavengers. Despite the fear gnawing at her, she pushed forward.

James made his way to Izzy's side and kept pace with her. "Looks like Shadow may lead us right to Audrey," he said.

Izzy nodded. "I'm impressed. He's only followed animals before now. I didn't know he could do this."

"Animals have an incredibly keen sense of smell," James said. "I used to be a police officer... you know, before all of this." He gestured at the abandoned buildings around them. "I had a K-9. His name was Ranger. We went through so much together. There was this one time we were called in for a bomb threat. Showed up at the building just as it turned into a giant fireball. Scary as hell. Anyway, the fire department was minutes away and if anyone was still inside the burning building, they'd be dead before they got there. So, when we showed up, Ranger immediately jumped out of the car and rushed inside. I couldn't even stop him. I tried calling him back, over and over again. I honestly thought I wouldn't see him again. Maybe thirty seconds later—although it felt like an eternity—he was dragging a body out the front door."

Izzy was wide-eyed, intently focused on James's story. She hoped Shadow would do the same for her.

"Ranger rescued three people before the fire department arrived," James continued. "He had second-degree burns on his face and body, and third-degree burns on his paws."

"Poor puppy," Izzy said.

"Yeah, poor puppy. But he rescued three people who otherwise would have died. He was a wonderful dog." He stopped talking and his expression turned sour.

"May I ask what happened to Ranger?" Izzy asked.

James sighed. "When everything started happening—when those creatures started showing up—he saved one more person. Me." Izzy could imagine his heartache. Shadow meant so much to her, especially now. She could only imagine how much Ranger had meant to James.

"Before a few of us formed this group, I was out roaming the streets with some people I used to know," James went on. "We were ambushed by two Drifters. I went running for my life. I've seen what those creatures can do. They'll cut you down in a heartbeat. Anyway, I was running towards what I thought was an exit until one of those *things* stood in my way. I turned to run in a different direction and Ranger, the brave dog that he was, charged at it. He tried attacking it. Maybe trying to give me the time to escape while he sacrificed himself for me—I don't know. I thought he was with me until I heard the yelp. The noise stopped me in my tracks. When I didn't see Ranger by my side... I knew."

"I'm sorry," Izzy said. It was all she could muster. She felt horrible for James. She'd had no idea he had gone through this. He always tended to keep to himself. She couldn't imagine losing Shadow like that. It would break her heart.

James nodded. "It's okay. He saved my life. If it wasn't for him distracting the Drifter for those few seconds, I may not have gotten away."

"How's Shadow doing?" Pete asked, poking his head between Izzy and James. "Are we catching up to them?"

"I don't know," Izzy said. "He's never tracked a human before." She glanced down at Shadow, whose nose was low, sniffing all around. "But he seems to be doing okay... I hope."

"Yeah," Pete said. "I hope so too."

They then reached a spot where Shadow stopped suddenly. He started sniffing in a circle, seeming confused. It looked like he was trying to find the scent again, but was lost.

"What's going on?" James asked.

"I don't know," Izzy said.

Pete knelt down and examined the street closer. "No footprints. There's nothing. It's as if they vanished into thin air."

"Footprints?" Matt asked.

"Yeah, at least there were faint dust prints left behind from the scavengers who took Audrey. Something even I could track," Pete said. "But here," he waved around, "there's nothing."

"Maybe they covered their tracks or went into a building and took a different route," Matt said.

Izzy watched as Shadow's nose twitched, trying to pick up a scent. But after a few moments of sniffing and circling, he stopped, dropping his tail in defeat. He walked over to Izzy and sat by her feet. She reached down to pet his head.

"Good boy, Shadow," she said. "It's okay. You got us this far."

"No!" Pete yelled. "It's not okay!"

"Pete, calm down," Matt said.

"No! I will not calm down. We need to find Audrey before anything happens to her," he insisted.

"We will," James said. He reached out and put a hand on Pete's shoulder. "We will." He turned to Matt. "Go see if you can see anything from above. Maybe a better viewpoint will help us."

Matt nodded and headed for the alley to his right. A ladder hung beside one of the buildings. He started climbing it and then disappeared from sight.

As Izzy waited for Matt to reappear and report back from above, she glanced around nervously. The desolate landscape seemed even more intimidating now than ever. They were vulnerable, out in the open, and the sun would be setting soon; after that, they would be in even more danger.

When Matt finally descended, his face was pale, his eyes wide with alarm. He didn't need to say anything; his expression said it all. A chill ran through her body. She knew what he'd seen.

"What?" Pete asked. "Did you find them?"

"No, we have another problem," Matt said.

"What?" Pete asked.

Izzy pointed down the street. "Run," she said.

Panic swept through the group at the sight of a group of three Drifters floating into the intersection a few blocks ahead. Their deathly howls rang out.

They quickly made their way inside a nearby building through a broken door.

Izzy swallowed hard, trying to steady her trembling hands. She gripped a banister as she rushed down a flight of stairs and into a basement. Had the Drifters seen them? Had they escaped in time?

Thoughts raced through her mind—thoughts of Audrey, of their lost weapons and supplies, and of the impending danger. Fear threatened to engulf her, but she knew she had to remain strong. For Audrey, for her group, and especially for herself.

The group huddled together in the enveloping darkness of the basement, their breaths shallow and quiet. Little light shined through down the stairs—barely enough for Izzy to see their surroundings. Blankets were tucked away in a corner. Two tables stood against the wall to their left. There was a locker of some kind to their right.

The silence from above was eerie. Izzy felt like she was in the eye of a storm, waiting for the onslaught to hit. What would happen if they were found?

"Is there another way out of here?" James whispered.

Everyone started looking around the basement. Walls enclosed them on all sides.

"I don't see one," Pete replied.

Suddenly, a soft thud came from above them. Everyone looked up at the ceiling. Izzy's blood ran cold as the realization hit her—the Drifters had entered the building.

She was overwhelmed with panic as the noises grew louder, coming closer to the basement door. With no escape route in sight, the group started grabbing whatever they could get their hands on to use as a weapon.

Izzy looked at Matt. He held a brick in his hand, pulled back and ready to throw. His face was pale, his eyes wide with terror, but there was a determination in them, a will to fight and survive.

Another thud, this time directly above them. And then, the sound Izzy dreaded—the creaking of the basement door opening. Matt stepped in front of her as she knelt down and held onto Shadow.

Something was coming down the stairs.

| 7 |

As the creaking of the stairs echoed ominously, Izzy braced herself for the worst. Her body tensed, ready to fight. But as the first foot came into view, followed by a pair of legs, her fear morphed into confusion.

Descending the staircase were not monstrous creatures, but five humans. Izzy's relief was short-lived, however, as she noted their hardened expressions and the guns they had pointed at them.

The standoff was tense, each group eying the other warily. A man stepped forward from the other group. His demeanor was stern, his eyes holding a mixture of suspicion and anger.

"What are you doing in our home?" he asked.

James stood firm, a folded chair still raised above his head. "We were just seeking shelter from the Drifters outside. We mean no harm."

The man took another step forward. He was tall and broad-shouldered, and a rough beard covered his jaw. Brown, shaggy hair emerged from under his dark green hat. A bandanna was wrapped around his neck. He was dressed in worn-out military fatigues and a pair of sturdy boots.

"Well, they're gone," he said. "I think it's time for you guys to pack up and head on out of here."

"I apologize for entering your home," James said. "We were only looking for shelter to escape the Drifters. We're actually looking for someone. Maybe you could help us?"

Izzy couldn't believe James was asking these people for help. What if they were associated with the scavengers from earlier? What if they were out to murder them? But then the logic side of her brain started processing the situation. If these people wanted to kill them, they would have already. They all had guns. Izzy's group held only bricks and chairs. They had no chance. And they had no supplies to hand over so it wasn't like they could be robbed. Maybe the threat wasn't as big as she had made it out to be.

Pete stepped forward. "Three scavengers, with a woman. Have you seen them?"

The leader lowered his weapon and turned to face the other members of his group. They were all shaking their heads.

"No," he said. "Sorry."

James put down the chair he had been holding. He gestured for the others in the group to do the same. Izzy watched Matt toss the brick on the ground a few feet away from him.

"These people took someone from us," James said. "They took our supplies, our weapons. We're just trying to find them and get our friend and supplies back."

The leader gestured for his group to lower their weapons, then pursed his lips. "Would you like something to drink?"

Izzy was confused. Seconds ago, they had been aiming guns at them, and now they were being offered water?

James stuttered for a moment before speaking. "W-We're not here for your supplies. You don't have to—"

The other man interrupted him. "Your supplies were stolen by scavengers. You say they took someone from you. You people clearly have nothing right now. You have no weapons. You're not a threat to us. And you look thirsty." He glanced at everyone of Izzy's group. "I insist."

He turned and nodded to one of the women behind him, who wore a faded tee-shirt and cargo pants. Her blonde hair hung far down her back. As she made her way to the locker, she pulled out a key ring and held a lock with her other hand. With a quick turn and a *click*, the padlock opened. She pulled it off the door and opened the locker, revealing jugs of water, and stacks of canned and bagged food.

"You're welcome to help yourself," their leader said. "But please be courteous—I have a group to care for as well."

James was the first to make his way over to the locker and accept the generous offer. Pete made his way over too, and Matt and Izzy followed.

The woman at the locker took out a small bowl and poured some water into it and placed it on the ground for Shadow. He immediately started slurping it up.

"Thank you for your kindness, sir," James said, after taking a sip of water from the cup that had been handed to him.

"My name is Chris," the leader responded. He gestured to the woman by the locker. "This is Jessica." He pointed to the remaining three people behind him. "That's Tom, Claire, and Damian."

James introduced his own group.

"What do you think?" Izzy whispered to Matt.

"They seem nice. Incredibly welcoming," Matt said, "But I've been taught not to trust people so easily. You tend to get taken advantage of."

"I don't blame you," Izzy whispered.

Izzy bent down to pet Shadow. He looked up at her and then went back to slurping his water.

"The sun will be setting soon," Chris said. "You guys are welcome to stay here for the night. The only thing I ask is that you leave in the morning."

"I appreciate your generosity," James said. "We all do. Any chance you can help us find our missing person?"

Chris sighed. "Look—I'd like to help. But we just can't. It's just us. This is all we have. We don't have the resources to help you. I'm sorry."

"You *have* to help," Pete said. "Audrey was taken from us. Our supplies were taken."

"I'm sorry," Chris said. "We're just not equipped for it."

Pete sat down in a folding chair and covered his face with his hands.

"Pete," Izzy said, moving closer to him. She knelt down and put a hand on his shoulder. "Can I ask you a personal question?"

He lifted his head. "What?"

"You keep bringing Audrey up," she said. "I know she's important to us. She's one of us. And we won't leave her behind. But you have been kind of obsessing over getting her back." Izzy knew something was up. She wanted Audrey back as well. She knew the rest of the group did too. But Pete was more insistent than the rest of them. "Is there something you're not telling us?"

Pete stayed quiet.

James perked up. He locked eyes with Izzy, giving her a look as if he knew exactly what she was talking about.

"We'll get her back, buddy," James said. "We'll find her. But Izzy is right. There's definitely something else going on."

"There's nothing going on!" Pete blurted.

"You don't have to hide it," James said. "Its obvious—you and Audrey are a thing, right?"

Pete sighed and put his head back into his hands. He sat there for a moment, taking a few breaths. Everyone just gave him his space, waiting for him to finally acknowledge the question.

Pete finally picked his head up and looked at James. He then glanced around at the rest of the group before speaking. "We've kept it a secret, but we've been together for a few months now."

"That's great," Izzy said.

Pete gave a slight nod. "Well, yeah. It is. But…" he trailed off. He was holding back something.

"But what?" Izzy asked.

James was hesitant, but finally spoke. "She's pregnant."

Everyone's eyes widened. Izzy even noticed expressions of surprise among Chris's people.

"That's incredible!" James said.

"Congratulations," Chris added.

Pete immediately became serious. "That's why we need to find her!"

"We will," James said. He made his way over to James and placed an arm around him. Izzy followed suit and did the same, followed by Matt. Pete tried pushing them away but eventually gave in, tearing up. His tough guy persona was abandoned and the tears started falling.

"I need to find her," he said, tears falling down his face.

James gave him his word that they'd find her. He promised him. Izzy knew James meant what he said. He was someone who could be trusted. Izzy just hoped he'd find Audrey. That was not a conversation she'd want to be a part of if things went wrong.

"I know you do," James said. "And we'll help you." He gestured to the rest of the group. "We're all family. We look out for one another. We'll get her back."

"We can't join you on your search, but I think I may be able to help," Chris said. "There's a camp a few miles north of here. It's based in an old prison. It's a big place, you can't miss it. I don't know if that's where these people went, though. We like to stay away from other groups—after a few unpleasant experiences."

"Let's go," Pete said, enthusiastically.

"The sun will be setting soon. It's a few hours hike from here," Chris said.

"We have to go now," Pete said.

Chris took a step closer to Pete. "I know you're eager to find her. But think about it. It's going to get dark soon. You'll never make it there before nighttime. And you don't want to be out there at night. Those things will creep up on you before you even know they're there."

"We have to try," Pete said. "She'd do it for us."

"Look, I don't even know if those scavengers even live there. We try to keep our distance from others. She may not even be there." Chris scanned the room. "Why don't you guys spend the night. Get some rest. Then in the morning, you can head out there."

"Chris is right," James said.

"You're taking *his* side?" Pete said. "You don't even know him. What happened to all the talk about us being *family*?"

"We are family. But how good are you to Audrey if you're dead?"

Pete's stern and determined demeanor changed. His stance softened and the anger flushed from his face. Izzy could tell he knew James was right. If Pete went out on the streets now, the darkness would make him an easy target for the Drifters.

Izzy took one of Pete's hands and wrapped both of her hands around it. "James is right. Please, Pete. Audrey wouldn't want you dying out there trying to get her back. Let's do it the right way. Let's do it as a group."

Pete's hand shook in hers. He was desperate. Anyone would be in his position. Immediately, Izzy imagined Matt disappearing—being taken away. Her heart sunk for a brief moment before she shook the thought out of her head. She wasn't even *with* Matt and she felt that heartache. She could only imagine what Pete was feeling. Missing someone he loved—the mother of his unborn child.

Pete's shoulders began to slump, but he looked at her with grudging acceptance in his eyes. "Fine," he said. "But the moment the sun comes up, we're out of here."

Izzy squeezed his hand. "I'll be right by your side."

"Me too," James said.

"And me," Matt said.

"No chance of you guys joining us tomorrow morning?" James asked, turning his attention to Chris.

Chris shook his head. "I'm sorry. It's not our battle to fight. I mean no disrespect. We found ourselves involved in too many issues that didn't concern us and unfortunately, we lost people we loved and cared about. We lost our homes too. We vowed not to get involved again."

"I'm sorry," James said. "We've all lost people we've cared about." He met Pete's stare. "And we don't intend to lose another."

Addressing Chris again, he said, "I'm sorry you won't join us, but I think I can speak for all of us when I thank you for your hospitality."

"It's no problem," Chris said. "And sorry for scaring you with our weapons earlier. We needed to make sure you guys weren't here to steal from us."

Izzy let go of Pete's hand and made her way over to Matt, who was sitting by Shadow in a corner of the basement, away from the group.

"Hey," she said, taking a seat next to him.

"James makes friends pretty easily, doesn't he?" Matt said.

"He certainly does." Izzy reached down to pet Shadow, who was lying on the floor beside her. He looked up at her and then placed his head back on the floor.

"You think we'll find her?" Izzy asked.

"Audrey? Yeah. Definitely," Matt said with confidence. "Pete's an excellent hunter. He'll be able to find something to guide us to her. And we have Shadow. And you."

"Me?" Izzy asked. "How can I help find her?"

"You and Shadow go out all the time, despite Jason not approving." He rolled his eyes, which made Izzy smile. "You guys find all kinds of stuff. You always seem to know where to go—where the adventure is. Maybe just being you is all we need to find her. And of course, it gives me someone cute to talk to. Burly men just don't do it for me."

Izzy found herself enjoying his flirtation. She could see something in Matt's eyes—a spark of something more than a friendship. Feeling a certain lightness in her heart, Izzy couldn't help but tease Matt further. She chuckled as she looked at him.

"Really, Matt? Cute?" She raised an eyebrow, her lips curling into a playful smirk. "I'd say I'm more of an 'adventurous and daring' type than 'cute.' But, I'm sorry burly men don't do it for you. I guess I'll take it as a compliment."

Matt laughed. "I like it. Cute *and* funny."

Izzy loved the compliment, but she knew she needed to pull back before this went any further. She liked Matt, a lot.

But.

Memories.

Too many terrible memories.

She slowly moved her hand up to her necklace and touched the ring. A sense of dread flooded through her. She glanced at Matt, whose head cocked to the side.

"Did I say something wrong?" Matt asked.

Izzy snapped out of it, shaking her head slightly, as if shaking the memory away. She tried to fake a smile, but then she looked into those eyes. Those handsome green eyes. She stared for longer than she should have. Next thing she knew, Matt was leaning in to kiss her.

Out of instinct, Izzy pulled away.

"Umm..." she stuttered.

"I'm sorry, I didn't mean—"

Izzy interrupted him. "No, it's okay. I... umm..."

She didn't know what to say. She knew she had blown a perfect moment. But the fear of losing someone else she cared about, maybe even loved—if she could feel that love again—consumed her. She never wanted to feel that again. She never wanted to go through that again. Keeping her distance was the only way to make sure it wouldn't happen again.

But at what expense?

She certainly didn't want to be lonely.

"Look, Matt," she said, finally finding the words.

"It's okay, Izzy. Really. I understand," Matt said.

"Understand what?" she asked.

"I see you holding onto the ring you keep around your neck." Izzy realized she still had a grip around it. She let go and dropped her hand back to her side. "You lost someone important to you. I get it. Maybe you're still grieving or something, I don't know. And if that's the case, I'm sorry, I didn't know."

Izzy looked at him. Those handsome green eyes of his, staring at her. She wished she could have just kissed him back. Why did she pull away?

So stupid, she thought.

"You don't have to tell me if I'm right or wrong, or even whatever it is you're holding back," Matt said. "It's your business. And if you ever want to talk about it, I'm here for you."

Handsome *and* sweet. What was wrong with her? Why couldn't she just rewind the last minute and try again?

Memories of her past life flashed before her eyes. Scenes played out like a movie behind her eyelids as she tried hard not to cry. But in the end, she couldn't help it. She opened her eyes and the tears appeared.

Matt pulled his chair closer to her. He placed his arm around her, pulling her close. Izzy placed her head comfortably on his shoulder, and he stroked her hair as she shed a few tears on his shirt.

Finally, Matt broke the silence. "So, back before all of this happened, I used to have this apartment. I was always running late to work. I always forgot to plug my phone in and it kept dying in the middle of the night. So I went to the store and bought this alarm clock that cursed at you." He paused for a moment. "It was a rude awakening."

Izzy thought about it for a second before the punchline clicked. She smacked his leg and started to chuckle. "A dad joke?" She continued laughing. "You're an idiot."

"An idiot that just made you laugh," he said.

She sighed and nestled into his shoulder again.

* * *

Izzy was jolted awake. The noise that had disturbed her slumber echoed loudly in the basement. She shot up instantly, trying to identify the source of the noise. Was it one of the Drifters? One of the scavengers from before?

She could feel Matt stirring next to her. She couldn't have been the only one to hear it. The faint light revealed Chris sitting up alertly, his eyes wide. A few others in his group had woken as well. Izzy noticed that James was still sound asleep.

"What was that?" Izzy asked Chris.

"The door," he said, looking around the basement, confused.

She glanced towards the stairs, waiting for something to make its appearance.

"Is someone coming down the stairs?" she asked, her voice barely a whisper.

"No," Chris said. "It's locked from the inside. That was someone leaving."

Izzy scanned the room to confirm her worst fear. Pete, who'd been sleeping a few feet from her, was gone.

Without wasting a second, Izzy scrambled to her feet. Matt was rubbing his eyes, still trying to wake up.

"Izzy, what's wrong?" he asked.

Already on her feet and heading towards the stairs, she said, "It's Pete. He left."

Matt's eyes opened wide, and he quickly got to his feet, following Izzy. They sprinted up the stairs and burst into the empty building above. They ran outside, scanning the early morning landscape for any sign of Pete. But he was nowhere to be found.

Pete was gone.

| **8** |

A cold knot of dread squirmed inside Izzy's stomach as she and Matt rushed back into the basement. The harsh reality of Pete's disappearance was a shock, but it hadn't been completely unexpected. She knew how much he wanted to get Audrey back. Izzy had hoped he would have waited for the rest of them. It would have been better to work as a team. A group of four people were better than three. They couldn't afford to lose anyone else.

"Pete's gone," Izzy announced, making her way down the stairs. "We can't find him."

James was already up and putting on his shoes. "We'll find him. Shadow can follow his trail. We'll catch up to him."

Izzy hoped he was right.

James finally stood up and made his way over to Izzy and Matt. He turned to Chris. "We could really use your help with this. Any chance you'd reconsider?"

Chris simply shook his head. "I'm sorry, we can't. We are done with all the violence," he said, his voice gentle yet firm. "We've been through too much."

Matt tilted his head and raised an eyebrow. "What about the guns yesterday, then? You guys seemed to have a violent streak when we all first met?"

A small smile appeared on Chris's face. "We don't go searching for violence. I can't help it if it shows up on our doorstep. And we need to protect our group and our supplies. I didn't know who you people were and what you were doing in our home." Chris paused, looking at each of them. "Look, I was a priest in another life... before all of this," he said. "I have a sense for people. I felt the sadness of your missing member. You are good people. I chose to help you, rather than harm you. And I'm glad I made the right decision."

Matt seemed taken aback, but satisfied with Chris's answer. "I, uhh... thank you."

James extended a hand. "Thank you."

Chris shook his hand. "My house is your house. I can't offer much, but if you ever need help or a place to rest your head, my door is open for you and your people."

"You're very kind, thank you," James said. "Alright, you guys ready?"

Izzy and Matt nodded and thanked Chris and his group. They all climbed the stairs, and with a final look back, Izzy, Matt, James and Shadow stepped into the abandoned building above the basement. They made their way through the building and stepped outside. The city streets stretched out before them, a maze filled with uncertainty and danger.

"So, where are we going?" Izzy asked.

"This way," James said, pointing to his right.

"How do you know?" Matt asked.

James pointed. "Because Shadow is already moving that way."

The group followed Shadow as he kept his nose to the ground, following what they hoped was Pete's scent.

* * *

As the group tracked Pete's movements, a strange sense of worry flowed through Izzy. She'd watched as Shadow kept his nose to the ground, following Pete's scent with unwavering focus.

But what if they didn't find Pete? What if they *did* find him, but he was dead?

Izzy tried to ignore the thoughts, but they consumed her. She wanted to find Pete *alive*. She also wanted to find and rescue Audrey. Maybe there was a possibility Pete had found Audrey already and rescued her.

Matt walked at Izzy's side in silence, his gaze fixed ahead of them. Izzy could sense his concern, too. As they traversed the city streets, she found herself thinking back to last night, to the moment they had shared… almost.

"Izzy," Matt said. "Look, I'm sorry about last night. I didn't mean—"

She interrupted him. "It's okay, really."

"I know, but I feel bad. I didn't mean to make things weird or anything."

She sighed, knowing she'd have to explain herself or else Matt wouldn't stop apologizing and talking about it.

"Anthony and I—" she started to say.

"Who's Anthony?" Matt asked, a tinge of jealousy in his voice.

A small smile crossed Izzy's face. "Anthony was my fiancée." She glanced over at Matt, and his eyes widened. "Yes, I was engaged a while back—maybe a year. Probably more. I don't know. I've lost track of time."

"*Was* engaged?" Matt asked. "What happened?"

"Death happened," she said.

"I'm—I'm sorry," Matt stuttered.

Izzy tried to push the pain away. "It's okay."

They walked in silence for a few moments before Matt said, "Don't hate me for this. I know I should just drop it, but I have to ask—did he die from the… the Drifters?"

Izzy shook her head. "No. Someone killed him."

"I'm sorry, Izzy. I had to ask," he said.

"It's okay," she said. "I understand the curiosity."

She reached for her necklace and curled her fingers around the ring dangling from it. The pain of losing a loved one overwhelmed her. Experiences she'd never get back—and new ones she'd never be able to make.

A hand touching her arm brought her back to reality.

"You okay?" Matt asked.

Izzy nodded. "Yeah, I'll be fine."

She noticed Matt glance at the ring that she held in her hand. "Is that your ring?"

"No. It was his." She took a deep breath, trying to work up the courage to talk about it again. "When I made it back home... after... afterwards... I started going through our stuff. I eventually came across the ring I had bought for him. I didn't want to leave it sitting around for fear someone would take it, so I kept it in my pocket. One day, I was gathering supplies and it must have slipped out of my pocket. I couldn't even begin to tell you the anxiety I felt. This was only days after I lost him. This ring meant the world to me. It was a small piece of him, the only thing I had left at that point. I went back and searched the building I was in from top to bottom. Just when I thought I'd lost it for good, this little puppy came strolling up to me. I start to pet him and he dropped something from his mouth at my feet. It was covered in slobber, but it was my ring."

"Shadow found your ring?" Matt asked.

"It's actually how I found him, too," Izzy said. "It was dark out. I could barely see anything. I was on the floor on my hands and knees, feeling around for this ring. And this dog just comes strolling out of the shadows with my ring, like he found it with no problem."

"I guess that's how you came up with his name?" Matt asked.

"No," Izzy said. "It was actually on his collar."

"Seriously?" Matt said, leaning forward to see if Shadow had a collar on.

Izzy laughed. "You're an idiot. Yes, of course that's how I came up with his name. He came wandering out of the shadows. Seemed fitting."

Matt shook his head, realizing how gullible he was. He smiled. "I can't believe I fell for that."

"Pretty easy too," Izzy said. "You went right for that imaginary collar."

"You two done flirting yet?" James asked. "We should be focusing on finding Pete and Audrey."

"Sorry," the two of them said at once.

* * *

The group continued forward for a few hours until the large prison came into view, perched atop a steep hill and surrounded by fences and concrete walls. From the distance, it looked like a fortress, impenetrable and foreboding.

They hid behind some trees, staying out of sight.

"You think Pete made it here?" Matt asked.

Izzy shook her head. "I don't know. But we need to get inside and find out. If we can work out how."

Matt peeked out from behind the trees and scanned the area. "I don't suggest we just knock on their front door. Maybe we can find a weak spot in that fence somewhere." He pointed towards the rear of the prison. "Over there. We may be able to sneak in there."

He started to move out from behind the trees, but Izzy grabbed him, holding him back.

"Wait," she whispered loudly. She pointed to the pathway leading up the hill towards the prison where three people were walking. They looked familiar. "That's them. Those are the guys who took Audrey."

"You sure?" James asked.

"I recognize those outfits. Yes, it's definitely them," she said.

"So, Pete's in there," Matt said.

"Maybe," Izzy said. "We don't even know if he made it here. We probably have a better chance of finding Audrey inside."

"Izzy's right," James said. "But at the same time, we don't even know if Audrey is in there either. Just because those three guys are heading towards the prison, doesn't mean she's in there."

"Only one way to find out, right?" Matt said.

James shook his head. "We wait."

"Why?" Izzy asked.

"How many people are inside?" James asked.

Izzy and Matt considered this in silence.

"Do they have weapons? Do you see any guards or people watching the prison?" James asked.

Again, both Izzy and Matt were silent.

"Exactly," James said. "We know nothing, other than those three scavengers who stole from us are heading towards the front door to the prison."

"So what do you suggest we do?" Izzy asked.

James watched as the three scavengers headed inside the prison walls. He looked up at the sky and then back at Izzy. "It'll be getting dark in a few hours. Let's use the darkness as cover and sneak inside. Matt had a good idea about finding a weak spot in the fence. I can go inside, get a quick look around and get out as quickly as possible."

"Wait," Izzy said. "You said, *I*."

James nodded. "We can't have three people wandering around in there, trying to stay hidden. That's too many." He looked at Shadow. "No offense, Izzy, but I can't trust a dog to remain hidden and quiet."

Izzy placed a hand on Shadow's head. She knew James was right. Three people and a dog would clearly stand out.

"I get it, but I'm coming with you," she said.

"This isn't a discussion, Izzy," James said.

Izzy knew she could sneak around the prison undetected. She'd been successful multiple times when gathering food and supplies for her camp. Even with Shadow by her side, she had been able to remain hidden.

"You need me," Izzy protested. "*You know* I can remain unde-tected. *And* what if you find Pete and Audrey? What if they're in-jured? What if you need another pair of hands to assist with an escape?"

James pursed his lips and shook his head. Izzy could tell he *really* wanted to say no. But he only pointed to Shadow and said, "He stays behind."

Izzy nodded. "Understood."

Her heart fluttered. She was going to help James with a rescue. This was huge for her. She knew she could handle it. This could be her moment to prove to James and Jason she was capable, despite what they had told her previously.

Once the sun had started to set, James said, "Let's move."

The group snuck out from behind the trees and cautiously be-gan making their way around the back of the prison, their eyes scanning the area for any signs of danger. They approached a dis-tant spot towards the rear of the building, which they had deter-mined was as close to an inconspicuous spot as possible. Shrubs and plant life surrounded the area, which gave them a little cover while they plotted their next move.

Matt grabbed the fence and started trying to pull it out of the ground, with little success. He let go and looked up.

"Maybe climb over it?" he said.

"That fence must be fifteen, maybe twenty feet high," James said. "Too much risk of getting injured, and we'll easily be seen climbing up it."

"So, what do we do?" Matt asked.

Izzy picked up a rock the size of her hand and dug it into the ground by the base of the fence. "We dig."

She took a chunk of grass and dirt from the ground and tossed it aside, then slammed the rock back into the ground and pulled more dirt away. Matt and James followed suit, finding rocks of their own and started to dig. Shadow pitched in and began digging as well, following what everyone else was doing.

"Good boy," Izzy praised him.

Having Shadow dig was much more helpful than she had imagined. His front paws pulled dirt away quicker than the other three of them combined. Eventually, they stepped back and let Shadow do his thing. They'd occasionally reach into the hole and pull dirt aside, making room for Shadow to continue his digging expedition.

After a few minutes, they could see the bottom of the fence. They brushed aside the dirt from the hole and started trying to make room to slide under.

"I'm going to try and go through," Izzy said. "Matt, grab the bottom and lift it up."

Matt grabbed the fence and pulled up, lifting the fence a few more inches. Izzy tried squeezing through, but it wasn't a big enough hole. James reached down and helped Matt pull up on the fence, giving Izzy the final inch she needed to squeeze through. She climbed out from the other side and looked around, making sure she hadn't been seen.

"Come on," James said.

Izzy reached down and pulled up on the fence with Matt, allowing James to crawl underneath. She let go once he had made it through the hole.

Shadow started to try and sneak down in the hole too, following James and Izzy, but Matt held onto him, holding him back. Shadow let out a soft whimper as he tried to wiggle free.

Izzy put her fingers through the fence, trying to touch Shadow. "I'll be back. Stay here, okay?"

Shadow let out another whimper.

"I'll be fine," Izzy told him.

"Come on, we need to move," James said.

Izzy gave one more comforting tap through the fence, then turned her back on Shadow, leaving him behind. She hated not having him by her side, but she understood James's concern.

The pair moved slowly along the concrete walls of the prison, trying to stay out of sight. The sun was beginning to sink lower in the sky, casting long shadows. They made sure not to be the ones casting those shadows.

They turned the corner to see a field surrounded by more fences. Inside was a collection of tents and makeshift shelters. Izzy could see the silhouettes of people moving around, and could hear the low hum of their voices.

"This way," James whispered, tapping Izzy on the shoulder.

Two guards stood to one side of the entrance of the prison. They each had a handgun stuffed in the front of their pants. As they were deep in conversation, James simply strode past them and entered the prison. Izzy followed him, tiptoeing past the guards, trying to be as silent as possible. She felt as if she was walking on a tightrope, one wrong step away from disaster.

They entered the dark prison. It was a labyrinth of darkness and uncertainty. The cold walls seemed to close in on Izzy. She suddenly felt nervous about the task at hand. Sneaking into an enemy camp was different. This was a rescue mission. She and James were unarmed and surrounded by countless people who had weapons.

She glanced at James. His eyes were scanning their surroundings with focused intensity. He gave a slight nod and moved forward with an eerie calmness.

As they crept along the cold, stone corridors, the only sounds were distant echoes of footsteps and voices. With each step, Izzy imagined someone would emerge from the darkness and catch them.

They approached the first corner.

James slowly peeked around it, before waving Izzy on. She followed him to a door. James reached for the handle and carefully turned the knob, then cracked open the door.

It was dark. It must have been unoccupied, because James slowly closed the door and continued along the hallway. Izzy's senses heightened in the darkness. She could hear the creak of an old door elsewhere in the prison, the rustle of her clothes as she took each step. Every noise seemed magnified, threatening to give them away.

Suddenly, the beam of a flashlight danced along the wall ahead of them. Izzy's stomach dropped in a gut-wrenching sense of impending danger. Someone was approaching, and they were out in this open hallway.

She glanced at James and could see the panic in his eyes.

The footsteps grew closer. The light became brighter.

They were exposed.

They were going to be caught.

| 9 |

Izzy turned to head back the way they had come, but she heard voices approaching from that direction too.

They were trapped.

She winced as a hand grabbed her arm.

"This way," James said, pulling her towards the wall and into a narrow alcove just as someone rounded the corner.

They pressed themselves against the cold, damp wall, barely daring to breathe. The guard's boots echoed on the stone floor, growing louder with each step. She glanced at James, who was holding an index finger to his mouth, signaling for her to be quiet. Izzy held her breath, praying the guard wouldn't hear or see them.

The light grew brighter; the footsteps grew louder. Izzy's lungs started to burn while holding her breath. She remained deathly still as the person in the hallway strolled past the alcove, making sure not to alert them.

Just when she thought she couldn't bear it anymore, the light and footsteps faded. The person had moved on. Izzy let out a sigh of relief.

"That was too close," she whispered.

"I know," James responded. He peeked out to make sure the coast was clear. He gave a slight nod and the two of them slowly made their way into the hallway again.

At the end of the hallway, they headed towards a slightly open cell door on their left. The door creaked as James pushed it open further, revealing a long row of cell doors.

Each prison cell they passed was a stark reminder of the grim reality they were facing. Izzy certainly didn't want to be placed in one of these cells and forgotten about to slowly rot away in the darkness.

So far, the cells had been empty, the bare floors and walls revealing nothing about their former inhabitants. But now they approached an occupied cell. Seeing the prisoner inside increased Izzy's fear of becoming trapped inside.

The prisoner was a woman, her long, dark hair draped over her face. She was using a jacket as a pillow as she slept on the cold, hard floor, her body curled up for comfort and warmth.

"There are people in here," Izzy whispered, pointing to the woman on the floor.

James peaked inside the sleeping woman's cell. "Must be a prisoner of theirs."

"Shouldn't we help her?" Izzy asked.

James moved onto the next cell, looked inside, and stopped. He sighed, staring inside.

"What?" Izzy whispered. Then she moved next to James and saw what he was looking at. A man was hanging from the ceiling grate, suspended from some kind of fabric and a belt. "Oh my God," she said, covering her mouth.

"Nothing we can do for him," James whispered. "Let's keep moving."

"Get me out of here," a voice said from the next cell.

Izzy and James moved on to find a man pressed up against the wall of his cell, his hands wrapped around the bars. He had clearly been locked up for a long time. The man's face was dirty and thin.

His worn clothing looked as though it belonged to someone much smaller. His pants only came about halfway up his shins.

"Why are you in here?" Izzy asked.

"Those damn people locked me up," he said. "They thought I was stealing from them." He looked around nervously. "You gotta get me out of here," he said urgently.

Izzy pulled on the cell door trying to open it. It didn't budge. "How?" she asked.

"I don't know. Maybe there's a control panel somewhere. They usually open a few of our doors at a time, so it's not something they use a key for," the man in the cell said.

"Izzy," James's voice alerted her. "Over here."

"I'll be right back," she told the man in the cell.

"No, don't leave me," he pleaded. He tried to reach out and grab her shirt, but she backed away quickly.

She made her way to James. The sight that greeted her took her breath away. There, on the floor of a cell, was Pete. His body was bruised and beaten. He appeared to be a shadow of the man they had only seen a few hours ago.

The sight of Pete, so vulnerable and hurt, filled Izzy with a mix of relief and dread. They had found him, but he was badly injured.

"Pete!" Izzy whispered loudly. "Pete!"

Slowly, Pete's eyes opened. "I... found her. She's here."

"Pete, relax," James said. "Save your energy. We need to get you out of here."

"I'll... slow you... down," Pete said, struggling to speak. "Save Audrey."

"No, we're not leaving without you," Izzy said.

"How do we open the cell?" James asked.

"The prisoner down there said there's some kind of control panel," Izzy said.

"Find it. Quickly," James said.

The two of them moved away from the cells, frantically searching the room for the controls that would open the cells. The search didn't last long. A chilling sound came by the entrance: the unmistakable clinking of chains and the ominous thuds of shoes against the concrete. A group of scavengers had entered the holding area, their guns pointed menacingly at Izzy and James.

The pair raised their hands in surrender. They had no choice. They were trapped, outnumbered, and outgunned. Izzy looked around, desperately searching for a way out of their dire predicament.

The sound of more boots came from behind the scavengers.

"What happened to our poor friend, Billy?" said a voice.

Izzy squinted. *That voice.* It sounded familiar. Where had she heard it before?

"Looks like he hung himself," one of the scavengers said.

"Who the hell let him keep his belt?" that familiar voice said.

She *knew* that voice. How?

"We'll take care of it," another scavengers said.

"Be sure that you do," that familiar voice said. Then the original group of scavengers parted to reveal him.

His appearance sparked a rush of memories in Izzy's mind—one of which had been just days ago. Memories of fear and insecurity when she was held hostage by him. His cruel smirk and cold eyes were etched into her memory.

He approached Izzy and cocked his head to the side. "Ahh, so we meet again."

"Hawk..." Izzy mumbled.

"That's me," Hawk said.

"I thought you died," Izzy said.

"You mean when that beast came charging through that hideout?" He gave a quick sarcastic laugh before continuing, "One thing you need to remember—someone ain't dead unless there's a body."

Izzy's mind flashed to when she had escaped one of the Reavers' hideouts with Shadow. She had stepped over a bloody mess of bodies, but she had never seen Hawk's body. She'd assumed he must have escaped, or was ripped apart by the Drifters somewhere else, but she never expected to find him again, especially not here.

"What are you doing here?" she asked.

"What am I doing here?" he repeated. He looked around before focusing on Izzy again. "I live here."

"What do you want?" James asked.

Hawk leaned to one side to see James standing behind Izzy. "And who might you be?" he said, ignoring the question.

"James. Now I'll ask again. What do you want?"

"I suggest your friend here dial down on the threatening nature," Hawk told Izzy. "We have all the guns, and they're all pointed at you two. You don't have any leverage. Oh, and speaking of leverage—we have plenty."

"What's that supposed to mean?" Izzy asked.

Hawk smiled. "In due time, little one. In due time." He turned around and waved two of his men on through. Someone must have flicked a switch because the door to Pete's cell immediately opened. The two scavengers made their way inside and picked him up. One of Pete's arms was wrapped around each of the scavengers.

"What are you doing with him?" Izzy asked.

"We're all going to take a little walk," Hawk said.

"I'm not going anywhere until you tell me what's going on," Izzy said.

"Again, I don't think you have any leverage to make demands," Hawk said. He pulled up his shirt to reveal a pistol tucked in the front of his pants. "Now, follow me, or I'll start killing your friends here, one by one."

Izzy nodded, giving in to Hawk's demands. She had no choice. The longer she played this out, the more time she would have to come up with a plan to escape.

She followed Hawk back through the prison. James walked beside her, a stoic expression on his face, his eyes darting for any sign of an escape route.

As they retraced their steps through the hallways, Izzy and James tried to converse quietly with Pete. Despite his beaten and bruised state, he seemed to regain some energy, though his voice was barely above a whisper.

"Why did you guys... come here?" he said.

"We were trying to find you," James answered. "You and Audrey."

"Where is she?" Izzy asked. "You said you found her."

"I don't know," Pete said. "I... wasn't able to... find where they held her. I heard... her voice. They... found me first."

"Why did they do that to you?" she asked, nodding towards his bruises.

One of the guards holding Pete up said, "This is what happens when you don't give us what we want to know."

"What does that mean?" James asked.

"They wanted to know... where we lived. They wanted... to know how many... of us there are. Our supplies..." Pete struggled to keep talking. "I gave them... nothing. Which is why I... look like this."

His cheeks were swollen, and there was dried blood underneath his nose and on his shirt. He seemed to have trouble opening his right eye fully. Izzy felt awful for him. None of this was supposed to happen. She suddenly wished she hadn't come on this adventure. Or maybe she should have just snuck out the night before and done this one on her own. Maybe she could have avoided all of this violence if she had just gone by herself.

"Save your strength, Pete," James said. "It's okay. We'll find Audrey. We'll all get out of this soon."

Whether or not James believed what he said, Izzy didn't know. She only hoped he had a plan. Because she surely didn't.

Hawk escorted them through the front door of the prison.

"Where are we going?" Izzy asked.

"You'll see," Hawk responded cryptically.

The uncertainty of what lay ahead made her wonder if he was going to kill them. Was he going to beat answers out of her and James, and make them look like Pete?

As Izzy stepped into the fields in front of the prison, a familiar bark echoed through the air, making her heart leap into her throat. Her eyes scanned the field and there was Shadow, tied to a flagpole next to Matt, surrounded by scavengers holding guns.

Izzy ran past Hawk, towards Shadow and Matt. The surrounding guards held their guns at the ready until Hawk told them to stand down. Izzy slid towards Shadow, then held him in her arms. He frantically licked her face. Izzy looked up at Matt and asked, "Are you okay?"

"Yeah," he said.

"What happened?" Izzy asked.

"Okay, okay," Hawk yelled out to Izzy. She turned to face him. "Now you can see what I mean when I spoke about you not having any leverage. Are you willing to listen now?"

"What do you want?" Izzy asked.

"Stuff. And more of it," he responded.

"What the hell are you talking about?" James asked.

"There's that threatening tone again," Hawk said. His eyes widened. "Oh! I almost forgot. Might as well just get it all out in the open, right?"

Hawk gave a slight flick of the wrist to someone behind him. "Bring her out."

A door opened by the main entrance of the prison, and two men brought out a woman who was kicking and trying to scream even though her mouth was covered with a cloth.

"Audrey!" Pete yelled.

Immediately, Audrey tried to make her way to Pete, who also had a spurt of energy, trying to tug his way free and reach Audrey.

Hawk laughed. "Well, clearly these two have a thing for one another. That's good to know."

"You son of a bitch! If you hurt her…" Pete said.

Hawk stepped close to Pete and pulled the gun out of his pants. "Go ahead. Finish that thought. What would you do? You're, from the looks of it, badly injured. You're held hostage. You have guns pointed in all your guys' direction. So, go ahead. What will *you* do if I hurt her?"

Pete winced at his words. Izzy could tell he wanted to say something to Hawk, but he knew better. Hawk was right. They were all trapped. At least if they followed his rules, maybe they had a shot at getting out of here alive.

Hawk leaned closer to Pete. "That's what I thought. All bark and no bite." He smiled at him before backing away and addressing the rest of the crowd.

"Now, back to the reason you're all here. We need stuff. And we have the guns to make sure you get us the stuff we need. I'm sure you're asking yourselves, 'But Hawk, what kind of stuff are you talking about?' Well, let me answer that for you all. Stuff as in supplies—medicine, food, water, clothing, weapons—basically anything we need, you go get for us. Understand?"

Everyone remained quiet until James spoke up. "And what if we don't agree to this?"

Hawk strolled up to James and placed an arm around him. "You don't want to *not* listen to my demands. I promise you, it won't go well for any of you."

"And where are we supposed to find this... *stuff* for you?" Izzy said, playing along.

Hawk removed his arm from James and suddenly got excited. "Good—you understand our arrangement. I knew I liked you, Izzy. Your first assignment is to go back to that building my guys found you in and clean it out. Bring everything back here. Whatever is there is now mine. Understand?"

Izzy knew she didn't have a choice. But at least she had a way out of this prison. If they followed his instructions, they could leave. Let him believe they'd do his bidding. Then when the time was right, they could make their escape.

"We understand," James said.

Izzy nodded. "Me too."

"No," Pete said, firmly.

Hawk turned and made his way over to Pete, who was barely hanging on to the two scavengers holding him up. Hawk scratched his head. "I'm sorry. I thought I heard you say *no*."

Pete stared right back at Hawk and repeated, "No."

Hawk smiled and faced the rest of the group. "Your friend here thinks he's funny." He spun around quickly and punched Pete in the stomach, knocking the wind out of him. The guards dropped Pete and he landed on his hands and knees.

"Pick him up," Hawk demanded. The guards bent down and held him up on his knees. Hawk then punched him in the face. Pete fell back to the ground and didn't move.

"Pete!" Izzy yelled.

Loud mumbles came from Audrey through the cloth around her mouth. Shadow barked twice and started to growl.

Again, Hawk issued his ultimatum to the group. "Now I'll ask again, does *everybody* understand me?"

Pete got up on his hands and knees, spat out blood, and said, "No."

Izzy knew what would happen next. Pete would get his ass kicked. She wished he would just put his ego and pride aside and agree to Hawk's demands. If only to buy them some time, to give them a chance to escape.

Suddenly, Hawk pulled out his gun. But instead of pointing it at Pete, he held it towards the ground, next to Pete. "You seem not to care about your life, so threatening you won't do me any good. Let's see what happens when I threaten those you love and care about." He looked in Audrey's direction. "Let's start with her." He left Pete's side and made his way over to Audrey.

"No!" Pete yelled.

"I see you're very fond of that word," Hawk said. He told the guards to hold Audrey still. He pointed the gun against her temple. Screams of protest rang out from the group, but Pete's voice rose above the rest of them. Audrey's eyes were wide with fear. Her own words of protests were muffled by the cloth tied around her mouth.

The standoff seemed to last an eternity, each second stretching out as Izzy watched, paralyzed with fear. If only Pete had just accepted Hawk's demands, all of this would have been avoided.

"Stop! Please!" Pete pleaded. "I'll do it."

Hawk smirked and slowly lowered the gun from Audrey's head. Her head sunk in a sigh of relief.

Hawk moved back to Pete, who was still on his knees. Hawk looked down at him. "I'm glad you finally saw things my way." He then took a deep breath. "But unfortunately, I can't have insubordination in my group. And there's really only one way to deal with that."

He aimed his gun at Pete's head and pulled the trigger.

| **10** |

The gunshot echoed through the field. Everything seemed to happen in slow motion.

Pete's body crumpled to the ground, lifeless. Screams of horror filled the air. The death of a friend was a shocking reality that none of the group had been prepared for. The two guards began to struggle as Audrey screamed through the cloth and tried desperately to free herself from their grasp.

Izzy's eyes watered up. Tears fell in between her screams of pain at losing a friend. She wanted to rise up and attack Hawk where he stood. She wanted to let Shadow loose on him. But she knew Hawk would shoot them if they tried to attack him.

"This is what happens when you don't respect authority," Hawk said. "Let this be a lesson for you all." His cold explanation shook Izzy at her core. His message was received, loud and clear.

Hawk turned to address the guards holding Audrey. He pointed back to the prison. "Take her away."

The guards struggled past, slowly dragging Audrey back to the prison doors. Izzy watched her friend being taken away.

"I'm keeping your friend here as a reminder that you have someone's life depending on you guys following through on your commitment," Hawk said. "Don't let Audrey wind up like your friend Pete here." He pointed at Pete's lifeless body. "Now… where were we? Ah, yes. You guys need to gather supplies for me. So, we're going to start small. I'm going to have a few of my men accompany you back to the facility where you were found yesterday.

I was told there's a lot of food and medical supplies still in there. You'll be leaving in a few minutes."

"But it's getting dark," Izzy said. "Wouldn't it be safer for all of us, including your men, if we go tomorrow morning?"

"Always trying to think ahead, Izzy," Hawk said. "And the answer is no. You'll be leaving once my men are ready. The quicker you get there, the quicker you can get back."

"You'll be putting all of us in harm's way," James said.

Hawk shrugged his shoulders. "So?"

"You seriously don't care? Not even about your own men?" Izzy asked.

"Oh, of course I care about the safety of my men. I also care about getting to that building before other people clear it all out. So, you're going tonight. Find a way to avoid the Drifters. I don't care how you do it, but make it work. Remember, your friend's life depends on it."

Hawk turned and walked away. His nonchalant departure was a chilling sight. How could someone just do what he had done and walk away like it was nothing? Pete's lifeless body lay only a few feet away from where she knelt with Shadow. She felt the cold ground beneath her knees, the gusts of wind biting at her face, but all she could do was focus on the haunting image of Pete's still form.

"Izzy," Matt said, trying to pull her out of her trance.

Forcing herself to move, Izzy stood up and looked at Matt. "Hey, sorry."

"It's okay. You seemed… distant," Matt said.

"Do you blame me? After what we just witnessed?"

"I completely understand. I was just checking on you—wanted to make sure you were okay."

Izzy sighed, attempting to push the pain aside before she responded. "I'm sorry. Yes, I'll be fine. We just need to get out of here."

Matt gestured at his arm, which was still tied to the flagpole. "You're telling me."

Izzy tried to free Matt from the pole as James made his way over to them. "What happened to you? How did you end up here?"

"They just snuck up on us," Matt explained. "Shadow was about to attack them, but I held him back. Didn't need anything happening to him." He looked at Izzy. "You'd probably never forgive me."

"He's a guard dog. He protects the ones he cares about," Izzy said. "I can't be mad at you for my dog trying to protect you."

Matt flashed a small smile before he continued, "So, one of the guys who snuck up on us recognized me from the building we were at earlier, and knew there were more of us. They assumed you guys were inside, trying to find Pete and Audrey."

"That's right," one of the men said as he approached. Izzy recognized him. He was the one who had held Audrey hostage and put a gun to her head back at the facility. "You guys thought you were *so* smart, didn't ya? Trying to sneak in and rescue your friends." He stepped over Pete's body. "If you guys don't want to end up like your dead friend here, you're going to listen to everything I say. Got it?"

Each member of the group nodded in agreement.

"Good." One of the Reavers walked over to Matt and pulled out a knife, cutting the zip ties from his wrist. When he bent down to cut Shadow free, Shadow started to growl. "You want to tell your dog to behave? Or do I have to cut it to show it who's boss?"

"Shadow, no!" Izzy ordered. "Sit."

Shadow obeyed.

The tall man with his shaggy brown hair bent down and freed Shadow. The dog took a few steps and cuddled up against Izzy's legs.

"Thank you," Izzy said.

"One wrong bark from that mutt and I'm putting him down. You understand me? We can't afford to be making noises out there at night. Those Drifters will find us in a heartbeat and we won't see them coming."

"You won't have to worry about him," Izzy reassured the man.

"I hope not," the man said. "Alright guys," he addressed the group, "let's go."

Izzy, Matt, James and Shadow followed the three remaining Reavers.

The first to walk by Izzy was leaner than the head guy. His hair was a sandy brown, kept neatly combed back. He wore a similar jacket to the first guy of the group, but wore a tight black tee-shirt underneath, which seemed to hug his muscular figure.

The next man was the most unassuming of the group. With his wire-rimmed glasses and neatly trimmed beard, he almost looked like a professional rather than a member of the Reavers. But the way he held his weapon, finger poised near the trigger, spoke volumes about his readiness. He was clad in a simple grey sweatshirt, a stark contrast to the other scavengers they'd come across from this group.

The last man was the shortest of the group. His bald head gleamed under the dim light, and a thick beard framed his square jaw. He wore jeans and a ripped jacket.

They followed the men to the gate and exited the prison yard with them. The journey out of the prison yard was a tense one. As Izzy and her group trailed behind the Reavers, their eyes constantly darted to the shadows in the distance. Visibility was challenging in the darkness. During the day, they could at least spot one of the Drifters from a distance, but now they were virtually blind. It was unsettling, knowing that while they were sneaking around in the dark, those creatures could hunt them with ease.

"Hey," James said to the closest man in front of the group, the one wearing the grey sweatshirt and glasses. "What's your name?"

"Why?" he asked.

"So I know what to call you," James asked. "What am I supposed to say if I see something and need to let you know? *'Hey, guy in front?'*"

"Technically, you shouldn't be saying anything," the lead man said.

The one with the grey sweatshirt shook his head. "The name's Dalton. Don't pay much attention to the asshole up front. That's Griggs. Pretty sure you met him already."

"Yes, you did," Griggs said. "Held that beautiful woman close to me. Boy, was she hot. Smelled like roses too."

"You're gross," Izzy said.

Griggs laughed.

Dalton pointed to the short one. "That's Knox." Then he pointed to the man with the ripped jacket. "That's Rourke."

"Introductions over yet?" Griggs said.

"Sorry about him," Dalton said quietly.

"It's fine," James said.

They continued to walk in silence as the sun completely disappeared over the horizon. With little to no lights in the area, the stars lit up the sky. Izzy looked up, wishing she was lying by a fire with her friend Sarah back home. She wished she was anywhere but here.

"You seemed to have a history with Hawk," Dalton said to Izzy. "He seemed familiar with you."

Izzy huffed. "You could say that. I've run into him a few times here and there—he always gives me shit. I saw him the other day. One of his guys knocked me out and threw me in a cage."

"Wait, what?" Matt asked. "You never told me that."

"Didn't feel the need to let others know I was captured," she replied, before turning her attention back to Dalton. "Hawk had a recent scar on his face during our last encounter. Well, more like a cut. Or a scratch. He was always so well kept. It seemed out of place."

Dalton smiled. "Yeah. He had a power grab the other day. Probably around the time he had his interaction with you."

"What do you mean?" Izzy asked.

"The previous leader, Rus, sent him and a few guys on what was essentially a suicide mission."

"A suicide mission?" James repeated.

Dalton nodded. "Rus apparently had no intention of any of them coming back. He sent them into the city to one of their local bases to gather some supplies. But when they got there, everything was cleaned out."

"How do you know someone didn't take the supplies stored there?" James asked.

"Because I was just there the day prior, and there was nothing there," Knox chimed in. "Rus knew it and sent Hawk, anyway. When Hawk came back after the bloodshed that was left after the Drifters attacked, he was furious."

Izzy remembered when the Drifters killed all of Hawk's men the day she was captured by him. Was this the moment Knox was talking about?

Dalton picked up where Knox left off. "He flew into Rus's office and started screaming at him, letting him know the entire crew was dead. Rus didn't seem surprised. It was almost like he expected it would happen."

"When Hawk mentioned about the supplies at the base," Knox said, "I spoke up and said there was nothing there when I went the day before. That's when Hawk knew he'd been set up. He flipped the table Rus was sitting at, and the two of them went at it."

"Why didn't you guys do anything about it?" Matt asked.

"Why would we?" Knox said. "Get between the two of them? No way."

"Yeah, wouldn't want to be on the losing side of that battle," Dalton said. "We defend the wrong guy and suddenly we're on the chopping block. No thank you."

"So, what happened?" Izzy asked.

"Rus went for his gun," Dalton said, "but Hawk was able to disarm him. The two of them threw a few punches before they smashed into one of the windows in the office. Rus grabbed one of the pieces of glass and swung at Hawk, which caught him in the face. Hawk charged at him and knocked the piece of glass free. After they tumbled to the ground, Hawk picked up the glass and stabbed Rus again and again, killing him."

"And now Hawk is the leader of the Reavers. History lesson over," Griggs said.

They approached the city limits and began walking between the large, abandoned skyscrapers. It was dark. The group avoided using flashlights to avoid giving away their position. They kept to the sidewalks, close to the walls of the buildings.

They approached a corner and stopped to peek around it.

"You see anything?" Knox asked.

"Yeah," Griggs said. "I see your mom pole dancing at the end of the block. What the hell do you think I see? It's pitch black, dumbass."

"I thought maybe—" Knox began to say.

Griggs cut him off. "You thought wrong. Now just shut up already." Griggs waved them on. "Let's go."

One by one, they turned the corner and continued down the block.

"We're going the wrong way," Rourke finally spoke up.

They all stopped in the middle of the block.

"What do you mean, we're going the wrong way?" Griggs asked.

"I mean, we're going the wrong way," Rourke repeated. "This building here," he pointed to his left, "is the old First Bank building."

Griggs shrugged his shoulders. "Yeah? And?"

"The abandoned factory is on the other side of the city. We're heading west when we should have been heading east."

"Why the hell didn't you say something then?" Griggs demanded. "Stop it with this quiet shit and speak up!"

"Guys, keep it down," James intervened.

"Shut the hell up," Griggs said. "You don't have a say in the matter." He turned back to Rourke. "So now we're how far away from our destination?"

"Maybe four or five miles," Rourke said.

"Four or five—are you kidding me? We're out in the open here and you're telling me we've been traveling in the wrong direction this whole time?"

"Why don't we just calm down..." Dalton said.

"Don't you start. This dumbass here doesn't know his left from right and now we're sitting ducks," Griggs said.

And then the howling began.

"Shut up," James whispered.

Everyone froze. Eyes quickly darted in all directions, trying to find the direction of the noise.

Izzy could feel her heart pounding in her chest. A Drifter was close by. It was coming their way. And in the dark, they had no idea where it was coming from.

Another noise from the creature. This time it was closer. Its eerie cry echoed through the still night air.

The four Reavers aimed their weapons into the darkness, turning in all directions.

"Where is it?" Dalton asked.

"We need to find shelter," Izzy said. "Now."

The group fell silent.

There was no more howling. No more noises. Had the Drifter gone away?

Izzy looked around but couldn't see anything in the darkness. She placed a hand on Shadow's head. She looked at Matt, who was staring back at her.

A scream.

Everyone turned to see one of the Reavers, Knox, being yanked into the air. His gun fire illuminated his shadow as he attempted to fire at the creature. Its black, slimy skin reflected in the gunfire. Its two giant black eyes were opened wide. It had Knox wrapped in one of its tentacles which extended from its large, black, slimy body. Its second tentacle flowed around Knox's head, crushing it with an audible *crunch*.

The creature let out a primal roar.

"Run!" James yelled.

| **11** |

They scattered like frightened birds, their frantic footsteps thudding against the pavement. The Drifter let out a deafening scream that seemed to vibrate the air surrounding them, making the hairs on Izzy's arm stand on end.

Griggs, Rourke, and Dalton turned back intermittently to fire at the creature. The gunshots rang out, possibly alerting other nearby Drifters. Each bullet seemed to do nothing other than irritate the beast. It just kept coming. It was like throwing pebbles at a mountain.

"Nothing hurts this thing!" Dalton yelled.

"Keep shooting at it!" Griggs shouted.

As the group rounded a corner, one of the creature's grotesque tentacles shot out, snatching Rourke in mid-stride. His terrified scream rang out in the distance.

Izzy turned as she ran and watched as the creature lifted him up and pull him behind the corner, disappearing from sight. His screams and pleas for help were soon cut off. The silence that followed was even more horrifying. It had killed another one of them.

"It's picking us off!" Matt yelled.

"Oh yeah? You think?" Griggs replied.

Suddenly, Rourke's lifeless body was tossed into the street, directly in front of the group, a gruesome obstacle in their path. The Drifter howled as it continued its hunt.

James darted to the right of Rourke's corpse, while Dalton veered left. Izzy instinctively followed James, with Shadow and Griggs close behind her. Matt trailed after Dalton.

James ran towards a building and pushed open its door, waving everyone through.

"Where's the rest of them?" he asked.

"Probably monster food," Griggs said. "Shut the damn door."

James glanced outside, then looked back at Izzy.

"They ran off in another direction," Izzy told him.

Why had Matt run off with Dalton? She wished he was with her instead. She hoped he would be okay.

James slammed the door shut.

"Why'd they run off another way?" he asked.

"Who cares? Let's just move," Griggs said.

"You don't care about one of your own?" Izzy asked.

"I care about saving my own ass and not dyin'. That's what I care about," Griggs said. He aimed his gun at James. "Now let's move."

James held up his hands in defeat and moved away from the door. Griggs waved the gun towards the hallway and James, Izzy, and Shadow followed him.

Shadow growled at Griggs.

"You better get a grip on that dog of yours, or else I'm putting a bullet in him," Griggs said.

"He won't do anything," Izzy replied. "He's protecting me."

"So, what's your plan?" James asked.

"To not die. That sounds like a pretty good plan to me," Griggs said.

A sudden howl sent a jolt through them, making them flinch.

"Yeah, not dying is a good plan," Izzy said, glancing back at the door through which they had entered, making sure the creature hadn't followed them.

The group surged along the hallway and entered a hotel lobby. The room was dark, despite the moonlight shining through the glass front doors. They looked around for a hiding spot in which to wait for the Drifter to leave the area.

Griggs flicked on a flashlight, its beam cutting through the gloom and cast an eerie glow over the dirty furniture and dusty counters. Sparks of dust floated within the beam of the light's path.

"No," Izzy whispered. "Turn it off."

Griggs frowned at her. "Why? I can't see."

"You idiot. Because it'll attract the Drifter," James interjected in a grim tone.

"You better watch your tone with me," Griggs said. "I'm the one with the gun."

"You keep saying that. But you do nothing about it," James said.

Before Griggs could respond, a thunderous crash reverberated throughout the lobby as the Drifter burst through the glass door. Shards of glass flew in all directions, glinting in the moonlight. The creature let out an ear-splitting growl, its monstrous form illuminated by Griggs's flashlight.

It was the first time Izzy had seen one of the creatures up close. Its black slimy skin looked like it was oozing out of itself. Its two large black eyes were locked on them. Its mouth opened wide, almost forming the shape of a triangle. Multiple rows of razor-sharp teeth extended from its mouth. Two long tentacle arms stretched out, appearing twice as long as the length of its body. It hovered by the front of the lobby, staring at them.

Panic surged through Izzy as she turned, sprinting in the opposite direction down the hallway where they had just come from. Griggs threw his flashlight at the creature and started running, too. He spun around after a few steps, attempting to stall the creature with gunfire.

"Stop!" Izzy yelled. "Save your bullets. They don't affect it."

Spotting a stairwell off to the side of the hallway, James pushed open the door and waved Shadow, Izzy, and Griggs inside. Izzy started climbing the steps, but James, in a desperate attempt to slow the creature down, began pushing a large metal toolbox in front of the door. Izzy came back down to help him create a barricade for the door. The two of them pushed desperately, sliding the large and heavy metal toolbox. As Izzy returned to the stairs, loud pounding came from the door. A monstrous howl came from the other side.

"What are you doing?" Izzy yelled at James, who was still standing in front of the toolbox, holding it in place. "Come on!"

James didn't answer. He continued to lean against the toolbox as the creature slammed into the door from the other side. He glanced up at Izzy, a scared, but determined look on his face.

"Go," he ordered. The moment the word left his mouth, a large tentacle smashed through the wall next to him, wrapping around him and the toolbox.

"No!" Izzy yelled.

She watched in horror as James was ripped through the door and into the hallway. The toolbox clattered to the ground, its contents scattering in the stairwell and outside.

Shadow barked furiously. Izzy wanted to run down the stairs and help James, but she knew it would be futile. If she went back, she'd be dead too. With a final glance at the broken wall where James had disappeared, Izzy turned, and she and Shadow sprinted up the stairs after Griggs, their footsteps echoing in the empty stairwell.

Izzy and Shadow finally caught up to Griggs on the fourth floor landing. Seeing him just standing there, as if nothing was wrong, made Izzy's anger bubble over. Her voice echoed around the stairwell as she let loose her pent-up stress and frustration.

"This is all your fault!" she accused him, pushing him. "We're in this mess because of you."

"What the hell are you talking about?" Griggs replied.

Izzy pointed a finger at him. "*You* attacked us at that building and took Audrey. *You* turned on that stupid flashlight that led that Drifter in here. And James died because of *you*." She pushed him again.

Griggs stared at her. His own anger seemed to be brewing. With a swift movement, he grabbed her and shoved her against the wall, his fingers digging into her arms. "Shut up," he growled.

Shadow leapt to her defense, his teeth sinking into Griggs's leg. The sudden attack caused him to release Izzy. His attention was now focused on the dog latched onto him. Seizing the opportunity, Izzy drew back her fist and punched Griggs in the face. He stumbled backwards, falling to the floor.

As he lay sprawled on the landing, Griggs managed to kick Shadow off of him. Instantly, the dog yelped, then rushed to attack again. As Griggs tried to shake the dog loose, he aimed his gun at Izzy.

"Get your dog off me now!" he yelled.

She contemplated ignoring his command, but she didn't want to end this fight by getting shot. She clenched her jaw, knowing she was stuck and he had the upper hand.

"Shadow, stop!" Izzy commanded. Shadow let go and backed up slowly. He growled, baring his teeth.

"Goddammed dog," Griggs said, rubbing his injured leg. He winced as he touched Shadow's bite marks. He pointed to Izzy. "That was your freebie," he sneered as he got to his feet slowly. "Next time, I'll shoot both of you."

Izzy had a feeling it was an empty threat, but she didn't want to push her luck. She knew Griggs wouldn't survive on his own. He needed her.

"So, what's your plan?" Izzy asked.

"My plan?" Griggs asked.

"You're the one with the gun. You're the one in charge here," she said sarcastically. "Unless you would like to hear *my* plan..."

"No, I don't want to hear *your* plan," he said, matching her sarcasm. "I already told you my plan earlier—not to die. Right now, we're going to wait until the sun comes up and then go gather the supplies."

"What?" Izzy asked, confused. "Wait here?"

"Umm... yeah? You want to get killed by that thing downstairs? Or outside. Or wherever it is now."

"No, I don't. But I would like to find my friend who ran off with one of your people."

"Screw them. They're on their own."

"Do you seriously only care about yourself?" Izzy snapped, her patience wearing thin.

"Yeah, I care about surviving. And they made their own choice going wherever they went," Griggs said. "That's their problem, not mine."

"You're such an asshole, you know that?"

"Yeah? Well, you're kinda bitchy yourself, *you know that?*" Griggs said, imitating her.

A startling howl distracted. Griggs aimed his gun down the dark staircase. "W-where is it?" he stuttered.

"Shut up, you big baby. It sounded like it was coming from outside," Izzy said. She opened the stairwell door and headed into the hallway of the fourth floor, then jogged to the window at the end of the hall and looked outside. Her eyes darted from one side of the street to the other, looking for any signs of movement. She heard Griggs come running up beside her. His heavy footsteps made him an easy target to listen for.

"Never snuck up on someone before, have you?" Izzy said.

"Huh?" he asked, clearly confused.

"You run like an elephant. I heard you all the way down the hallway."

Griggs huffed. "Whatever. Your dog bit my leg. I'm walking heavily because I'm limping."

"Aww, poor baby."

"Shut up. You see anything?"

"There!" Izzy said, pointing out the window. A quick flash of black was zooming down the moonlit street. "It's heading away from here."

Griggs sighed. "Good." He turned and leaned against the wall behind him and slowly slid down to a sitting position. "Now we know we'll be safe here for the night."

"Fine. Your weak ass can stay here," Izzy said. "I'm going to find the only person I have left on this trip."

He aimed his gun at her. "You're going to stay here until morning."

She stared at him. What would he have to gain by killing her? Nothing. Griggs needed her—especially because of that limp of his. He wouldn't last on his own. He wouldn't pull the trigger.

At least, Izzy hoped he wouldn't.

"No, I'm not," she told him. "I'm leaving. Come on, Shadow." They walked side by side towards the door leading to the stairs.

"Stop! I'll shoot!" Griggs yelled.

"No, you won't," Izzy said, and reached for the handle.

"Wait! Wait!" Griggs said. Izzy turned and watched as he used his rifle as a makeshift crutch to help push himself to a standing position. "I'm coming too." He limped towards her.

"Oh, so now you're joining me? I thought you wanted to shoot me?" She couldn't resist adding sarcasm to her tone.

Ignoring her comment, Griggs limped past her and began making his way down the stairs, slowly taking them one at a time. Izzy and Shadow brushed past him and descended to the first floor. The gaping hole in the wall and the missing door were grim reminders of James bring ripped through it.

Izzy felt a lump in her throat as she carefully navigated through the debris. She braced herself for the sight of her friend's lifeless body, possibly torn apart and bloodied. But, to her surprise, there was nothing. No body, no blood, just remnants of the destruction she had witnessed.

"What's up?" Griggs asked as he finally made his way to the first floor.

She waved at the debris in front of them. "James is gone. There's no body."

"Maybe the Drifter ate him." Griggs's voice was flat and emotionless. "Or dragged him somewhere else. I mean, that thing threw Rourke half a block. Maybe his body is just somewhere else."

Izzy hoped she didn't find him. She didn't want to remember him as lifeless. She also didn't want to remember him being pulled through the wall by a giant tentacle.

They walked down the hallway and exited the hotel the same way they had entered. Izzy looked across the street, making sure the Drifter wasn't anywhere to be found. They made their way onto the street where Rourke's lifeless body laid.

"Over there." Izzy pointed in the direction Matt and Dalton had fled. "That's the last place I saw them."

"You want to tell me again *why* we're going after them when we could be safe inside that hotel?" Griggs asked.

"Because Matt is the *only* one I have left here," Izzy responded harshly. "And I *refuse* to let another one of my friends die out here. Maybe you're so selfish you can't comprehend that, but I *will* find my friend—with or without your help." She turned and began to walk towards where she had last seen Matt.

"See? There's that bitchiness again," Griggs said.

She ignored the comment and continued walking, letting him fall behind due to his injured leg. It brought a smile to her face knowing that Shadow had been the cause.

As Izzy stepped into the building, her eyes darted around the dark interior. It was an old, abandoned restaurant, its once-bustling atmosphere now replaced by dust and decay. Chairs were upturned and tables strewn haphazardly around the room, but there were no signs of Matt and Dalton.

Griggs limped through the door after her. "Are they here?" he asked, his voice echoing off the peeling walls.

"No," Izzy responded. "We need to keep looking."

Griggs let out a grunt of frustration, but said nothing more. Instead, he limped around the restaurant before sitting down in a booth. Izzy watched him for a moment before breaking the silence.

"Why are you working with Hawk, anyway?" she asked.

He let out a heavy sigh and slouched over the table, folding his arms and resting his head on them. "I'm not talking about this with you."

"Look," Izzy said, refusing to let it go. "If we're going to be stuck together, then we're going to talk. I'm not walking around in awkward silence. And I want to know why you're working with that *monster*."

Griggs raised his head and leaned back against the red cushions of the booth. "You're unbelievable," he grumbled. He shook his head in frustration. "The prison... it's safe. There's shelter, protection, food."

"And you're okay with what you have to do in return for him?" Izzy asked. "Kidnapping. Stealing. Killing."

He shrugged. "So what if I have to do some bad things? At least I'm alive. Better than the alternative."

Izzy could barely comprehend his words. The idea of only thinking about oneself was alien to her. She couldn't live like that, *wouldn't* live like that. She had friends back at camp whom she cared about and who cared for her. She had a friend out here somewhere. She couldn't just give up on them.

A noise from the kitchen startled them—it sounded like a utensil of some kind dropping on the floor. Shadow let out a shallow growl and lowered himself closer to the ground, staring intently at the door leading to the restaurant's kitchen. Izzy followed his gaze just in time to see a face appear in the small window in the door.

Her muscles tensed up as she watched the door swing open, revealing four men. They were rugged, with evil smiles. In their hands, they held an assortment of weapons—bats and knives. They waved them around as they stepped out onto the restaurant floor.

Griggs slid out of the booth and held up his gun, pointing it between the four men. Izzy found herself taking a step closer to

Griggs. She felt weird doing it, but he was the one with the gun, after all.

"What do we have here?" one of the men said. He was wielding a knife and sported a plaid red and black button-up shirt.

"Looks like a disabled dude and one hot chick," another one of them said, spinning a baseball bat in his hands. Chains on his black jacket jingled as he moved around.

"We don't want any trouble," Izzy said. "We're just looking for our friends."

"We can be your friends. We're all friendly," the man in the plaid shirt said, with a creepy smile.

Shadow's growl grew louder as the men slowly approached Izzy and Griggs.

"Back up," Griggs said. "I'll shoot." Izzy thought about all the times he'd used that threat. She hadn't really believed him, but then again, he hadn't been in a situation like this. She hoped he'd pull the trigger if need be. She wished she had her own gun.

"What? Come on..." the man in the black jacket said. "We can all be friends. Especially *you.*"

He stared at Izzy, his eyes moving up and down her body. The uncomfortable sense of knowing what he was thinking about made her skin crawl. She had to get out of here, fast.

"We need to go," she whispered to Griggs. He nodded his head.

"Okay, guys. Here's how it's going to go," he said. "We're going to leave now, and you guys can just pretend we were never here. Sound fair?"

"Nope," the man with the plaid shirt said. "You ain't leaving."

The man with the bat stepped closer, slamming his weapon into the palm of his hands.

Griggs aimed his weapon at him. "One more step and I'll shoot you."

The man holding the bat stopped walking. He stared at Griggs with a giant smile on his face. "It ain't *my* bat you have to worry about."

"What the hell does that—"

Griggs words were cut short as a baseball bat connected with the back of his head with a sickening *thud.* He crumpled to the ground, his rifle clattering onto the floor beside him. The room filled with the men's cruel laughter.

Before Izzy could react, firm hands gripped her arms from behind. She struggled, pulling and twisting, but the grip only tightened. Out of the corner of her eye, she saw one of the men scoop up Shadow and instantly disappear into the kitchen, another man trailing behind them. Shadow's barking became fainter. Izzy heard a door slam shut, and she could barely hear the barking anymore. Had they locked him inside the freezer?

The men made lewd comments about Izzy, their leering faces twisted in ugly anticipation. A wave of revulsion washed over her as they spoke about taking her back to their hideout. She knew what that meant. She gritted her teeth, trying to block out their words.

Two men dragged her through the restaurant. She kicked and tugged, trying to free herself from their grip, but it was no use.

"Griggs!" Izzy screamed, her voice full of fear and desperation. "Get up! Help!"

Her pleas echoed through the abandoned restaurant, bouncing off the grimy walls and empty tables. But there was no response from Griggs. His body lay motionless on the dusty floor. She was dragged away, further from Griggs, further from Shadow, towards an unknown fate.

"Griggs! Help me!" Izzy screamed one more time, before losing sight of him and being dragged out into the streets.

| 13 |

The men's laughter filled the air as they dragged Izzy away, their crude comments leaving no doubt about their intentions. Each word made her stomach feel nauseous, filling her with dread and disgust. She screamed a desperate plea for help, her voice echoing around the empty streets.

Suddenly, one of the men stepped in front of her, pulling out a knife and pressing it against her throat.

"Shut the hell up!" he commanded. "We don't need that Drifter coming back. You scream again, I'll cut out your tongue." He stuck out his own tongue and placed the knife on it for a moment. "We don't need your tongue to have fun with you." He placed the knife back against her neck. "Do you understand?"

Izzy felt utterly powerless. A sense of vulnerability overwhelmed her, silencing her. She could feel the cold steel against her skin, the man's hot breath on her face. She had no choice but to comply.

"Yes, I understand," she said.

Just as she was losing hope, a gunshot rang out. One of the men fell, a bullet hole in his head. Izzy turned just in time to see Griggs, his face contorted with rage, firing his rifle at the remaining men. Two more fell, their bodies hitting the street with dull thuds.

Two men scrambled for cover while one of them grabbed Izzy, using her as a human shield. "Drop the gun or I'll kill her!" he yelled, his voice trembling.

Griggs' response was emotionless. "Go ahead, kill her. She means nothing to me.

Izzy's heart pounded in her chest. She could feel the man's grip tighten around her, his body shaking with fear. She could smell his sweat, hear his ragged breathing. He was scared. And that gave her an idea.

"I'm serious! I'll kill her!" the man yelled.

"Go for it," Griggs said. "What's stopping you?"

The man's grip loosened ever so slightly, and Izzy took advantage of it. Summoning all her strength, she raised her heel and stomped on the man's foot. He let out a grunt of pain, loosening his grip even more. Seizing the opportunity, Izzy kicked backwards, hitting him square in the groin. He then released her completely, doubling over in pain.

With a burst of adrenaline, Izzy sprinted away from him, giving Griggs the clear shot he needed. Another few gunshots rang out behind her. Without turning around, she knew Griggs had killed the man who had held her hostage.

She ran towards Griggs and stood beside him. The two remaining men had taken cover—one behind a rusty dumpster and the other crouched behind an abandoned car in the middle of the road.

"Come out and let's end this quickly," Griggs said. The men remained hidden, their voices echoing back in defiance.

"Go to hell!" one of them said.

Without another word, Griggs fired his rifle at the car. Multiple bullets hit the metal with loud bangs, causing the man behind it to jump up in surprise. He tried to make a run for it, but panicked, and Griggs took aim. Another three gunshots rang out, followed by the thud of a body hitting the ground.

"One left," Griggs declared, his gaze now fixed on the dumpster.

The last man finally stood up, his hands raised in surrender. "Look man, I give up. Don't shoot me." His voice was trembling with fear.

Griggs kept his rifle trained on him. "I don't accept your surrender," he told him. "You swung a bat at my head. And I don't take kindly to people attempting to hurt or kill me."

"I didn't know what they were going to do!" the man said.

"I don't care. It's not my problem," Griggs told him.

With a quick motion, the man went to throw his knife at Griggs, who simply sidestepped it. The knife bounced off the street somewhere behind him.

"You people are so stupid—bringing a knife to a gunfight." Griggs pulled the trigger. The man grabbed his chest and fell to the ground.

Griggs limped over to the man, who was barely breathing, and reached into the man's pockets.

"What are you doing?" Izzy asked.

"Looking for whatever they have that we can use," Griggs said.

He made his way over to another of the men on the ground and grabbed the knife he had held in his hand, then offered it to Izzy. "Here. Clearly, you need this."

Izzy was shocked. First, this man was holding a gun at her, and now he was handing her a knife for protection.

She took the knife and put it in her cargo pants pocket.

He just saved my life.

He's still your enemy, though.

Shadow!

Izzy's eyes widened. She raced back to the restaurant and pushed through the back door of the restaurant. She could hear barking from behind the kitchen door. She pushed through the door and into the kitchen. Immediately, she pinpointed where the barking was coming from—a giant steel door in the far corner.

She rushed over to it and opened it up. Shadow came rushing out, knocking Izzy to her knees, then jumped into her arms. He began licking her face.

"I got you," she told him. "You're safe now."

Griggs had wandered into the kitchen and stood by the entrance. Izzy pushed Shadow off of her and stood up.

"Thank you," she said, not believing the words she just heard leaving her mouth. Thanking *him*? Griggs? What was happening here?

"For what?" Griggs asked.

"Saving my life."

"Your life wasn't in danger."

Izzy huffed. "What do you mean, my life wasn't in danger? Those guys were dragging me away with them. They kidnapped me."

"Yeah—to rape you. Not to kill you."

Izzy rolled her eyes. "Regardless, thank you."

"I didn't do it for you," Griggs said. "They swung a bat at my head." He reached behind his head and winced as he touched it. When he brought his hand back around, it was stained with blood. "I did it because they deserved it for attacking me."

"It really is all about you, isn't it?" she asked.

"I told you that earlier. Whatever it takes to survive." He swung the strap of his rifle over his shoulder. His gait was uneven, his limp from Shadow's bite still bothering him. He moved out of the kitchen and back into the restaurant.

"Pretty sure my plan wouldn't have included shooting six men and getting smacked in the head with a baseball bat," he said. "We'd be sitting safely and quietly inside a dark hotel right about now. But *oh no*, we just *had* to go look for your friend." The sarcasm in his voice was obvious, and Izzy could practically feel his mocking gaze on her.

Izzy rolled her eyes. Griggs's selfishness was almost as chilling as the cool breeze she felt as she stepped back outside onto the deserted street. He had rescued her, yes, but by his own admission, he had done so for himself. She wasn't sure if she fully believed him, yet there was a part of her that was grateful that he had saved her, and that she was alive.

Griggs was right, though, to an extent. Izzy's insistence on finding Matt had led them into this mess. Yet she couldn't shake off her gnawing worry for her friend. The thought of leaving Matt behind was unbearable. And the memory of the Drifter that had attacked James gave her a sense of unease. She hoped Matt hadn't had the same fate.

Izzy shook her head, trying to clear her mind of the conflicting thoughts. She needed to focus on the task at hand—finding Matt. She and Shadow joined Griggs on the street.

"Where are we going?" Izzy asked, catching up with Griggs.

"To that building, to gather our supplies," Griggs responded.

"But we're supposed to find Matt," Izzy said.

"Look, we tried your way already. Now it's my turn. We're continuing to that building. And maybe your friend will be there. That's where I'd go to meet up with someone I lost in my group."

He gave her hope. Why was he being so nice all of the sudden? Izzy didn't let her guard down that easily, though. She decided to go along with it, at least for now. And he had a point—maybe she would find Matt there—at least she hoped.

| 14 |

The silence hung between them. Each step they took sounded like loud thuds in the quiet streets. Finally, Griggs put an end to the silence. "You wanted to talk earlier and not walk in awkward silence. Now you're silent. What gives?"

Izzy glanced at him, her brows furrowed in thought. "I'm trying to figure you out," she admitted.

Griggs laughed. "Oh, don't hurt that pretty little head of yours. You'll be trying for a long time and not get anywhere. Psychologists couldn't figure it out back in the day."

"But you could have just left me back there," Izzy said. "Instead, you rescued me."

"I told you, they attacked me. It was payback for this awful headache they gave me," Griggs said.

Izzy continued asking Griggs questions because she just couldn't understand the concept of being only out for oneself. It was foreign to her. They bickered back and forth until they were approaching the building they were looking for. Izzy recognized the large air duct on the roof that she had climbed into and fallen through just days ago.

"Looks familiar," Griggs said.

"Yeah, I bet it does," Izzy said. "You took Audrey from us here."

Griggs smiled. "Yeah. Yeah, I did. But hey—the past is behind us, right?"

Izzy's face flushed. Her lips curled in disgust. "No! The past is not behind us. You may have saved my life. And I'm grateful for that. But you are the reason we are in this mess right now. It started when you walked inside that building there and took my friend, our weapons, and our supplies." She curled her hands into fists. "You don't know how badly I want to hit you right now." She reached into her pocket and grabbed the knife that he had given her. "Better yet, maybe I should just use this instead."

Griggs leaned closer to her, as if trying to tempt her. "But you won't." He smiled and pulled away.

Izzy stood motionless as he limped away from her. She held back screams of frustration. He had called her bluff just as she called his earlier. As much as she wanted to use that knife on him, she knew she couldn't. Her hatred for someone didn't mean he deserved to die. Plus, he had saved her life. As much as she didn't enjoy having Griggs around, he was a benefit.

In defeat, Izzy put the knife back in her pocket and caught up to Griggs. As they approached the building, a surge of energy raced through her veins. The thought of finding Matt inside excited her. She was praying he was there.

Griggs swung his rifle around as he got ready to enter the building. He looked at Izzy. "I'll open the door and you can go check inside."

"Or how about *I* open the door and *you* check inside, since you're the one with the gun," Izzy told him.

Griggs rolled his eyes. "Such a girl. Are you ready?"

Izzy nodded. She grabbed the handle and pulled open the door. It creaked loudly on its hinges. Griggs entered and aimed his gun in all directions. Izzy and Shadow followed him inside.

"See anything?" she asked.

Griggs shook his head and lowered his rifle.

The sudden sound of a gun cocking made Izzy jump. Griggs reacted instantly, raising his weapon again in defense. He swung around, trying to find the source of the noise.

"Izzy?" a voice said.

Izzy instantly found the source of the noise. "Matt!"

They both stood in silence for a split second before they ran towards each other. Her heart was bursting with joy. She had found him. They embraced, their bodies colliding with a force that nearly knocked her off her feet. Matt picked her up in an enormous bear hug.

Finally, they released each other. Shadow, eager to say hi to Matt, nudged his way in between them, his tail wagging furiously. Matt smiled, kneeling to give the dog the affection he craved. Shadow responded by jumping on Matt, his front paws on his shoulders, and licked his face.

"Okay, buddy. I missed you too," Matt said, in between licks. He gave Shadow a small shove to get him off of him. Then Matt stood up, looking around. His gaze landed on Griggs.

"Where's James?" he asked in a quiet voice.

Izzy felt a weight press down on her chest her at the mention of James's name. She swallowed hard, trying to keep her emotions in check. Matt's face fell as he saw her reaction.

"He didn't make it, did he?" he asked.

Izzy shook her head. "The Drifter followed us inside the hotel. James tried to block the door but... it took him."

He wrapped his arms around her once again. "I'm sorry you had to go through that. I should have been there."

"It's fine," Izzy told him. "It was just an awful experience."

"I can only imagine," he said.

She pulled away. "You don't understand. Watching him be ripped through the wall like that... it was terrifying."

"Those things can be terrifying," Matt said.

"That's not even all that happened," Izzy said. "I was kidnapped, too."

"By Griggs?" Matt asked.

Izzy shook her head. She explained how she had been kidnapped by some men, and how Griggs was attacked, but had come to rescue her. Matt's expression changed as she spoke, a hint of jealousy flashing in his eyes. His eyes narrowed as he glanced at Griggs, who was engaged in conversation with Dalton.

"I don't trust him. I should have been there for you," Matt said, a hint of resentment in his voice. "I'm glad you're okay, though." His gaze was still fixed on Dalton and Griggs. He pulled Izzy further aside, out of sight of the two of them. "We need to talk."

"What's going on, Matt?" Izzy asked.

"Dalton and I had a lot to talk about on our way here. He's not too fond of Griggs."

Izzy peeked back at Griggs and Dalton. "They look like they're friends to me."

"Dalton said the guy is *only* out for himself. He doesn't give a shit about anyone else. The only reason he's in Hawk's group is because he's a survivor—he'll do whatever it takes."

Izzy contemplated Matt's words. They made sense. Griggs was out for himself—he had even admitted that to her earlier. Nothing Matt said surprised her.

"I'm aware of who Griggs is," Izzy said. "He basically admitted this all to me earlier."

"But you said he saved you," Matt said.

Izzy shrugged. "He said it was because they attacked him first, and it was payback for hitting him with a bat."

Matt checked on Dalton and Griggs, then glanced back at Izzy. "Did you say anything to Griggs about our camp?" he asked urgently.

Izzy raised an eyebrow. "No. Why?"

"Good." Relief fell upon his face. "Because Dalton said his job here is to get us to reveal where our camp is. He said Hawk will make Griggs his number two guy if he can get all these supplies for him, and get us to bring him back to our camp."

"Why our camp?" Izzy whispered.

"Why *not* our camp?" Matt said. "We have supplies, food, people. What's stopping Hawk from just sending all his people with weapons to take us all out?"

As the gravity of the situation settled upon her, Izzy could only nod, her mind reeling with this new information. She thought about everyone back at camp. She thought of her friend, Sarah, who wouldn't be able to fight back against these kinds of people. They had weapons, and a lot of them. And they were ruthless, based on what she had experienced with Hawk earlier and with Griggs just a few hours ago.

"Hey, what are you guys doing over here?" Griggs asked.

"Just talking," Matt replied.

"Okay, well, you can talk and pack at the same time." He tossed one of the empty bags at Matt and another at Izzy. "Get moving."

Izzy and Matt busied themselves with packing up the supplies. Canned goods, medical supplies, anything that seemed essential were placed inside their bag. Dalton and Griggs packed up the drugs that remained inside the building. *This is the expensive stuff* Izzy and Matt were told.

Izzy opened one of the plastic containers of pre-packaged chicken nuggets and took a whiff of its scent. Hunger consumed her. Her stomach grumbled at the sight and smell of the chicken. Shadow sat by her feet and started whining.

"I know, I know—you're hungry," Izzy said. She bent down and dumped a few nuggets onto the floor. "Here you go. Eat up."

"What are you doing?" Griggs asked.

Izzy stood up and tossed the empty sleeve onto a nearby desk. "I'm feeding my dog. Is that okay with you?"

Griggs huffed. "Just that one. I don't need you wasting my food on your dog."

"*Your food?*" Izzy said.

"Did I stutter?"

"No. But I can clearly see where you get your asshole personality from," Izzy said, remembering Hawk claiming everything as his.

"You know, it was your dog who was the one who injured me to begin with. You're lucky I'm allowing you to get away with that one can." Griggs limped away and left Shadow to eat in peace—which didn't last long, as by the time Griggs left, Shadow had slurped up everything that Izzy had given him.

"Hungry, huh?" Izzy said, petting his head.

"I'm packed up here," Matt said. He dumped his heavy backpack on the desk. "How's everything going here?"

"Oh, just peachy," Izzy said.

"You guys ready?" Dalton asked, walking by Matt. "Griggs is ready to leave. Grab your stuff and let's go."

Izzy zipped up the backpack containing supplies and tossed it onto her shoulder. She followed Matt to the front door, where Griggs was waiting.

"I see your dog is done *eating*," Griggs said.

Izzy ignored the comment. "Let's just go."

Griggs held up his hand. "Not just yet. Need something answered first."

"What's that?" Izzy asked.

"How far is your camp from here?" he asked. "I mean, it can't be that far from here, right?"

"Why would I tell you where our camp is?" Izzy asked.

"Because we're all tired," Griggs said. "We need a safe place to rest. I haven't slept in over twenty-four hours. I'm sure you guys haven't either."

"I'm fine," Izzy said, masking her tiredness with defiance. She glanced at Matt. "You tired?"

Matt shook his head.

"See? We're fine. We just want to get this trip over with and get our friend back," Izzy said.

Griggs smiled. "I'll let you in on a little something. First, a question—do you have a doctor at your camp?"

"Yeah, why?" she asked warily.

Griggs rolled up his pants leg. "You see this wound here? You know, the one caused by that mutt of yours—"

"Shadow," Izzy interrupted.

"Whatever. Anyway, I would like to get it bandaged up and treated before it becomes infected," Griggs said.

"*If* it becomes infected," Izzy said, squinting her eyes at the wound. "Doesn't look that bad anyway."

"I'm sorry. Who's the one with a giant bite mark on their leg? Oh, that's right, me. And I don't think you're a doctor either, so I suggest you keep your medical recommendations to yourself."

Izzy shook her head. "Can't you just get treated back at your camp instead?"

"I have a reputation there," Griggs said. "And if I were to go back to camp injured, it wouldn't be a good look."

"People get injured, so what?" Matt said.

"Can't show weakness around some of those people. So, that means we're going to your camp to get patched up." Griggs opened the door and held it open. "Lead the way."

"No," Izzy said.

He shut the door. "No? I'm sorry. I don't think you remember who's in charge here." He raised his gun and aimed it at Matt. "Either we go to your camp, or he dies. Don't forget, it's *your* fault we're in this position anyway. It was *your* dog who attacked me."

"Because you attacked me!" Izzy shouted back at him.

"Griggs attacked you?" Matt asked.

"Wasn't talking to you," Griggs said. "And you," he addressed Izzy, "if I recall correctly, started it by pushing me and blaming me for everything. So, again, we're in this situation because of you."

"And again, I blame you," Izzy said. "Remember, *you* took Audrey. *You* turned on the flashlight that brought the Drifter to us, which killed James."

"Okay, look, there's clearly enough blame to pass around for the both of us," Griggs said. "But for now, this wound is *your* fault and we're going to your camp."

He kept the gun trained on Matt. Izzy couldn't risk Matt's life anymore than she already had by arguing with Griggs. She knew human life wasn't a concern for him, based on the way he had treated those people earlier—killing them with such ease. She had to protect Matt's life now. Maybe there was something she could do back at camp. After all, it was just Griggs and Dalton against a camp full of her friends. At least at the camp, they had numbers on their side.

"Fine," she agreed, her voice barely above a whisper. She saw the triumphant look in Griggs's eyes and felt a surge of anger. But she pushed it aside. Now was not the time.

They gathered their belongings and left, heading towards Izzy and Matt's camp. The journey ahead was uncertain, but Izzy knew one thing—she would do whatever it took to protect her friends.

| 15 |

The building was behind them now, a grim silhouette against the early morning orange sky. Izzy led the way, guiding the group towards the camp. Matt was trying to keep the mood light, tossing a stick for Shadow to fetch.

"So, what's your plan, Griggs?" Izzy finally asked. She looked at him, her gaze steady despite the anxiety gnawing at her. "This is my camp. My people. They have weapons too. What's stopping me from ratting you out when we get there?"

Griggs didn't miss a beat. "You haven't forgotten about your friend back at camp, have you? Audrey?"

"What about her?"

"If anything happens to me or Dalton, Hawk will kill Audrey," Griggs said. "Before we left, that was the arrangement that was made."

"And what if you guys had been killed by that Drifter earlier? What about those other scavengers?" Izzy asked.

Griggs shrugged. "Didn't think that far ahead. I guess Hawk thought we'd be fine because you guys knew we had one of your friends held hostage back at our camp."

"So if you guys didn't return, regardless of what happened… he'd kill her anyway?" Izzy asked.

"The price you pay having to work with a madman like Hawk," Griggs said.

His words did little to comfort her. She felt like a traitor, leading these men to her camp. But she didn't have a choice.

Griggs fell back to speak with Matt. Izzy moved closer to Dalton. She asked him, "Are you okay with this plan?"

"Just do what he says," Dalton replied. "We all want something here. I don't want to be here any more than you want me here. Let's just get this over with so we can all get out of this mess."

Izzy couldn't shake her feeling of unease. She had to protect Audrey. She had to protect her friends at the camp. The weight of her decision weighed heavily on her, but she pushed forward.

* * *

As they made their way up the hill, the large watchtower of the camp appeared ahead.

Griggs moved next to Izzy. "Don't forget, make sure you're convincing. Be a good liar. We're here to rest and for medical attention. Remember, your friend's life depends on this going right."

"And what if they find out who you are when you're here?" she asked. "What happens then? I mean, we can get a group together to go after Audrey before you get back to your camp to warn anyone."

"Maybe I'll just kill you then," Griggs said.

"That'll be suicide," she told him. "They'll kill you too."

"Probably. But you'll be dead. And I'll take a few others out with me before I go down. Do you really want that?"

Izzy wanted to avoid the violence at all costs. If all he wanted was medical attention and then they'd leave, maybe following along was the best option for now.

"No killing anyone," Izzy said.

"Good," Griggs said.

As they approached, one of the guards greeted them.

"Can I speak to Jason?" Izzy asked him.

"Sure, Izzy," the guard said. "I'll get him for you." He nodded, glanced at the two unfamiliar people she had with him, then walked off.

The group stood in silence, looking around.

"Nice place," Dalton said.

"Izzy?" said a familiar voice. Turning, Izzy saw Sarah sprinting towards her.

"Sarah!" Izzy managed to say, before they crashed into each others arms, holding on tightly.

Shadow barked excitedly and his tail began to wag furiously. Izzy released her grip on Sarah and pulled away. Sarah bent down to hug Shadow. Her smile didn't fade even as he licked her face. "Okay, Shadow," she said. "I missed you too."

Sarah stood back up, and Izzy noticed her gaze landing on Griggs and Dalton. "Who are these guys?" she asked, her brow furrowing. Izzy felt a lump form in her throat as she introduced them, hating the lie that slipped so easily from her lips.

"Where's everyone else?" Sarah's asked.

The sudden image of James's face as he was pulled through the wall by that long, black tentacle flashed through her mind. She forced herself to keep her composure.

"They're helping some other people we found. Griggs needed medical attention, so we brought him back here to get him some help," Izzy told her. She wanted to tell Sarah everything, to confide in her, but she couldn't. Not when Audrey's life was at risk.

As Jason approached, Izzy quickly ended the conversation with Sarah. "We'll catch up later, okay?" she promised, giving her friend a reassuring smile. "Can you take Shadow for me? There's a few things I have to do."

"Of course!" Sarah said, her face lighting up with excitement. "Come on, Shadow! Let's go!" The two of them ran off into the camp together.

As she turned to face Jason, Izzy hoped she was making the right choice—lying to keep her friend safe.

"Welcome back Izzy," Jason said. "And Matt," he added, nodding to him. "Where is the rest of your group?"

"We ran into another group and this man needed medical attention," Izzy said. "We brought him back here while the rest of the group stayed behind."

Jason raised one eyebrow. "Why did they need to stay behind? Are there more people injured?"

Izzy had to improvise. She had known Jason would ask questions, but she had hoped the simple lie would do.

"We—" she began, before Griggs cut her off.

"My group ran into a Drifter the other day," Griggs said. "It's been hunting us. Your group saved me, but not before I was almost taken out by it. Your girl here distracted it so I could get away—unfortunately, not before I was injured by it."

A small smile appeared on Jason's face. "Looks like you were lucky my team was there to help. But before I take you gentlemen any further, I need to ask for your weapons."

Izzy noticed Griggs and Dalton's look at each other.

"Don't worry," Dalton said. "We mean no harm."

"I understand," Jason said. "But you are guests in our home. We don't know you. You can get them back when you leave."

Griggs shot Izzy a concerned look. She gave him a slight nod, letting him know it would be okay. Hopefully Jason hadn't noticed.

"Alright," Griggs said. He took the strap off his shoulder and handed Jason the rifle. Dalton did the same.

Jason placed both of the weapons over his shoulder. "Thank you both for understanding." He put out a hand in a gesture of welcome. "This way. I'll bring you to our doctor so she can take a look at your wound."

"Thank you," Griggs said.

Jason escorted Griggs and Dalton to the camp medic, a few yards away. As he opened the door to let them inside, Griggs shot Izzy a murderous look, a silent reminder of their agreement, before he disappeared inside the building.

"Let's go talk, shall we?" Jason said to Izzy and Matt. He ushered them through the camp and into his office. He shut the door behind them and placed the weapons on a small table by the door.

Izzy and Matt stood before Jason's desk. Jason stepped past them and sank into his chair behind his desk, studying Izzy and Matt.

"Where is the rest of the team?" he asked, his voice quiet but firm. "Audrey, James, Pete—why aren't they with you?"

Izzy opened her mouth to repeat the lie, but Jason cut her off. "Don't," he said, his eyes piercing through her. "I can see it in your eyes. You're hiding something." He turned to Matt and asked him the same question: "Where is the rest of the team?"

Matt and Izzy locked eyes, a silent conversation passing between them. Izzy's resolve crumbled as a single tear escaped from her eye.

"Talk to me!" Jason exclaimed. "I can't help you if you won't tell me what's going on."

Izzy couldn't bear the weight of the lie any longer. Jason deserved to know. Even if she didn't see eye to eye with him on most things, he deserved to know. Audrey's safety was at risk. Maybe Jason would be able to help. He had Griggs and Dalton's weapons, so she and everyone at the camp would be safe, at least for now. And at this point, he knew something was already going on.

She took a deep breath and began to speak. The words tumbled out, almost too fast for Jason to follow. She told him everything—the Reavers attacking them at the building, the kidnapping of Audrey, Pete's murder at Hawk's hands, the Drifter that had killed James and two of the Reavers' own team.

"And these two men that are here now, they're part of this group?" Jason asked.

Izzy nodded. "The injured one—he was the one who took Audrey."

Jason's face turned a fiery red, and his eyes blazed with fury. "How could you let them into our camp?" he yelled, slamming his fists on the table. "We're all in danger now! What if more of them start showing up?"

"I didn't have a choice!" Izzy shot back, her voice trembling. "They would have killed Matt if we didn't do what they asked. I couldn't risk losing anyone else. We already lost so much."

Jason rose from his chair. "I'm going to kill them," he growled as he moved towards the door.

"No!" Izzy and Matt shouted in unison, rushing to block his path.

"They still have Audrey," Matt said.

"Griggs said if they don't return to their camp, they'll kill her," Izzy told him.

Jason halted. He closed his eyes for a moment before opening them back up. Slowly, he released the tension in his face and exhaled. He returned to his chair and sat down, rubbing his temples.

"We need a plan," he finally said, his voice heavy with resignation. "Can we try to rescue Audrey from their camp? You guys know where it's located, right?"

Matt shook his head. "We tried that already. We were all caught, which got us into this mess."

"Can we just take those two guys hostage and trade them for Audrey?" Jason suggested.

"I don't know if you've met Hawk or not, but he wouldn't care," Izzy said. "He'd probably sacrifice them to prove a point."

"Why don't we just attack their camp?" Matt asked.

"Out of the question," Jason said. "We don't want to start a war. We lost two people already, and a third is held hostage. We don't need any more loss of life."

"So, what do we do?" Izzy asked.

"Why don't we just return to the camp with all the stuff Hawk asked for and maybe he'll let Audrey go," Matt said.

"You don't know Hawk like I do," Izzy said. "He'll just use her as leverage for something else he wants. He may not let her go."

Jason sighed and shrugged his shoulders. "I guess there really isn't much we can do. I think our safest option is to just let this play out."

"Let this play out?" Izzy exclaimed. "How can you say that? These people are the cause of everything wrong that has happened over the last day or so. They're the cause of the deaths of two of our friends."

"Izzy, we don't have another choice right now," Jason told her. "I'm just as angry as you. Moments ago, I wanted to walk out there and put their heads through a window, remember? I understand your frustration, but we need to try to get Audrey back with as few issues as possible. If they still think you told me nothing, let's just play this out. They don't know that I know."

"But what good does that do if we don't have a plan?" Izzy replied.

"How about this," Matt said. "Send someone out to their camp to scout it out. Hell, you do it yourself. Get a feel for the land and their base of operations. Maybe once we know more, we'll have a better idea of how to get Audrey back with no one else getting injured."

Jason sat in silence, pondering Matt's suggestion.

"Do you know where their camp is?" Jason asked.

Matt leaned forward and spun one of the maps on Jason's desk to face him. "We're here," he said, pointing at the map. "Their camp was north of the city—a few miles, maybe." He made a circle around an area with his finger. "Probably somewhere around here."

Jason spun the map back around, then stuck a pin in the area Matt had indicated to. "Here. You sure?"

Matt nodded.

"Alright, then," Jason said. "I'll head out there once you guys leave. I'll make sure to stay out of sight. I'll scope it out and see what they're working with. With what the two of you know about the Reavers camp already, and what I can find out when I get there, we should be able to figure out a way to sneak in and get Audrey out of there."

"Okay," Izzy said, reluctant to move forward with the plan. She wished there was a better way. She wished none of this had happened in the first place.

"Now that it's settled, let's go check on our guests," Jason said. "We don't want to give them reason to be suspicious."

He stood up from his chair and escorted Izzy and Matt to the front door, picked up the weapons from the table, and then left, shutting the door behind him.

They arrived at the doctor's office as Griggs and Dalton were walking out. Griggs had a white wrap around his leg where Shadow had bitten him earlier.

"Everything go okay for you guys?" Jason asked.

"Yeah. Thank you for your help," Griggs said. He tossed his big backpack over his shoulder again. "We good to go now?"

"You gentlemen are free to leave whenever you'd like," Jason said.

Dalton held out his hand. Jason reached forward and shook it. A smile appeared on Dalton's face. "I was asking for our weapons back."

"Ah, yes," Jason said in embarrassment. He took the straps off his shoulder and handed the guns back to Dalton and Griggs. "Sorry for taking them in the first place. Rules…"

"Rules," Griggs said, agreeing. "I understand."

They all began to make their way back to the entrance of the camp. Izzy spotted Sarah, her face glowing with joy as she played with Shadow. He was barking as he chased her in circles. Guilt overwhelmed Izzy. She wished she could have told Sarah about the danger they faced. She hated having to lie to her friend like that.

Idle chatter filled the air as they continued to walk. Everyone around the camp was busy with some form of contribution for the group.

"Welcome back, James," a voice said.

Suddenly, Izzy's ears pricked up at the sound of James's name. She experienced a jolt of confusion.

She turned towards the entrance, her eyes widening in disbelief as she saw a figure stumble through the camp entrance. The figure was muddy and disheveled, but there was no mistaking who it was.

"James?" Izzy said. "I thought…" She trailed off, her mind struggling to process what she was seeing. She remembered the creature pulling him through the wall. She'd assumed he was dead. There was no way he could have survived whatever happened next. Although, she never found his body…

"I thought you said James died?" Jason asked.

"I thought he did too," Izzy replied.

Before she could comprehend the situation, the world erupted into chaos. James pulled a handgun from under his shirt and started firing into the crowd of people.

<h1 style="text-align:center">| 16 |</h1>

The moment instantly exploded into a symphony of screams and gunfire. Izzy watched in horror as James—once her friend, now a living nightmare—unleashed a hail of bullets into the crowd of people. Her mind screamed at her to do something. Anything. But her body was frozen in shock.

"James!" she yelled, but her voice drowned out by the chaos.

Suddenly, she was knocked off her feet. Jason had lunged at her, pulling her behind a massive tree trunk for cover. She started to awaken to the surrounding destruction. She glanced around and spotted Matt ducking behind another tree not far away.

People were screaming, and gunshots were ringing out. Then a new sound alerted Izzy—more gunfire, but much louder and closer. Someone was shooting back.

Whipping her head around, she saw Griggs firing at James from behind the door of the houses.

"No!" Izzy cried out, her voice raw with desperation. But even she didn't understand why she was screaming no. James was shooting at everyone in the camp. He was a threat, and Griggs was doing what anyone with a gun would do: he was returning fire to the threat. It was kill or be killed.

Griggs's bullets pierced through James, and he dropped to the ground. Izzy pushed herself away from Jason and scrambled to her feet. She rushed over to James, who was lifeless on the ground. As she neared him, she noticed a strange grayish liquid oozing from his wounds.

"What the hell is that?" she muttered, recoiling in horror.

Before she could investigate further, Matt grabbed her and pulled her back. "Don't touch him," he warned, his eyes wide with fear.

"What is it?" she asked.

"He's infected," Matt explained. "I don't know if touching that stuff infects you or not, but I'd stay away if I were you."

She had only heard stories about the infected. She had never experienced one before. Why did it have to be James, though? She hoped he hadn't suffered.

"Do all your friends bleed weird?" Griggs asked.

Izzy punched him in the chest.

Griggs took a step back and raised his rifle slightly. "I swear to God, you're already on thin ice with me," he said, but then he seemed to remember where he was, and calmed himself down before anyone else noticed.

"You killed him," Izzy said.

"He was already dead," Jason said.

Izzy turned to face him. "There was no way to save him?"

"If he's infected, he's already dead," Jason said. "They infect us somehow. I've never been able to figure that out. But they use us as a host of some kind. It's like they have access to our knowledge and memories. They use it to find us."

"How do you all of know this?" Izzy asked.

"Remember when I told you about that story on our walk to the building a few days ago?" Matt reminded her. "The one about how me, James and Jason were the original ones left of this group. I told you about how one of the people James thought was dead suddenly came back and attacked everyone?"

Izzy nodded.

"I don't think James would just walk up and shoot everyone," Jason said.

"I wouldn't think so either," Izzy agreed.

"Help!" someone from the crowd yelled.

They all turned and headed towards the direction of the cry for help.

"Don't touch that body!" Jason told Griggs as he ran past him.

Izzy's heart stopped as she spotted Sarah leaning against a rock. A dark red stain was spreading across her shirt. Shadow was by her side, whining.

"Sarah! Oh my God!" Izzy said. She looked at the woman sitting next to Sarah. "Is she okay? What happened?"

"She was trying to grab the dog and rush back inside when the shooting started," the woman said. "Looks like she got hit in the stomach somewhere."

Izzy knelt next to Sarah and placed a hand on the top of her head, brushing her fingers through her hair. Sarah opened her eyes.

"Hey, Sarah," Izzy said. "You're going to be okay." She gazed down at Sarah's hands, which were both pressed against the wound on her stomach.

"Matt, go get the doctor," Jason said. Matt ran off immediately.

Izzy's hands trembled as she tried to comfort her friend. The sight of the bullet wound in Sarah's stomach and her blood-soaked shirt were instant reminders of how easy it was to lose people you cared about.

"Stay with me, Sarah," Izzy pleaded, her voice trembling. "You've got to stay awake. The doctor is coming. You're going to be okay."

Sarah managed a weak smile. "I'm not going anywhere," she managed to say. "I still need to hear about this adventure of yours."

Izzy couldn't help but let out a small chuckle. Despite the grim circumstances, Sarah's spirit remained unbroken.

The sound of hurried footsteps rang out behind her. Izzy looked up to see Matt rushing towards them, the doctor trailing behind. Once she had made her way to Izzy, she stepped back to let the doctor work. Matt stood next to her, unfolding a makeshift stretcher. He placed it on the ground beside Sarah.

"We need to get her on the stretcher and to my office," the doctor said. "Now!" Matt leaned over and grabbed Sarah's arms while the doctor slid her feet onto the stretcher.

"Someone grab this side for me," she said.

The doctor stood up and moved out of the way as Jason stepped in front of her and grabbed the foot of the stretcher, while Matt picked up from the other side.

Shadow started to bark as they lifted Sarah up.

"It's okay," Izzy told him, rubbing his head. "They're going to take good care of her." Izzy watched Jason and Matt carry the stretcher towards the doctor's office, then disappear inside. She wished she could have had a few more moments with her. She wanted to follow her into the office and be by her friend's side. She prayed that Sarah would be okay.

Izzy knelt down and hugged Shadow. He nestled his head onto her shoulder as Izzy finally let it all come out. All the pain, frustration, anger, and sadness she'd felt over the last few days came pouring out. She couldn't contain it anymore. Tears rolled down her face. Shadow pulled back and started licking her face. Izzy broke down and started laughing. Shadow suddenly pushed himself into her and knocked her over. He stood over her and continued licking her.

"For someone whose friend was just shot, you seem to be doing just fine," Griggs said.

Izzy pushed Shadow out of her face and saw Griggs standing over her.

"Shut up," she said as she pushed herself back up.

"I'm sorry about your friend," Dalton said.

Izzy stood back up. "Thank you," she said, before addressing Griggs. "Your friend here has a little more sympathy than you do."

Griggs shrugged his shoulders. "Ehh."

Matt finally emerged from the doctor's office and approached Izzy. "Sarah's in good hands," he assured her. "The doctor is getting her prepped."

"Thank you," she said, wrapping her arms around him. She held him for longer than she expected. Once she realized it, she pulled away. "Will she be okay?"

A smile appeared on Matt's face. He nodded and said, "The doctor seemed hopeful, so that's what we're holding onto."

Before Izzy could respond, Griggs interrupted. "Okay, before you two start gushing over each other again, we need to head back to our camp. You two can continue to *undress each other with your eyes* while we get a move on."

"Yeah," Dalton added. "I'd prefer not to stick around for another infected, or a Drifter, to show up."

"Me neither," Griggs said. He waved them on. "Let's go."

Griggs and Dalton started walking away while Izzy stood motionless with Matt by her side. Eventually, the two men turned and noticed that Izzy and Matt weren't following.

"Did you not hear me when I said, let's go?" Griggs said.

"I heard you," Izzy said bluntly. "I want to stay with my friend. You know, the one who was just shot and you didn't care about?"

Griggs pointed at her. "There's that bitchiness again." He strolled up to her. "You're really good at that. Keep it up. Seriously. I can't wait until I can smack that smug look off your face."

Matt stepped forward. "Hey, don't speak to her like that."

"Aww, the boyfriend to the rescue," Griggs said.

Izzy reached up to place a hand on Matt's shoulder. She stepped in front of him to speak to Griggs. "You don't need us. Take your shit back to Hawk and let us be."

"Have you forgotten about your friend back at our camp?" Dalton reminded her. "Hawk isn't going to let her go unless you guys come back with us."

Jason stepped outside the doctor's office, interrupting the argument. "Everything okay out here?"

"All good," Griggs told him. "We were just getting ready to head back out there. Isn't that right, Izzy?"

Izzy's gaze went back and forth from Jason to Griggs. Jason held his stare at her until she locked eyes with him. He gave her a slight nod and wink, to show he understood what was going on.

Izzy regained her clarity and pushed away the anger. The plan that they all agreed on popped back into her head. She had to find a way to save Audrey. There was nothing she could do for Sarah here. She had to let the doctor do her thing.

"Yes," she said finally. "We're getting ready to leave." She saw Shadow sitting by the door to the doctor's office. "Come on, Shadow." He laid down and whimpered. "Do you want to stay and watch over Sarah for me?" His tail started to wag and he barked once.

"I'll watch him for you," Jason said. "He'll be great company for me and Sarah."

Izzy thanked him, and she and Matt joined Griggs and Dalton. With a final glance, she looked at Jason and Shadow standing outside the doctor's office. She hated leaving the camp with everything that had just happened. Her thoughts were with Sarah, but she knew what had to be done—she had a plan to follow and a friend to rescue.

| **17** |

The journey back to the Reavers' camp was a somber one. The forest around them seemed to echo the grim mood of the group, the trees standing like silent sentinels in the fading light. The four of them walked in silence before Izzy broached the subject that had been gnawing at her since the incident back at their camp.

"How did James get infected?" she asked Matt.

Matt shrugged. "I don't know, Izzy. I've only ever seen the aftermath where they're already infected."

"Do any of you guys know?" Izzy asked Griggs and Dalton.

They both shook their heads.

"I heard a rumor once that they basically eat you whole, and then spit you back out as a new person," Dalton said.

"That makes no sense," Griggs said. "I heard they shoot some kind of liquid at you and it seeps into your skin."

"That actually makes more sense than the idea he just told us," Matt said.

"Clearly. I mean, eating someone and then spitting them back out? How the hell would that work? Sound like an idea a five-year-old came up with," Griggs said.

"Look, that's what I heard, okay?" Dalton said. "I never said if it was right or wrong. I personally don't know how those things infect us. And honestly, I don't want to find out."

"I don't think any of us do," Griggs said.

"Izzy, what happened with James when you were with him?" Matt asked.

Immediately, an image popped into her head. The quick motion of that long, black tentacle bursting through the wall next to James, wrapping around him and pulling him into the blackness of the hallway.

She shook the thought from her head.

"He was pulled through the wall and that was it," she told them. "He was gone after that. Never saw him again until he strolled into our camp and started firing that gun." Her thoughts immediately went to Sarah, slumped over, holding her wound covered in blood.

"Izzy?" Matt asked in concern.

"What?" Izzy's eyes widened. She realized she hadn't been paying attention.

"I asked you how you think those creatures infect us," Matt said.

"Oh." Izzy realized thoughts of Sarah's wellbeing were consuming her. She was distracted and, given that they were on their way back to the Reavers' camp, she *couldn't* let herself be distracted. She told herself Sarah was okay. She had to make herself believe it.

"Everything okay?" Matt asked.

"Yeah, sorry," Izzy told him. "I'm just worried about Sarah."

"I know you are, but I think you need to be optimistic," Matt said, trying to reassure her. "The doctor seemed to know what to do and she was able to assist her quickly. She's in good hands."

"I know. I just wish I was there for her," Izzy said.

"Try to think of it this way—are you a doctor? Do you know how to operate on her? Do you know how to treat a bullet wound?" Matt asked.

Izzy shook her head.

"Then there's nothing you can do for her right now," he told her. "Leave it to the professionals. Just as others are leaving what we're doing up to us."

"And what's that?" Griggs asked.

"Assisting you guys and getting our friend back," Matt said.

"Good answer," Griggs said.

Matt let Griggs get a few steps ahead of them before he spoke again. "Idiot," he whispered under his breath, loud enough for Izzy to hear. A small smile appeared on her face. "I saw that," he told her.

"Thanks, Matt," she said.

"For what?" he asked.

"For being here—through this whole thing. It's been a lot," Izzy said.

"Not like I had a choice, right?" Matt said. "But if I had to do it all over again, I'd absolutely be here by your side."

Izzy was happy to have Matt with her. He made her feel more comfortable, even if they were in a world of trouble. She reached out and took his hand, and he glanced down as she interlocked her fingers into his. He looked up at her and smiled, then gripped her hand tighter.

* * *

After making the trek across the many miles, the familiar sight of the large walls and fences came into view. Hawk's camp was not far away. Relief swept through Izzy as she was happy to get out of the open and safe from any potential creature attacks. Unfortunately, that meant getting close to another monster—Hawk.

The guards opened the gate and let the four of them through. They proceeded through the yard outside the prison. Once they made their way inside, Izzy started looking around for Audrey, trying to remember the path she and James had taken in relation to the path they were currently following, trying to mentally map out the hallways of the prison.

"Where are we going?" she asked. Her inquiry was met with silence. She spoke up again, "Hello?" But Griggs and Dalton ignored her as they continued to guide her and Matt through the hallways.

They came to a staircase and went up the stairs. There was a long hallway of doors, all closed, but at the end of the hallway was an open door. Izzy could see a few men standing in the room beyond, but couldn't make out who they were. It wasn't until they walked in that she saw who was standing in front of her—Hawk.

"Ah, my favorite girl returns," he greeted her. "Welcome back." He glanced around their group and then his eyes narrowed. "Where's the rest of you? Pretty sure when you left, there were seven of you. And a dog."

Griggs dropped his bag on the floor. "We ran into a situation."

Hawk moved around the few other men in his office and took a seat at his desk. "Excuse me gentlemen, but I have a story to listen to," he said before waving off the men in the room. Once the door had shut after them, he leaned back in his chair and said, "Let's hear it. What happened?"

Griggs and Dalton took turns explaining their interpretation of the series of events. Izzy noticed Griggs embellishing some details to make himself look better. She rolled her eyes when he mentioned how he was able to take out the group that had attacked him—except for the fact that he left that part out where he told Hawk the group had only tried to steal from him and Izzy, and that's what had sparked his retaliation.

The two of them continued to describe their time away, from their detour away from the Drifter attack, to packing up their bags and heading off to Izzy and Matt's camp. They ended their story by telling Hawk how they were attacked by an infected at the other camp. Griggs, of course, let Hawk know that he was the one who had stopped the infected.

Hawk listened intently, nodding every now and then at their harrowing tale. "Sounds like you were quite the action hero, weren't ya, Griggs?"

"Just doing what I had to do," he replied.

Izzy rolled her hands into fists, trying to contain her frustration. She wanted to scream out what a liar he was, but what good would that do? She dug her nails into the palms of her hands to try and hold in the outburst.

A slow smile spread across Hawk's face as he addressed Dalton. "So, the plan worked then. Is that what I gathered from this drawn-out story?"

Dalton nodded. "Yes, sir. I can give you exact coordinates to their camp."

"Wait, what?" Izzy asked in total confusion. "Dalton? I thought Griggs was the one who wanted to know where our camp was?"

"Hold on," Griggs said. "What the hell are you talking about?"

"Oh, calm yourself down, Griggs. You're too much of a lone wolf," Hawk said. "I couldn't task you with this. Had I known I'd lose half of you guys on this simple trip, I probably would have included you on the plan."

"What plan?" Griggs asked.

"I had Dalton tasked with trying to find where these guys' camp was," Hawk said, gesturing with his hand at Izzy and Matt. "I wanted to know where this one was hiding." He pointed to Izzy. "You have given me headache after headache every time our paths seem to cross."

"Maybe you should just get out of my way, then," Izzy said.

Hawk chuckled. "Oh, Izzy. I've waited for this moment. And you can't take it away from me."

"What are you talking—"

Hawk slammed his fists on the desk. The loud and sudden noise made everyone jump in the room. "Shut up!" Hawk exclaimed. "Just. Shut. Up." He took a deep breath and leaned back in his chair again. "As I was saying, you've caused a lot of frustration for me over the many interactions we've shared together. Honestly, I thought you were dead the last time I saw you."

"You mean when you left me in a cage when the Drifters attacked?" Izzy replied.

"You've got an excellent memory," Hawk said.

"How could I forget? It was the time I thought *you* died too," Izzy said.

Hawk shrugged. "Sorry to disappoint you. Anyway, when you strolled up into my camp, and I realized I had two of your friends, I knew this was too good of an opportunity to pass up. I could manipulate you into gathering those supplies for me. I could lure you into thinking you'd get your friend back. And the best part, I could finally find out where *your* camp is, and take *everything* from you."

"For what?" Izzy responded. "Taking some stuff from what you claimed was *your* area? Big deal. Not like I broke into a hideout of yours and stole from a safe or some kind of storage that's literally *yours*. I was scavenging from within the city. There's no territory there. We all have rules, remember? We don't take—"

"From other people. Blah blah blah. I know the rules," Hawk said. "Doesn't mean *I* follow them. I live by my own rules, but I'm glad you have the honor bestowed from the old rules—thou shall not steal. But anyway, I digress. The point is, there are consequences from stealing from me—like we discussed a few days ago. You steal from me, I take everything from you. Now I know where you live and soon my men will go there and take everything from your camp."

"Sir, I suggest you hurry," Dalton said.

"What did you just say?" Hawk answered angrily.

"What I mean is we should send people over to their camp soon," Dalton replied.

"And why should I do that?" Hawk asked.

"An infected was at their camp," Dalton said.

Hawk had a confused look on his face. "So?"

"One of the guys there, I think their leader, he said something along the lines that the Drifters know where their infected are, and it uses their knowledge and memories to find them," Dalton said.

"Is that true?" Hawk asked, addressing everyone in the room.

They all remained silent.

"Griggs," Hawk said, "you're awfully quiet now. Is it true what Dalton said?"

Izzy noticed a bulging vein on the side of Griggs's head. He looked like he was about to explode.

"Yes. That's what was said," he said finally.

"Then we need to give the green light to our team," Hawk said. "Dalton, go get them ready. Griggs, take our two new residents to their rooms."

"You're not keeping us here," Matt said.

"Oh, I'm sorry. I forgot to mention you don't have a choice in the matter," Hawk said.

"Hawk, this is between you and me," Izzy said. "Leave my people out of it."

"Aww, sweetheart. If it was only that easy," Hawk said.

"Don't call her that," Matt said, inching towards Hawk.

"And what are you going to do about it?" Hawk threatened.

Matt took a quick swipe at Hawk's head, but Hawk ducked just in time and charged into Matt's side. The two of them fell on the ground, Hawk on top of Matt. He wrapped his hands around Matt's neck and started to squeeze.

"What did you think was going to happen?" Hawk said.

"Let him go!" Izzy yelled. She went to approach Hawk, but Dalton drew his gun and aimed it at her, shaking his head.

Izzy watched as Matt struggled to break free. He tried pulling Hawk's hands off his neck and wiggle free, but nothing worked.

"Stop!" Izzy yelled again. "You're killing him! Please!"

Matt's face turned red as he struggled to breathe. Just when he appeared to lose consciousness, Hawk released his hands. Matt began coughing up a storm, taking in all the oxygen he could. Hawk stood up and got off Matt. Izzy rushed over and got down on the ground beside him. She helped him sit up.

"Are you okay?" she asked, in between his coughing fits. He nodded as he began to gain his strength back.

"What the hell, Hawk?" Izzy exclaimed. "You could have killed him!"

"And I probably should have," Hawk said. "But I needed you guys to realize who's in charge here—me. And he seems like an able body I'd like to have on my team. I can't just go around killing all of you guys. I also need to grow my group. And I can't do that with all of you dead."

"You're a psycho," Izzy told him.

"Ehh. Not the worst I've ever been called." Hawk turned his attention to Griggs. "Take them to their quarters. I have to get the team together to take their camp." Hawk gestured towards the hallway with his hand. "Let's go."

Griggs sighed. "Get up, guys. Come on."

Izzy helped Matt stand up and make his way into the hallway. He placed his arm around her. "Thank you," he said.

When Griggs walked out into the hallway, Hawk remained in the room, shutting the door. "Jackass," he said, moving past Izzy and Matt.

"Excuse me?" Izzy said.

"Not you. Him—Hawk," he said, pointing back at the door. His face darkened in anger. "He used me. The asshole used me."

"He used all of us," Izzy said, trying to help calm him down.

"But you don't do that to *me*," he said. "Let's go. Follow me."

Griggs led Izzy and Matt through the corridors of the prison. Izzy saw the jail cells where they had originally found Pete. Her heart sank as she was reminded of what had happened to him.

Izzy was inundated with a flurry of questions in her mind. Where was Griggs leading them? What was his plan? Was she going to be trapped here? She finally spoke up, her voice bouncing off the walls of the empty hallways. "Where are we going?"

He remained silent and continued guiding them through the never-ending maze of hallways until they reached the front of the prison. He opened the door and checked outside to see a few guards stationed throughout the field between them and the fence. Griggs closed the door and gestured for Izzy and Matt to follow him. He navigated the hallways again until he reached another door. He opened it. It seemed to lead to the back of the prison.

"This is where we part ways," he said simply, pointing towards the break in the fence that Izzy and James had previously used to enter the prison. "You're going to go back to your camp and warn your group that Hawk is coming with a team to take everything. And knowing him, death usually follows. So, I'd hurry."

As Matt and Izzy walked past Griggs, Izzy stopped and asked, "Why are you doing this?"

Griggs's eyes filled with bitter rage. "Hawk needs to pay for betraying me. For manipulating me. For using me. That asshole told me *I* was in charge—that *I* was running things. That the group I went out with was *my* responsibility. He told me *I* was his close confidant." He shook his head. "I don't like it when I'm lied to—when I'm used like that."

"Sounds like someone is a little jealous," Izzy said.

"I'm letting you go. Don't start with me," he told her.

"Sorry, you're right," Izzy admitted. "Thank you for doing this."

"Isn't Hawk going to know that you let us go?" Matt said. "If we're gone and you were the last to see us, wouldn't he know you let us go?"

"That's why I want you to hit me," Griggs said. "Give me a black eye."

"Seriously?" Izzy asked.

"Don't make me change my mind. Use all that hatred you have. All of that anger." He pointed to the corner of his eye. "Hit me."

Izzy hesitated for a moment before winding up and delivering a punch. Griggs flinched slightly, then teased her about her lack of strength.

"Seriously, Izzy? That's all you got?" Griggs said. "You hit like a girl. Come on and put some—"

Matt swung his fist, landing a punch right where Izzy had previously hit. Griggs stumbled backwards, caught off guard by the unexpected punch, and fell against the wall.

Matt grabbed Izzy's hand. "Let's go," he told her, and pulled her outside the prison and sprinted towards the break in the fence. They both quickly climbed underneath the hole they had previously made. Once through, they made a beeline for the trees, blending into the shadows.

They both leaned against a tree. Izzy suddenly started laughing.

"What's so funny?" Matt asked.

"You completely knocked the crap out of Griggs," she said, and started laughing again.

Matt joined in with the laughter. "It felt good getting a punch in after dealing with Hawk."

"Izzy? Matt?" a voice came from within the forest.

Jason appeared from behind a tree along with Shadow.

"Shadow!" she said excitedly. She got down on her knees and gave him a hug when he ran up to her, his tail wagging.

"How'd you find us so quickly?" Matt asked.

Jason smiled. "I have to hand it to you, Izzy. It was Shadow. That dog knew exactly where to go."

She petted Shadow's head and back as she stood back up. "He's the best dog."

"What are you guys doing out here?" Jason asked. "I thought you were inside with those guys?"

"We were," Matt said. "Griggs let us go."

"Hawk is sending a group to attack our camp and take our stuff," Izzy said.

"Are you serious?" Jason asked.

"He wants our supplies. He also has a grudge against me. Says I need to pay—so he's going to take all of our stuff as punishment," Izzy told him.

"A grudge?" Jason asked. "For what?"

"He claims I stole from him. Remember when I was out a few days ago and came back with some weapons?" Izzy began to say before Jason nodded. "Well, he thinks I stole from him. I was in the middle of the city. No one has territory there."

"Right. *And?*" Jason said.

"And he thinks it's his territory," Izzy said.

"That's ridiculous. Did you tell him that?" Jason started shaking his head. "Nevermind. The guys sounds like a psychotic moron. No point in trying to understand his flawed logic. If they're heading for our camp, we need to get back and get our people out of there."

"Lead the way," Matt said.

| **18** |

Jason, Izzy, Matt, and Shadow sprinted through the city to reach their camp. Their breaths were ragged as Izzy and Matt relayed to Jason the events in the Reavers' camp while running.

"How much time do we have?" Jason asked.

"I don't know," Matt said. "Depends on how quickly they realize Izzy and I aren't there anymore."

"Hawk is going to be pissed," Izzy said. "We may have an hour on them. Maybe two. I doubt they'll be running like we are, so I'm sure we'll have put some distance between us and them. But he'll send his team out as soon as possible."

"Our people are already aware we have to move because of the threat of the Drifters showing up after James came back infected," Jason said. "We may just have to speed them along when we get back."

* * *

They had finally reached the outskirts of their camp. Her joy at the familiar sight of their home was marred by the impending threat.

Jason took charge the moment he passed the guard watching the entrance at the camp.

"Everybody, I need you all at the pavilion immediately!" he yelled. "Make sure everyone knows. Now."

The members of the camp started spreading out and spreading the word. Izzy followed Jason to the pavilion.

"What are you going to tell them?" Izzy asked.

"The truth," Jason said. He climbed up on the makeshift stage consisting of three large boulders and waved for everyone to come in closer. "Pack it in here. I want everyone to hear me." He gave the group another minute to make their way over before he spoke.

"I know that just hours ago, we experienced a tragedy right in front of our eyes. James came back to our camp infected and shot one of our people. Luckily, he was taken out before he could harm anyone else. If it wasn't tragic enough losing James, the infection he carried communicates to those creatures and lets them know where we are."

People in the crowd started mumbling. Questions were shouted out.

"Are the Drifters coming?"

"How long do we have?"

"Are we going to die?"

Jason held up his hands and yelled for everyone to quiet down so he could continue. "Guys! I know you're all scared. But we'll be out of here before they come for us. Unfortunately, we have another more pressing matter at hand." He looked down at Izzy and extended his hand to her.

Was he asking her to come up and join him?

Izzy reached up and took Jason's hand, and he pulled her up onto one of the boulders.

"Izzy was instrumental in gathering this information for us," he said. "Tell everyone what you learned."

Izzy was stood there paralyzed in shock. She was utterly confused. "What?" was all she managed to say.

Jason spoke softly. "Izzy, you got this. Just tell them what's happening."

Izzy looked out at the crowd of people. She inhaled and pushed aside her fear of public speaking. This was important, and she needed to warn the others.

"There's an old prison, just past the city limits, and their leader has a group of people coming here to take everything we have," Izzy said.

People started mumbling. Izzy couldn't make out any one conversation.

"Why are they coming here?" someone in the front yelled out.

Izzy looked down at the woman who spoke out. Her brown eyes stared at Izzy. The woman held a small child in her arms, who couldn't have been older than two.

"Their leader—his name is Hawk—he's not a good person," Izzy began. She glanced at Jason, who nodded and mouthed *Tell them*. "This man—their leader, Hawk, he's an evil person. He murdered Pete."

Gasps came from the crowd. She pressed on.

"He is still holding Audrey hostage. We need to rescue her," she told them.

"How?" someone yelled out.

"We're in the process of figuring that out," Jason stepped in to say.

"If he's coming here, how do you know he won't kidnap or kill any of us?" someone else shouted.

Jason faced Izzy for a moment before addressing the crowd again. "We don't. And that's why I need everyone to pack up whatever you can as quickly as possible. We need to move."

Everyone started conversing and began shouting questions. Izzy couldn't hear half of them, but she knew they weren't happy. They were uprooting everyone from their homes. This camp site had been their home for the better part of a year. Everyone was safe. It had been quiet and peaceful.

"Guys," Jason yelled, trying to get everyone's attention. "I know this is a stressful situation. But we're all in this together. And we will be fine. We just need to leave before Hawk's group gets here."

"Or the Drifters," Izzy added.

"Or the Drifters," Jason said to the group. "I need everyone to pack what you can. We will be leaving within the hour."

His words were met by an eruption of a frenzy of activity.

Jason hopped off the rocks and reached out to help Izzy down.

"The orders extend to both of you as well," he said, addressing Izzy and Matt. "Go to your homes. Pack what you can, then assist anyone else who needs help."

Izzy and Matt nodded and headed towards their homes, with Shadow by their sides.

"That surely didn't make too many people happy," Matt said.

"No, no really. I don't think anyone is going to be happy about leaving," Izzy said. "I don't have much to grab. I'm just going to load up my backpack and then pack up some stuff for Sarah."

"Alright, I'll meet you at your place when I'm done," Matt said. "Then we can go prep Sarah to move."

"Thank you," Izzy said.

"Of course." Matt smiled at her before heading towards his home.

Izzy pushed open the door of her home. She and Shadow stepped inside and Izzy closed the door behind her. The room felt empty without Sarah around to constantly talk to and gossip with. Her best friend was gravely injured, and Izzy didn't know if she'd be okay.

She sat down on her bed. Shadow jumped up and laid down next to her, placing his head on her lap. Acting on instinct, Izzy petted his head.

"Thanks for sticking with me, buddy," she told him. "We've been through a lot, haven't we?"

Shadow let out a gigantic sigh before picking his head up to look at Izzy. He began panting.

"It's okay," she told him. He placed his head back on her lap, and she continued to pet his head. Her eyes began to water up. The events of the past few days had been weighing on her. Everything that she had been holding inside came out now that she was alone.

"I miss Audrey. I miss Pete. I miss James." She wiped a tear away. "I hate that Pete and Audrey's relationship was cut short because of that asshole, Hawk. I hate how Audrey will have to have that baby by herself." She felt a deep-seated anger towards Hawk, a burning resentment and hatred for the chaos he had caused—for the lives he had ruined.

Another tear fell. She used her sleeve to dry her eyes. The faces of Pete and James were stuck in her head, frozen in time. "I hate how I watched two of my friends die. I hate that my best friend was shot. Why is all of this happening? Why can't things just be normal again?" A sob escaped her lips as she yearned for the simplicity of her former life.

Shadow slowly rolled onto his side and Izzy began petting his stomach. He then tried rolling onto his back while on Izzy's lap, almost falling off the bed. Izzy let out a brief laugh as she caught him. "Everything going on and all you can care about is getting your belly scratched." Shadow rolled back over and looked up at Izzy, panting in her face. He reached up and licked her. She pushed him back and wrapped her arms around him. "I love you too, Shadow," she said.

A knock at the door jolted her back to reality. Shadow let out a quick bark and jumped off the bed. Wiping her tears hastily, Izzy opened the door to find Matt standing there. His eyes widened slightly upon seeing her.

"Are you okay?" he asked.

Izzy nodded quickly, attempting to mask her vulnerability. "Yeah, I'm good."

"You sure?" Matt asked. "You look like you've been crying."

"Just a little distracted. I'm good now," Izzy said, trying to force herself to believe the lie. "Give me a minute to get my bag together, then we can go get Sarah."

"Go ahead," Matt said, bending down to pet Shadow.

Izzy quickly opened her drawers and stuffed some clothing and supplies into her backpack. She didn't have much, so there wasn't much to pack. She found Sarah's backpack by her bed and begun stuffing Sarah's own clothes in it.

Then something floated to the ground. Izzy leaned down to pick it up. She stood up again, holding it in front of her. It was a photo of Izzy and Sarah after their first run together. Sarah had found an old Polaroid camera in an abandoned house. She had been playing with it, and had wrapped her arm around Izzy and taken a selfie of the two of them, not realizing there was film still in the camera. When the picture developed after a few seconds, the two of them burst out laughing at the photo. Sarah had her tongue sticking out and one eye open, while Izzy had a look of confusion on her face. Izzy remembered how the two of them hadn't been able to stop laughing at how funny the picture looked. Once they had calmed down, they went to try and take another one, but the camera had no more film. This was the only picture left, and it was of the two of them.

Izzy smiled as she stared at it.

"What's that?" Matt asked.

Izzy swung Sarah's bag over her shoulder, then moved over to Matt and handed him the picture. "It's a photo of me and Sarah." He took it from her and looked at it. A slight giggle left his mouth.

"You two look... well, you look like your personalities," Matt told her. "She's being goofy and you're being your serious self." He laughed and handed the picture back to Izzy. "It's a cute picture. How'd you get it, anyway?"

Izzy told him the story of how they found a camera and they used the last polaroid in it.

"You're lucky to have gotten that," he said.

Izzy nodded and put the photo in her back pocket. "Ready?"

"Yup," he said. He picked up Izzy's backpack for her and they made their way out of the house and towards the doctor's office. Izzy walked in silence, her heart beating erratically as she prepared to find out what was happening with Sarah.

* * *

"Oh, hey there," the doctor said as they entered.

"How is she?" Izzy asked immediately.

The doctor smiled. "Sarah will be just fine."

Izzy breathed a sigh of relief. "Thank God."

Matt placed an arm around Izzy. "Are we able to move her?"

"I don't think moving her is a good idea yet," the doctor said. "Her body has just experienced trauma. Luckily, the bullet only nicked her stomach lining, so the damage was minor. But she needs to heal."

"Did you not hear Jason earlier?" Izzy told her.

The doctor looked at both of them in confusion. "What do you mean?"

"We need to go," Izzy said. "There are people coming for us and those creatures may show up at any time."

"We'll help you prep Sarah to move," Matt said. "We need to get you both out of here soon."

"Okay," the doctor said. "Let me handle getting her situated. I'll come get you when I'm ready."

Matt and Izzy nodded and walked back outside with Shadow. Izzy dropped her stuff and wrapped her arms around Matt. He had to take a step back to catch himself as Izzy just planted herself onto his body. He placed his arms around her as she started to cry.

"What's wrong?" he asked.

Izzy had finally had the first piece of good news—her friend was going to be okay. She told Matt how she felt about everything—Audrey's abduction, the death of Pete and James, her hatred for Hawk. Matt listened silently to every word, his arms around her providing a pillar of strength.

"We'll get through this, Izzy," he said. "One step at a time. I promise."

His reassurance soothed her. They stayed like that for a while, locked in a comforting embrace. Izzy pulled back slightly and looked at him, their faces inches apart. As they stared into each other's eyes, Izzy found herself drawn to him. She felt a pull, a desire to bridge the gap between them.

Caught in the moment, Matt leaned in. Izzy moved closer, too. Just as their lips were about to meet, a sudden gunshot distracted them and ruined the moment.

They immediately pulled away from one another, their eyes wide with shock. A voice echoed through the camp—a voice Izzy recognized.

"Ohh, Izzy..." Dalton taunted. "I know you and your friend are in there. Aren't you going to welcome us back?"

| 19 |

The camp was a whirlwind of fear and panic as the people scurried about, their faces etched with terror. Dalton's taunting voice echoed around the camp. His calls for Izzy made her hairs stand on end.

Why me? she thought.

She stood rooted in place, Matt at one side of her, Shadow on the other. She quickly tried to make sense of the events unfolding around them.

"How are they here this quickly?" Izzy asked.

"They must have found out we escaped sooner rather than later," Matt said.

"Dammit!" Izzy exclaimed. "I thought we had more time."

"Me too," Matt said, agreeing.

Suddenly, Jason appeared and shouted, "We hold our position! We're going to defend this camp until everyone is out safely. None of those assholes get in here, understood?"

Matt and Izzy both nodded in agreement.

"Matt," Jason began, "I need you to take up position on top of the guard's tower with a rifle." Jason turned to one of the guards by his side and gestured towards Matt. The guard handed him a rifle with a small bag of ammunition. "Watch my ass, got it?"

"Yes, sir," Matt said.

Izzy looked at the guard, waiting for him to hand her a weapon of some kind. Nothing came her way.

"Ohh, Izzy?" Dalton taunted. "Come out, come out wherever you are…"

Izzy stuck out her hand. "Jason, where's my gun?"

"Izzy, I need you to assist the group and get them out of the camp and to safety," Jason commanded, his tone leaving no room for argument.

A flash of anger surged through Izzy. She had proven her capabilities time and time again, yet here she was, being sidelined once more.

"I can help!" she protested.

"You *will be* helping," Jason said. "You'll be helping everyone get to safety."

"You know what I mean. I can fight," Izzy said.

"No." Jason was adamant. "That's an order, Izzy." He then turned on his heel and told the few guards nearby to follow him as he headed to the entrance of the camp.

Izzy watched him go. There was a bitter taste in her mouth. Just when she thought he had finally accepted her as an equal, he had pushed her aside again. It was infuriating, but she knew there was no time for arguments now.

Matt tried to reassure her. "It'll be okay, Izzy," he said softly. But his comforting words were cut short as Jason called for him to get into position. Izzy experienced a pang of fear as Matt prepared to leave.

"Be careful," she told him.

"Always," he said, and then turned and disappeared towards the entrance of the camp.

Izzy took a long, deep breath and pushed aside her frustration. She told Shadow to follow her, and they headed for the group making its way towards the rear of the camp.

"Hey, Emily," Izzy said as she approached the woman who was directing everyone. "Jason asked me to help get everyone out."

"Really? He asked me to do that," Emily told her.

"Are you serious?" she asked.

"Yeah," Emily said. "Why? Dan is helping lead people towards the exit now and Christine is running around the camp making sure everyone is accounted for."

"Jason told me to help with this. Unbelievable," Izzy said. Then she noticed the bow around Emily's shoulder. "Emily, can I borrow your bow?"

"Uh, yeah, I guess?" Emily said. "What do you need it for?" Her fingers trembled slightly as she took it off her shoulder and handed it to Izzy.

"I'm going to the gate to help," Izzy said. "I *have* to help." She reached out for the arrows in the quiver behind Emily's back. "Arrows too, please."

"Oh, sorry," she said, taking them off and handing them to Izzy. "Are you sure this is the right thing to do?"

Izzy slung the quiver of arrows behind her back and hung the bow on her shoulder. "Yes, I need to help them. No one knows the Reavers better than I do. Maybe I can stop this." She turned to Shadow. "Let's go," she said, and the two of them sprinted towards the entrance of the camp.

They slowed as they approached the entrance gate, hiding behind trees and shrubs as they approached. Izzy could hear voices, but their words were inaudible. She had to get closer. She glanced around and saw Matt stationed in the guard tower. He held his rifle, aiming into the fields beyond the gate. Izzy decided to join him up in the tower.

She hurried towards the ladder and told Shadow to stay while she climbed up to join Matt. With each rung she climbed, the voices beyond the gate became clearer.

"...walk in here and act like you own everything?" Jason was saying.

"Not my call," Dalton responded. "I have my orders. And if we have to, we will take everything by force. But I don't think you want that. Do you?"

Izzy made it to the top rung and climbed into the observation deck. Matt spun around and aimed his gun at her.

"Jesus… Izzy," he said. "I could have shot you. What are you doing here?"

She made her way next to Matt, overlooking the group of Reavers surrounding the camp's entrance.

"I'm here to help," she told him. "What's happening?"

"Dalton has been threatening Jason," he told her. "He's been telling him that if he doesn't let his group in, they have orders to enter by force."

"Dalton is going to kill them?" Izzy said.

Matt nodded.

"So what's it going to be?" Dalton asked.

Jason stood in silence, staring at the group of fifteen or more Reavers. Izzy gripped the bow tighter, her knuckles turning white. She readied herself in the event she needed to act quickly.

"I'm going to give you to the count of five to leave our campground," Jason said. "If you don't, I'll take it as an act of war and we will use all means necessary to defend ourselves."

"Are you threatening *us*?" Dalton said.

"I have people in high ground ready to take you guys out. We are well defended. You guys don't stand a chance. I'll only ask this once more. Leave now, or face the consequences," Jason said.

Izzy knew he was bluffing, but he sounded plausible. His tone suggested confidence. Did he really have people stationed in places she didn't know about?

Dalton looked at the gate. Izzy had been making sure she remained hidden, but she swore Dalton had seen her, as if he was capable of staring right through the wall she was hiding behind.

"Well," Dalton started to say, "I guess we have nothing more to talk about."

He quickly pulled a handgun from behind his back, aimed it at Jason, and fired.

"No!" Izzy and Matt yelled in unison.

As Jason fell backwards, Matt began unloading his rifle into the crowd of people below. Izzy pulled back the string of her bow and aimed at the closest member of the Reavers, and quickly released. The arrow dropped right next to his foot, missing its target. Izzy dropped below the wall and covered her head as bullets erupted on her location. Matt ducked next to her, lying on top of her to protect her.

Gunshots continued to be fired, but not at their location anymore. "Are you okay?" Matt asked.

Izzy was seething with rage. Even though Jason had disrespected her multiple times, he was still a part of her family. And because of Hawk, another one of her family members had been killed.

"I'm fine," she snarled. "Dalton needs to die."

"You don't have to tell me twice," Matt said. He peeked above the wall, then quickly ducked back down. He looked at Izzy. "On the count of three, I'm going to stand up and fire at the few Reavers at the tree line. Another of them is directly below us. When I start firing, you take out the one below us, okay?"

Izzy nodded.

"One. Two. Three."

Matt stood up and starting firing his weapon. Izzy quickly brought an arrow from behind her back, placed it in her bow, and pulled the string back, aiming below her. The man below her looked up, ready to shoot, but Izzy had already let go of the bowstring. The arrow shot straight down, striking him in the chest. He screamed in pain and fell to the ground.

"Good shot," Matt said, before a stream of bullets was unloaded in their direction. "Go!" he yelled, pointing to the ladder.

Izzy moved to the ladder and started climbing down as quickly as she could. She reached the bottom and looked up for Matt, calling out to him. She heard a few more shots come from the guard's tower before he leaped over the side and slid down the ladder, landing next to her.

"Come on," he said, grabbing her arm. "They just shot the guards outside with Jason. They're coming through the gate."

"Shadow, come!" Izzy yelled as she and Matt ran across the path. Bullets whizzed past them as they sprinted, darting between trees and finding shelter behind a cabin. Their breaths came out in ragged gasps as they pressed their backs against the cabin.

"I'll head to the other side of the entrance," Izzy said, her voice just loud enough to be heard over the gunfire. "I'll watch the tree line to the left of the entrance while you cover this side."

Matt's eyes widened. "That's suicide, Izzy," he argued. His gaze flicked to the simple bow she held in her hands. "You're not equipped for this."

Izzy bristled. She was more than capable, and she intended to prove it. With a swift motion, she plucked an arrow from the quiver on her back and placed it onto her bow. She pulled back on the bowstring and released it. The arrow whistled through the air and embedded itself in a dark knot on a distant tree.

Izzy turned back to face Matt, a smirk appearing on her face. Silence fell between them as Matt stared at the arrow, his earlier doubts seemingly proven wrong. "I stand corrected. I didn't know you could handle a bow like that."

"I can do a lot more than you guys think I can," she said.

Matt smiled. "Duly noted." He stared at her for several seconds. "Be careful, Izzy," he said finally, his voice filled with concern. "I'll watch your back from here until you get into position."

"Thanks, Matt," she said, offering a quick nod before moving to the tree to retrieve her arrow. She stuck it back in the quiver behind her back, then she and Shadow stealthy trekked through the camp to the other side of the entrance. They moved quietly, slipping between cabins and keeping a low profile.

From her vantage point behind the cabin she hid behind, Izzy watched as two of the Reavers sauntered into the camp, their guns swinging. Anger surged through her when one of them took down a camp member with a single gunshot.

Izzy moved silently to a nearby tree, her hands trembling slightly as she prepared herself for what was to come next. She signaled for Shadow to stay put while she took aim. She nocked the arrow in her bow and aimed at one of the Reavers. The arrow sang as it left her bow, finding its mark in the chest of one of them. He collapsed, his hat falling off his head as he hit the ground.

Without missing a beat, Izzy nocked another arrow, ready to unleash it on the second man, but he noticed her. She let the arrow fly, hitting him in his upper thigh. He crumpled to the ground, his gun falling from his grasp. As Izzy reached for another arrow, the fallen man reached for his gun. She nocked the arrow as he grabbed his weapon and aimed it directly at her. Izzy froze. There wasn't enough time to aim and release the arrow before he could pull his trigger.

Suddenly, a gunshot rang out, and the man jerked and fell, dropping the gun.

Matt emerged from behind a tree close to Izzy. He gave her a reassuring nod, which she returned with a grateful smile. Gunfire distracted her. Izzy darted towards the trees for a quick escape.

From her new position, she saw one of the Reavers chasing one of the members of her camp. Her fingers moved instinctively, pulling an arrow from her quiver and nocking it onto her bow. With a deep breath, she released the string. The arrow flew through the air and struck the Reaver's leg. He tumbled to the ground, his weapon skittering out of his reach.

As he went to retrieve it, Izzy commanded Shadow, "Get him!"

Shadow, ever alert, sprang into action. He darted out from the trees and lunged at the fallen man, his teeth sinking into his arm, preventing him from reaching for his gun. The scavenger screamed in pain, his fingers inches away from his gun.

Izzy quickly nocked another arrow.

"Shadow, move!" she called out.

The dog obeyed instantly, releasing his grip and running back to her side. As soon as Shadow was clear, Izzy let loose another arrow. The man grunted in pain as the arrow struck his chest. He writhed on the ground for a moment before falling still.

A gunshot echoed nearby, a bullet tearing into the tree behind her. Izzy ducked instinctively and then moved, but was met with sharp pain as something had hit her head. She stumbled, her vision blurring as she fell to the ground. Through her hazy vision, she saw Shadow spring into action again, latching onto the hand of the man who had struck her. His growls echoed around her as one of the Reavers screamed, trying to shake Shadow off, but the dog held on fiercely. The chains on his black jacket and belt rattled as he shook the dog.

"Get this thing off of me!" he yelled in between screams of pain.

Slowly, Izzy regained her strength and saw another member of the Reavers, one with a white tee-shirt and ripped jeans, with his arms wrapped around Shadow's chest, trying to pull him off the other man. She shook her head to clear her vision and picked up her bow. Quickly, she nocked another arrow and pulled the bowstring back.

"Shadow, down!" she yelled.

Both Reavers looked in Izzy's direction in surprise. The one holding onto Shadow let go of him. Shadow instantly released the man's arm and laid down, giving Izzy a wide-open shot. She held her breath and let the arrow fly. The man gasped as the arrow struck him in the chest, his eyes widening in shock as he went to feel the arrow sticking out of his chest. He slowly slumped to the ground.

Izzy went to nock another arrow, but not before the remaining man took out his pistol and aimed it at her. Before she could even pull the bowstring back, a gun went off.

But it wasn't his.

The man went to turn around but lost his strength and fell down. Izzy would have never imagined the person she'd see standing behind him.

"Jason?" she gasped, her mind reeling. She had thought he was dead. She had watched him get shot, yet here he was, standing tall and grim, a smoking gun in his hand. "How?"

Jason smiled and unzipped the sweatshirt he was wearing, revealing a bulletproof vest. "My chest hurts like hell, but I'll be fine," he said. "Where's everyone else?"

"Matt and I were holding our ground here, trying to defend the entrance," Izzy said. "How did you get away from Dalton? Where is he?"

Jason shrugged. "I don't know. Once a few of them moved away from me, I collected myself, took two of them out and entered the camp again. I was actually hoping you took out Dalton."

"I haven't seen him," Izzy told him.

"Where's Matt?" Jason asked.

"He and I split up," she said. "He's on the eastern side of the camp, and I took the west side."

He nodded. "Alright, let's head back to get him. Then let's find the rest of our group and get out of here."

"What about Dalton?"

"I'd rather live to fight another day than hunt him down right now. We're lucky we took out as many as we did. Let's just get—" He was interrupted by the chilling howls of the Drifters. His eyes widened in fear. "We need to leave—now!"

"But we have to find Matt," Izzy said. "And we have to get Sarah out of the medical building."

One of the Reavers with baggy clothing screamed as he ran into the camp. Another followed. Suddenly, a giant black beast rammed through the entrance, knocking down the guard tower Izzy and Matt had been in earlier. One of its long tentacles stretched out to snatch the man with baggy clothing in mid stride. The creature brought the screaming man to its black, slimy face. Its mouth dropped open, its sharp, razer-sharp fangs glistened in the sunlight. In one bite, it chopped him in two. The Drifter tossed the lower half of the body over the wall of the camp and chewed what was in its mouth. Izzy heard the crunching of bones.

"We need to leave," Jason said, his voice tight with fear.

Izzy couldn't believe what she had just witnessed. She knew Jason was right—they had to leave.

But she couldn't.

Not yet.

Izzy shook her head. "We can't leave without Sarah and Matt," she insisted.

Jason nodded. "You're right. We won't leave anyone behind," he agreed. The sounds of the creature's roars and the Reavers' screams flowed through the camp. "Follow me," he said.

Stealthily, they made their way through the trees within the camp to return to the cabins.

"We need to split up," Jason whispered. "I'll go find Matt. You go get Sarah and the doctor from the medical building." Izzy nodded in agreement. "Let's meet at the rear entrance, okay?"

"Sounds good," Izzy said.

"Be careful," Jason said, then disappeared into the shadows behind the cabins, leaving Izzy and Shadow alone.

The Drifter's howls grew closer, the sound sending goosebumps rippling across her skin. She spun around and crouched down, holding Shadow close to her to muffle his whines.

She sensed the presence of the creature on the opposite side of the cabin, its foul stench of death making her gag. She held her breath, praying it wouldn't detect them. It let out a high-pitched scream that pierced her ears. It was so loud that it sounded as though it was right next to them. Izzy tucked herself into a ball, hoping it wasn't as close as it seemed. Her chest started to hurt, her lungs burned. She slowly released the air from her lungs.

She heard a breeze of air as the Drifter floated away. It was followed by another scream in the distance. Carefully, she peeked around the corner of the cabin, scanning the area for any signs of the creature. When she was sure it had moved away, she whispered to Shadow to follow her.

They sprinted across the open field as quickly as they could. Izzy didn't want to give the Drifter a reason to come back. They burst into the medical building, slamming the door behind them. But the sight that greeted them froze Izzy in place.

The doctor laid lifeless on the ground, in a pool of her own blood. Her once blonde hair was now stained of red and brown. Standing over Sarah on the operating table was Dalton, a malicious grin on his face as he held his gun to her head.

Fear gripped Izzy, but she told herself she had to stay strong. She couldn't afford to lose anyone else today.

"So nice of you to *finally* join the party," Dalton said.

Dalton towered over Sarah, his gun pressed against her temple. Sarah was awake. Her face was pale, and her breathing came in shallow gasps. She clutched at her stomach and winced in pain every few seconds.

"Don't hurt her," Izzy pleaded, her voice barely a whisper for fear of alerting the Drifter outside.

Dalton's eyes darted towards Izzy, a cruel smile curling his lips. "This girl clearly means something to you. So, if you want to keep her safe, you'll get me out of here alive," he demanded, his gaze never leaving Izzy's. "Is that clear?"

"And what if I don't agree to this?" Izzy countered. She didn't want him to leave this room. She wanted to kill him where he stood. He was threatening her best friend with a gun to her head. She tightened her fingers around the bow. Hatred filled her. She wanted this nightmare to end.

Dalton shrugged, his smile widening. "Then I'll kill both of you." Izzy didn't have a choice. His gun was quicker than her bow—she wouldn't stand a chance. She was cornered, with no choice but to comply.

He aimed his gun at her. "Put down the bow," he ordered.

Izzy hesitated at first, but then slowly uncurled her fingers from the bow, letting it slip from her grip.

The haunting sounds of the Drifter echoed outside. Sarah whimpered quietly. Dalton aimed his gun towards the door. Izzy rushed to Sarah's side, her hands hovering over her wound.

Dalton swung his gun towards Izzy. "Stop," he demanded, "or I'll shoot."

"I'm checking on Sarah," she told him. "Relax." Shadow moved slowly to Izzy's side, growling at Dalton and showing his fangs. "No, Shadow. Stop," Izzy commanded.

Gunfire erupted outside. Izzy and Dalton rushed to look through the window in the door. A female camp member and one of the Reavers were running, their faces distorted with terror.

"Oh, no. Charlotte," Izzy said.

She lunged for the door handle, desperate to help, but Dalton grabbed it and held it shut.

"We need to help," Izzy insisted.

"I'm not opening this door," Dalton said. "The Drifter is right outside. I'm not dying."

Their voices were soon drowned out by the terrifying howl of the creature. It was too late. The Drifter swooped forward, its tentacles snaking around the man and Charlotte, lifting them both off the ground. The Reavers' member fired at it, but the bullets merely bounced off. The Drifter roared and its tentacle tightened around him, crushing him. Izzy could hear the sounds of his bones crunching from behind the door. The man went limp and the Drifter discarded the lifeless body with a careless flick of its tentacle, turning its attention to Charlotte, who was screaming at the top of her lungs.

Izzy tried pulling on the door again. "We need to help," she pleaded.

"Do you see what's happening out there?" Dalton asked. "How do you plan on helping her?"

Izzy knew Dalton was right, but she still felt a need to try to do something.

"She'll be dead by the time you step outside," he told her. "And then you'd be next."

Charlotte was lifted high into the air. Izzy watched in horror as the creature brought her up to its mouth, and with one swift motion, bit down, silencing her screams. The Drifter threw the dead body aside, and it thudded as it connected with a nearby tree. It let out a triumphant roar before floating away, leaving behind a scene of devastation.

Dalton turned back to Izzy, his eyes cold and calculating as he pointed his gun at her once again. "Get your friend. We're leaving," he ordered.

Izzy moved to Sarah as Dalton continued to stare out the small window in the door.

"Are you okay?" she asked. Sarah's hands were trembling as Izzy helped her off the table.

"I think so," Sarah said. "Just don't let me die out there."

Izzy wrapped her arms around her. "I won't let anything happen to you," she promised. She let go of Sarah and extended her hand. "Ready?"

Sarah nodded and took Izzy's hand. Izzy helped her off the operating table. As they stepped over the lifeless body of the doctor on the floor, Sarah squeezed her eyes shut to avoid the gruesome sight.

Dalton opened the door cautiously, scanning their surroundings for any sign of the Drifter.

"Just keep your head down and listen to everything I tell you, okay?" Izzy said.

"I will," Sarah responded.

Dalton turned and waved them forward. "Come on," he said. Izzy wrapped her arm under Sarah's arms, supporting her weight as they ventured outside, Shadow by their side. Clouds were beginning to cover the sun, reducing the light in the camp. Izzy could hear screams in the distance, but couldn't distinguish between the cries of the Reavers or her friends. She forced herself to focus on the task at hand: getting Sarah to safety.

Dalton stayed in front of them, aiming his gun in all directions. They moved quickly from the medical building and into the open landscape, heading in the direction of the camp's entrance. Bodies were scattered all over. The broken guard's tower had been knocked over and lay in pieces. The wall that provided a barrier against the outside world was in ruins, knocked down in multiple sections. Izzy's home had been destroyed.

The trees in the distance began to move, and a rustling sound grew louder. The howling seemed to get closer. A wave of rotten air hit them instantly, and suddenly, the trees parted. A Drifter burst through, its grotesque form towering over them. Its mouth opened wide, letting out a deafening roar that curdled Izzy's blood.

"Run!" Izzy shouted.

A tentacle shot out, wrapping around Dalton and lifting him off the ground. Izzy tried to move as fast as she could whilst still supporting Sarah's weight, but they were too slow. She turned just in time to see the creature's other tentacle curling towards her. She let go of Sarah and shoved her aside, then dove out of the way—but she wasn't quick enough. The tentacle latched onto her foot, dragging her across the ground towards the creature.

Shit. Shit. Shit.

A wave of terror instantly overwhelmed Izzy. Was she going to die? Was this it? Her mind then went blank as she stared death in its dark and slimy face.

Shadow growled and barked nonstop at the Drifter as it held onto Izzy. He looked as if he was about to attack the creature, but sensibly kept his distance.

As Izzy was being dragged, her leg brushed against something hard in her pocket. It slipped out, bouncing on the dirt.

The pocketknife.

The one Griggs had given to her earlier when they were attacked. She reached out to grab it, but her fingers only brushed against the cold metal as she was pulled away. Panic surged through her as she clawed at the ground, her fingers scrambling for the knife.

"Izzy!" Sarah yelled

With every passing second, Izzy was dragged further away, the Drifter's monstrous form looming closer. With one last burst of energy, she clawed with all her strength, and reached out for the knife, her fingers barely touching the handle. Before she was dragged again, she was able to grip the handle of the knife.

"Help!" Dalton yelled in between screams of terror.

As Izzy was dragged closer to the Drifter, something caught her eye that froze her blood. Dalton was suspended in the air, screaming as it held him captive. The monster's gaze was focused entirely on him. The end of its tentacle blossomed open, like a flower blooming in the sunlight. It screamed at Dalton in a scream Izzy had never heard before. Then, with eerie precision, closed its tentacle around Dalton's head. His body jerked violently for a few seconds before going limp, his screams coming to an abrupt end.

She couldn't let this happen to her. Not to Sarah, and not to Shadow. She clutched the pocketknife tighter; her knuckles were white. With a loud battle cry, she stabbed the Drifter's tentacle. Again and again, each stab a desperate plea for freedom.

The creature shrieked, a sound so horrifying and unlike anything Izzy had heard before. She stabbed it again, this time twisting the knife into its black, slimy flesh, then sawing back and forth. As she fought for survival, white, gooey liquid leaked from the Drifter's flesh.

It's bleeding, Izzy thought. *I'm hurting it.*

The tentacle released its grip on her foot. Izzy scrambled back to her feet with a renewed determination to fight on and defeat this beast. She sprinted towards Sarah and Shadow, the creature's enraged howl echoing behind her. Izzy reached Sarah and got her ready to move. She watched as the Drifter released its grasp on Dalton's head and tossed him aside like a rag doll, its focus now solely on Izzy. She could feel its rage as it dropped its jaw and screamed in her direction. She had a fraction of a second to determine her next move.

Before she could do anything, a voice cut through the chaos. "Get down!"

Without thinking, Izzy pulled Sarah to the ground and laid on top of her. Shadow immediately understood, and laid down next to Izzy. Something whizzed past her, colliding with the Drifter in a fiery explosion. Wind and heat blew towards Izzy. So much heat.

After the explosion, a ball of smoke lifted into the air. The Drifter roared in pain, but before it could react, another projectile whizzed above Izzy, striking it again. Another explosion erupted in front of her. The Drifter roared one last time before disappearing through the entrance of the camp and into the distance.

As Izzy regained her bearings, she looked up and saw a figure standing amidst the chaos. She had to blink a few times to make sure he was really there.

"Griggs?" Izzy's voice came out as a whisper.

He stood holding a rocket launcher. He approached her as she climbed back to her feet.

"What the hell are you doing here?" she asked, a mixture of confusion and relief in her voice.

"Apparently, saving your ass again," he said. "I think the next words out of your mouth should be something like, *thank you.*"

Izzy gritted her teeth as frustration built inside her. She hated owing him anything. He was one of *them.* The enemy. But he had let her and Matt go earlier so that they could warn everyone of the impending attack. Had it been another trap? Though she couldn't deny the fact he had just saved their lives. If it was a trap, he could have just let her die.

Swallowing her pride, she muttered a begrudging, "Thank you." Then she turned back to help Sarah to her feet.

"See? That wasn't so bad now, was it?" Griggs said.

A dark bruise was forming on his cheekbone where Matt had hit him earlier. A small smirk played on Izzy's lips as she pointed it out. "I like your beauty mark," she said sarcastically, pointing to her own cheek.

Griggs rolled his eyes. "Always with the sarcastic remarks," he grumbled. He turned his attention to Sarah. "How are you doing?" he asked her, seeming genuinely concerned.

Izzy interrupted him. "Hold on. Why the nice-guy routine? What are you trying to get at here?"

Griggs smiled. "Have you learned nothing about me yet?"

"What's that supposed to mean?" Izzy asked.

"I'm here for revenge," he stated. "How can you be so smart, yet so dumb at the same time?"

"Dumb?" Izzy said angrily. "Why don't I give you a matching beauty mark on the other side of that face."

"Guys, stop. Please," Sarah said, from her position on the ground. She winced in pain again, holding her abdomen.

Izzy rushed over to her, dropping to one knee. "Are you okay?"

Sarah nodded. "Can we just get out of here before that thing comes back?"

"Of course." Izzy stood up and offered her a hand, then helped her stand up and placed an arm around her for support.

"So, where to?" Griggs said.

"Where to?" Izzy said. "Sarah and I are leaving. You can go wherever *you* need to go, but it's not going to be with us."

"He just saved our lives, Izzy," Sarah reminded her.

"Sarah, this guy kidnapped Audrey. He held me and Matt captive. He manipulated us into leading him back here to learn where our camp was, then caused this." She waved her free hand around, gesturing at the destruction around them.

"First of all, this was Dalton, not me," Griggs said. "Second, that Drifter did most of the damage."

"You're just as much a part of Dalton and all those Reavers, whether you were a part of this plan or not," Izzy said.

"Izzy, listen to me," Griggs said, taking a step closer to her. "The one you should be mad at is Hawk, remember? *He's* the one who's behind everything here. *He's* the one who's currently holding Audrey captive. *He's* the one who killed your friend. And *he's* the one who betrayed me. Why would I let you leave the camp and come back here to warn your friends? Why would I then come all this way and then save your life if I was trying to betray you?"

Izzy considered Griggs's words. Fear and suspicion were hard feelings to shake. She had been betrayed before, and the sting of that was still fresh. She could see the results of that betrayal within the camp. She couldn't allow it to happen again, and she couldn't shake the feeling that this could be just another one of Hawk's elaborate schemes. But in the back of her mind, the thought of Griggs genuinely seeking revenge kept creeping in.

"You guys are my best bet at taking revenge on Hawk. And who knows Hawk and that prison better than me?" Griggs added, his voice steady and confident.

They were sitting ducks out in the open. They had to make a decision soon, in case the Drifter returned. She knew she was taking a gamble here. Trusting Griggs was not without risks, but he did have valuable insider information about Hawk. That could turn the tide in their favor. She took in a deep breath, meeting Griggs' gaze.

"Fine," Izzy said firmly. "You can come with us. But I'm keeping an eye on you."

A smirk spread across Griggs's face, his eyes twinkling with amusement. "I don't think Matt would appreciate that too much." His comment caught Sarah off guard, making her chuckle.

Izzy shot her a warning stare.

"What? It was funny," Sarah defended herself, her lips curving into a small smile.

"Don't encourage him," Izzy said, shaking her head slightly. The tension in the air seemed to lessen a bit, but Izzy knew they were far from safe. "Let's go," she said.

| 21 |

Izzy walked back to the medical building and grabbed her bow. She slung it over her shoulder and led the way, navigating through the wreckage of what was once her home. Griggs and Shadow followed close behind, while Sarah used Izzy for support.

The stench of burnt wood and flesh made Izzy's stomach churn. Bodies lay strewn about, some of them Reavers, others were friends and people she knew. Some of the trees had been knocked down by the Drifter as it passed, their branches twisted at grotesque angles. Some homes had been reduced to rubble, their remains scattered around the campsite like pieces of a jigsaw puzzle. Supplies that had once promised sustenance and survival were now destroyed.

This was more than just a camp for her. It was a sanctuary, a place they had called home. Now, it was nothing more than a graveyard.

"I can't believe it," Sarah said. "All this from the Drifter?"

"Probably both the Drifter and the Reavers," Griggs said. "They were sent to take what they needed from here and destroy the camp."

"You never did tell us how you wound up here," Izzy said.

"You never asked," Griggs replied.

Izzy rolled her eyes. "Fine. What happened after Matt and I left?"

"Well, after your boyfriend got his cheap shot in," Griggs started, acknowledging his bruise on his cheek, "I went back and saw Dalton gathering a group together. I kind of followed him and then joined in and listened. He mentioned how Hawk gave the order to head to your camp and basically to just take everything. He gave Dalton the order to destroy the camp and kill anyone that stands in his way, especially you." His eyes narrowed at her. "Dalton specifically said that Hawk would pay to have your head presented to him on a silver platter."

"You missed your opportunity," Izzy told him. "How come you didn't kill me back there and walk back into his good grace?"

He shrugged. "Money is meaningless. I mean, look around us. What do you need to survive around here?"

"Food and shelter," Izzy mumbled.

"Exactly," he said. "I also like being respected and not taken advantage of. And Hawk broke that agreement when he used me the way he did." Griggs shook his head. "I won't let anyone take advantage of me like that. So, once Dalton and his gang of misfits left, I snuck into the armory and grabbed a gun for myself."

"But you're carrying a rocket launcher," Izzy reminded him.

He stuck up a finger. "Let me continue. As I was saying, I grabbed a gun for myself. Then I saw the backpack and loaded some extra ammo into it. Then I saw it—the rocket launcher. I had to have it. I never fired one before, and it just looked so lonely on the table. I picked it up and walked out. I snuck out the back door while Dalton and his group went out the front. I made sure to stay a few miles behind him since I didn't want to run into any of them on my way here. Which was why I showed up when I did."

"Well, if Izzy doesn't appreciate it, I definitely do," Sarah said. "Thank you."

"*You're* welcome," Griggs said, smirking at Izzy. "Which leads me to you. You clearly want Hawk dead. And so do I. You work with me to do that, and when it's done, we can go our separate ways, never to be heard from again."

"We kill Hawk, and, what, you take over the Reavers?" Izzy asked.

"Hell no," Griggs said. "I don't want that responsibility."

Izzy pondered Griggs's offer. She hated Hawk. She certainly wanted him dead, especially after he had killed Pete right in front of everyone. She had to put an end to his reign of terror.

"Look, Griggs," Izzy said, "I'll help you with stopping Hawk, as long as you keep your word and we go our separate ways once things are done."

Griggs nodded.

"Then we have a deal," Izzy said. She reached out a hand, and they shook on it.

* * *

They reached the rear entrance of the camp and saw Jason and the rest of the group in the distance. Izzy realized there were fewer people than she had hoped. But then there was one face she had been waiting to see—Matt. His gaze met hers. Relief washed over her as she rushed towards him. He pulled her into a tight hug.

"I'm so happy to see you," he said. "I saw the explosion. I thought maybe..." He trailed off, leaving the implication hanging.

"I'm okay. Actually, it was thanks to him," Izzy said, nodding to Griggs.

"Griggs?" Matt asked.

Izzy nodded.

"I mean, I guess I'm happy he was there to help," Matt said. "Any sign of Dalton?"

"He's dead. The Drifter killed him," Izzy said.

"Good riddance," Matt said.

Jason's eyes narrowed at the sight of Griggs. "*Him*? Why is *he* here?"

"He saved our lives," Izzy said. "That explosion you saw, and probably heard, was Griggs and his little toy there." She pointed to the rocket launcher dangling from his shoulder.

"No. Absolutely not. He's too dangerous and unpredictable," Jason said. "What if he's still working with Hawk and the rest of the Reavers?"

"You know I can hear you, right?" Griggs said.

"I don't give a shit what you can or cannot hear," Jason said. "What just happened at my camp, to my people, is because of you." He approached Griggs and got up in his face. "If it wasn't for you and your people," he said, prodding Griggs's chest, "none of this would have happened."

"Don't touch me," Griggs said, and pushed Jason back.

"What are you going to do about it?" Jason said. "Do you have more troops coming to wipe the rest of us out?"

"Stop it!" Izzy said.

"It's just me. And if you don't stop it with your bullshit and listen, then I'll shut you up and make *sure* you stop," Griggs said.

"Are you threatening me?" Jason asked.

"Guys, stop!" Izzy exclaimed again.

"No," Griggs said. "It's a promise."

"Asshole," Jason mumbled. Then he charged at Griggs. The two of them became locked in each other's arms and tumbled to the ground.

"Stop!" Izzy yelled again.

Jason landed on top of Griggs and went to throw a punch, but Griggs moved away and made Jason lose his balance, falling to the ground. The two of them rolled around in the dirt for a moment before Izzy, Matt, and a few of the camp members ran over and pulled Jason away from Griggs, who then climbed back to his feet quickly, ready to attack. Izzy stepped between the two of them.

"Guys! Stop!" she exclaimed. "Jason, listen to me. Griggs and I worked out a deal."

"You can't trust him!" Jason yelled. "He's the enemy."

"Listen to me!" Izzy yelled back. "First of all, calm the hell down. Second, he wants Hawk out of the picture just as much as all of us. He's willing to give us information about Hawk and the prison."

"How do you know what he's telling us is true?" Jason asked.

Izzy shrugged. "I don't. But he didn't have to come back and save my life. He didn't have to come back at all. He doesn't have to offer any information to us. But he is. We can keep a close eye on him and still hear what he has to say."

Izzy seemed to reduce the tension between Jason and Griggs. Both men stared at each other for a moment before Jason returned his attention to Izzy as he pondered the deal.

"Fine," he said grudgingly. "But he's *your* responsibility. Anything happens, and it's on *you*." He pulled himself away from the camp members who were holding onto him and walked off.

"No pressure," she mumbled.

Matt released his grip on Griggs. "Don't make me give you another black eye," Matt told him.

"Don't make me choke you out like Hawk did to you," Griggs replied.

"Guys, stop," Izzy said. "No more of this. We're on the same team now, whether you like it or not. Okay?"

Both Griggs and Matt nodded.

"Good." Izzy took a deep breath before letting it out like a pressure valve. "Now, start talking, Griggs."

"Well, you guys clearly don't want to go through the front door, so we'll have to go in through the back. They don't cover it all that often, so we should be able to sneak in with no problem. Plus, you took out about fifteen or so of their men, so they're probably short-staffed anyway," Griggs said. "Once we're inside, I can guide you around the prison. We can access the armory and anything else you need."

"Do you know where Audrey is being held?" Izzy asked.

Griggs nodded. "I do."

"Besides taking their weapons, getting Audrey back is a priority," Izzy said.

"We'll get your friend back," Griggs said.

Jason made his way back over. "Look, I don't trust you. But if you're truly here to help get Audrey back and take down Hawk, then you're welcome to join us. But keep in mind, I will have my eye on you. And I won't hesitate to take you out at the slightest sign of betrayal."

Griggs held up his hand with three fingers extended. "Scout's honor."

Jason shook his head in frustration. "Whatever. Anyway, we need a place to go. We obviously can't use our camp. It's destroyed, and who knows if those Drifters will come back. Anyone have an idea where we can go?" He looked up at the sky. Dark clouds were rolling in. "It's getting darker, and a storm is probably coming through. We'll need shelter soon."

The group fell silent. No one had any idea where to go. Izzy felt tiny drops of water on her arm. They were going to need a shelter soon.

Then a thought hit her.

"I think I know where we can go," she said.

| **22** |

As the drops of rain had become steadier, Izzy found herself standing before a building nestled in the heart of the city. Jason moved up next to her and stared at the building.

"What's in here?" he asked.

"A friend," Izzy replied. She stepped into the deserted opening and headed for the door.

The steady, soothing drone of pattering rain hitting the walls of the building reverberated through the empty hallway. The sound was punctuated by the occasional drip-drip from leaks in the ceiling. A drop hit Izzy on the head as she approached the large metal door. Her knuckles banged against it.

After a moment, the door creaked open, revealing a familiar face.

"Izzy?" Chris asked. He opened the door wider and welcomed her with a friendly smile. "I'm glad to see you're alive and well." His gaze roved over her ragged appearance. He corrected himself with a smirk. "Well, maybe just alive." His attempt at humor did little to dispel the tension.

"What are you doing here?" he asked, his voice filled with genuine concern.

Izzy swallowed hard. She had one chance to make the impression she needed. She didn't know Chris all that well, but at this point, he was her only hope.

"We were attacked," she said. She explained how the Reavers attacked her camp and how one of the Drifters attacked soon afterwards.

Chris's face fell at her words. He opened the door wider as an invitation. "I'm so sorry, Izzy. Come on in," he offered.

Her instinct to get out of the open made her take a step forward before she stopped herself. She hesitated for a moment. She felt awful asking him to help her entire group. Just a few days ago, Chris and his group had held them at gunpoint when she had entered their basement hideout without notice. He had helped her group get on their feet before Pete went running off the next morning. It was only four of them then. Now she had an entire camp with her.

"I'm not alone," she admitted. "The survivors from my camp are with me."

Chris blinked in surprise. "Oh," he said, his brow furrowing in thought. "How many are you?"

"Maybe thirty?" Izzy said. "I was hoping you would be able to provide us all a place to stay," she added, her heart pounding in her chest. "I know you don't have a large place, but I was hoping you could help in some way."

Chris's expression was unreadable as he considered her request. The silence stretched on, making Izzy eager with anticipation.

Finally, Chris nodded. "Of course," he agreed, his voice warm and welcoming. "They're absolutely welcome here."

A surge of relief swept through her. "Oh my God, thank you so much," she said. "I didn't know where else to go."

"It's okay, Izzy. You and your friends were respectful and friendly. If the rest of your camp is like that, they're welcome here," Chris said.

"Thank you," she said again. She waved behind her. "The others are outside. I'll introduce you to them."

Chris followed Izzy outside. The rain was beginning to fall harder now. He followed her towards the huddled group, and she introduced him to Jason, whose wariness softened at Chris's friendly nod.

"It's nice to meet you," Chris said, extending his hand.

Jason shook his hand, accepting the welcoming gesture. "You too."

"Chris has opened his doors to us," Izzy said to the group. "All of us." There was a happy commotion amongst the group.

Matt stepped up and offered his hand. "Nice to see you again. Thank you for helping us... again."

Chris smiled. "It's good to see you too."

Shadow moved to Izzy and looked up at her. She rubbed his head. He barked once at the sight of Chris.

"I haven't forgotten about you either," Chris said. He got down on a knee and patted his head. "Here," he said, standing back up. He reached into his pocket and pulled out a granola bar. He opened the wrapper and broke it in half, then tossed a piece to Shadow, who caught it in midair.

As the rain started to come down harder, Chris gestured towards the building and said, "Let's get you all inside and out of this horrible weather." He led them through the narrow hallway and towards the metal door that led to the basement. Chris made his way downstairs first and welcomed each and every member of Izzy's camp as they made their way down.

Izzy and Jason helped Sarah and were the last to enter. Izzy shut the door behind her and descended the stairs. She looked around. The basement was smaller than she had remembered, but at least it was dry and warm.

She helped Sarah sit down and get comfortable.

"Are you okay?" Izzy asked.

"Yeah," Sarah said. "I'll be fine. How did you find this place?"

"It's kind of a long story," Izzy responded.

"Where are the other two people you were with before?" Chris asked. "Did you ever find the guy who ran off after… Audrey? Was that her name?"

Izzy nodded. "Yes, Audrey." Her heart sank at the thought she was still being held captive by Hawk and the Reavers. She could only imagine what she must be going through.

"Pete and James unfortunately didn't make it," she told him.

Chris's brows furrowed as he frowned. "I'm so sorry for your loss," he said.

"Thank you," Izzy said. "It was just—" Izzy lost her train of thought as the image of Pete being shot in the head and James being pulled through the walls by the Drifter's tentacles jumped to the forefront of her mind. She shook the thoughts away. "I'm sorry. It's just been a very crazy and emotional past few days."

Chris nodded. "I understand. I know how difficult it can be. I'm sorry again for your loss."

Izzy gave a polite smile. She noticed Jason next to her, looking around and taking in their new surroundings.

"It's a little cramped in here, don't you think?" he murmured, leaning closer to her.

Izzy nodded in agreement. She watched as members of her group were shoulder to shoulder, squeezing past each other, the tightness of the space becoming more apparent with each passing moment. "Yeah, but would you rather be out in the open?"

"No. Definitely not," he said.

Their quiet exchange didn't go unnoticed by Chris, who was quick to speak up. "Don't worry about the space," he said. "I have something to show you." He was already moving away and beckoning one of his own members to follow him. They navigated through the crowd of people to the metal cabinets at the far end of the room.

Izzy watched as they pulled the cabinets away from the wall. A gasp rippled through the crowd as a gaping hole was revealed. Everyone gathered around it. Izzy weaved her way through the crowd to see what everyone was looking at.

She couldn't believe it. It wasn't just a hole in the wall—it was a passage. And beyond that passage was another group of people, peering back at her and her group.

Chris looked at her, a smirk on his face and his eyes twinkling. He gestured at the passage.

"Welcome to my home."

| **23** |

Izzy peered into the tunnel, her eyes widening at the sight of an unexpected group of people looking back at her. The flickering candles and weak beams of flashlights from her side of the tunnel cast long shadows on their faces, giving them an eerie, otherworldly appearance. It was as if she were staring into a mirror that reflected another world—a world that was just as distressed and disoriented as hers.

"Who are... How... What is that down there?" she stuttered. She turned to Chris in confusion.

Chris simply smiled, his eyes sparkling. "*My* people," he said, his voice echoing slightly in the confined space.

Izzy felt a knot in her stomach. This made no sense to her. "You never mentioned any of this before," she replied. Why all the secrecy? What else was Chris hiding from them?

"Why would I? I didn't know who you people were when we first met," Chris said. His calm demeanor added to Izzy's frustration.

A hand was placed on Izzy's shoulder. She turned to see Jason beside her. He looked down the tunnel, his curiosity piqued. "What is this place?"

Chris stepped into the narrow opening. "Follow me," he said.

As Izzy climbed into the narrow passage, it occurred to her that this could be another trap. But why? Chris and his people had been so nice to them. Maybe that was the point—to gain her trust. She shook the insane thought away, but it still lingered. She had to remain vigilant. She didn't know what she was getting herself into.

Chris stepped out of the way, making room for Izzy to pass through the opening. She took a deep breath, preparing herself for what lay ahead. As she emerged from the tunnel, her jaw dropped at the sight that greeted her.

The tunnel opened up into a gigantic warehouse-like space. Possibly twenty bunk beds lined the walls, some of them occupied. Tables and chairs were scattered around, creating a makeshift dining area. Children ran around, their laugher echoing in the vast expanse, adding a touch of normalcy to the bizarre scene.

"What is this place?" Izzy asked, her voice barely audible. She felt a strange sense of awe and fear, her mind struggling to comprehend the situation.

"We think it was an old military bomb shelter of some kind," Chris replied nonchalantly. Izzy turned to him, her eyes wide with disbelief.

A bomb shelter? Here? How? She had so many questions.

"How did you guys get inside?" Jason asked, his practicality cutting through Izzy's shock. "Aren't these places supposed to be really secure?"

Chris shrugged. "I'm honestly not sure. The hole was here when we got here."

"Holy shit," Griggs said as he stumbled through the opening. "Look at this place. It's amazing."

Matt emerged from the tunnel with Shadow and moved to stand next to Izzy. "I can't believe it," he said.

Izzy shook her head. "Neither can I."

Shadow barked and ran into the depths of the shelter. "Shadow, come here!" Izzy yelled. Then she noticed what he was running towards. There were two other dogs in the distance—a black

Labrador and a golden retriever. The dogs all sniffed at each other before running around to play with the kids. It brought a smile to Izzy's face. She felt at peace. This place felt like a home.

"Thank you," she said to Chris. "This means a lot."

"To be honest," Chris said, "I think my people were getting bored. We haven't interacted with any other groups since…"

He trailed off.

"Since what?"

"Since we were attacked by the Reavers," Chris said. "We used to live peacefully within the city. We made ourselves at home in one of these small apartment buildings. But then this guy and his band of goons came kicking down our doors telling us they owned that area and we were on their territory."

Izzy's eyes narrowed. The story sounded quite familiar. "Do you know who it was who told you that?"

Chris shrugged. "Not sure. A big guy. He had black hair. Oh! The other people in the group called him by some kind of a bird name. Falcon? Eagle?"

"Hawk," Matt said.

"Yes, that's it. Hawk," Chris said. He sighed. "What an asshole he was. I mean, who just comes in and claims everything as his own?"

"Ask this one," Jason said, nodding to Griggs. "He's buddy-buddy with him."

"What?" Chris asked.

"*Former* buddy-buddy. He's dead to me," Griggs said. He stuck out his hand. "The name's Griggs. It's nice to meet you."

Hesitantly, Chris shook Griggs's hand.

"Ignore him," Jason said. "Continue your story."

Chris continued, "So, they came in to just take our stuff. Well, we weren't going to just let that happen. We sent one of our guys back to their camp to negotiate some kind of deal. We didn't want a war. We didn't want to fight."

"What ended up happening?" Izzy asked.

Chris shook his head. "No deal. We were told we had to leave since we were on their territory."

"Did you leave?" Jason asked.

"Hell no," Chris said. "I told my team to stand our ground. The one who went to negotiate fought me on it. He told me I was going to get my people killed. He just wanted me to give up everything to these people. Would any of you just give up your home to someone who wanted to take it?"

"That's kind of why we're here," Jason said. "We fought against those Reavers for our camp. They wanted to come take it from us."

Chris nodded. "Izzy told me. I'm really sorry you had to deal with them too."

"What happened when the Reavers came back?" Izzy asked.

Chris's faced soured. "We lost. And it happened just like how I was warned. We lost people. Good people. We eventually retreated. I had to do something to protect the group we had left. We grabbed whatever we could as we rushed out of there."

"I'm sorry," Izzy said.

"It's okay. I mean, I know we all lost people. It's the nature of the world we live in now. But look at where we are because of it. It's horrible, what had to happen for us to get here. But, I guess, sometimes you just have to look on the brighter side of things."

Griggs chuckled.

"What?" Chris asked.

Griggs shook his head. "Sorry. You guys—you seriously think there's a *brighter side* to all of this?" He gestured around the shelter. "*This? This* is a brighter side?" He dropped his hands back down to his sides. "You guys are so sheltered. It's no wonder you were so easily taken over."

"Griggs, stop!" Izzy snapped.

"No, it's okay," Chris said. "What do you mean by that, Griggs?"

"I know you guys want to think you're the *good* guys," Griggs said. "You want to care about people's *feelings* and treat people fairly. But you know who doesn't care about that? Hawk. The rest of the Reavers. Probably many other groups out there too. You know what they *do* care about? Survival. Power. Supplies. Food. You want to beat these groups? You need to march into their camp and take them all out. Drop the feelings crap. They don't care about you. Why should you care about them?"

"Because that makes us no better than them," Izzy said.

"Who gives a shit?" Griggs said. "Look around, Izzy. Look at where you are. Look at the state our world is in—those creatures roaming around up there, killing people at will and with ease. It's about survival now. You want to go back to your cellphones, social media, TV, bar hopping, whatever little world you grew up in... you may need to start thinking about how to get to tomorrow. Advocating for a group who will kill you in a heartbeat will not give you a long lifespan in this current world."

"I'm not advocating for the death of all of them," Izzy said. "I only want to take out Hawk."

Griggs smiled. "See? You do want death. It's in there, isn't it?" He leaned in closer to her. "You know I'm right."

She wanted to hit him. Knock him on his ass where he belonged. But for some reason, she couldn't. She stared at Griggs with such anger, but not because he had just freaked out at her, but because he was right—again. And she *hated* when he was right.

"He's right," Chris said. "The Reavers don't care about anyone but themselves. They're ruthless, selfish, and only care about their own survival."

"See? He understands. They even back stabbed you guys," Griggs added, his gaze shifting between Izzy and Jason. "They don't care about you. Why would you give one ounce of energy to caring about them?"

The accusation stung, but it also sparked a defiant flame within Izzy. She stepped closer to Griggs, returning his glare. "Because I refuse to believe not every one of them is as evil as Hawk is. I honestly believe there are good people there who are just caught up in it all."

Griggs scoffed, stepped back and waved her off. "I'm telling ya, Izzy. It's going to be your downfall." He turned his back on her and disappeared into the depths of the shelter.

His warning echoed in her mind, filling her with doubt. It was the same doubt Chris had been left with when his friend had warned him of the Reavers. Was she wrong to hold on to hope? Should she adopt a more ruthless approach, becoming like one of the Reavers herself? The thought made her stomach churn. No. She couldn't do that. She wouldn't. She was better than that. There had to be a better way.

Her thoughts were interrupted by Matt's voice. "Now what?" he asked.

"Well, at this point, the buckets we have outside may be filling up with water from all the rain," Chris said. "Care to assist me in replenishing our water supply?"

"Of course," Matt said. As Chris moved back into the tunnel, Matt turned to Izzy. "Are you coming?"

Izzy nodded. "Yeah, I need some fresh air anyway."

"Don't let him get to you," Matt said, noticing Izzy's somber expression.

"He's right, though," Izzy said. "That's the thing—*he's right*. In order to get to Hawk, we'll have to take out everyone else in our way. That could be a few of the Reavers, or it could be all of them." She turned back to look at the group in the shelter. "What if some of the Reavers are people like them? Just there to make a home for themselves."

"Maybe they don't have a choice," Matt said. "Maybe by us taking out Hawk, we can free them of his reign." He reached out for her with his hand.

"I hope so," she said, taking his hand as he led her through the tunnel and back into the small basement.

Chris gathered a few others and had already begun making his way up the stairs. Izzy and Matt trailed behind Chris and the rest of his group as they marched up the stairs and into the dark hallway. The rain outside had transitioned from a gentile drizzle to an unforgiving downpour.

Chris led them through the hallways to the back of the building. His voice cut through the pounding rain, "Ready to get wet?" There were nods from all around. "Let's go!"

When they emerged into the open, they were immediately drenched by the pouring rain. They each grabbed one of the large buckets scattered around the alley behind the building. Izzy's hands were slippery, and she struggled for a moment to get a good grip on her own bucket. Once she had lifted it up, she made her way back to the door.

Suddenly, a name rang out, causing Izzy to freeze in her tracks. "Dalton?"

That name—he died. She had thought she would never hear that name again.

Turning around, she saw a figure slowly walk through the pouring rain. Once he got closer, she saw that it was truly Dalton. He was supposed to be dead. She had watched him die, watched as the Drifters had attacked him. Then the realization of what had happened dawned on her. He was infected. That Drifter... its tentacle...

Dropping her bucket, she went to warn the others. But it was too late. Dalton raised his arm—his hand was clutching a gun—and opened fire.

| 24 |

Deafening gunshots rang out. A woman screamed, falling to the ground, her life extinguished in an instant. Chris's voice cut through the chaos, issuing a desperate command.

"Run!"

Suddenly, Izzy was hit with a force that knocked the breath out of her. She hit the wet ground hard, the cold ground-water seeping through her already soaked clothes. Matt's body covered hers, forming a human shield against the bullets flying their way. His heavy breathing mirrored her own fear.

Izzy looked up, watching Dalton continue to fire, his face contorted with a twisted snarl on his lips. Bullets continue to whiz by as people tried desperately to escape. Then, just as suddenly as it had started, the gunfire stopped.

Chris had pulled out his handgun and shot at Dalton, who had dropped his gun and collapsed onto the rain-soaked ground.

Matt rolled off Izzy, and she pushed herself up, watching as Chris ran over to Dalton, kicking the gun away from his reach. He barked orders at the remaining members of his group, his voice filled with urgency. "Check on everyone. Makes sure everyone is okay."

Izzy found herself drawn to Chris, her legs moving almost on autopilot. He knelt over Dalton's body. The man's breathing was shallow and ragged. With his last bit of strength, Dalton reached for Chris, his hands shaking. Then, his arms fell to the side, his body going limp. He was dead.

Chris brushed his hand over Dalton's face, closing his eyes.

"Lori is dead," a woman said behind Izzy. "Tom was shot in the arm, but should be okay. We're going to take him inside to see Charles."

Chris nodded. "Okay."

The woman left and Izzy was left with Matt and Chris, who was still kneeling over Dalton's body.

"What the hell was he doing here?" Matt asked. "I thought you said he was dead?"

"He was," Izzy replied. She was trying to make sense of what had just happened. She knew he watched him die. When that tentacle latched onto his face, that must have been how they infect others.

"How do you know Dalton?" Chris asked, looking up at them. His question was met with a shared look of confusion between Matt and Izzy.

"How do *you* know Dalton?" Izzy countered.

Chris sighed, his gaze dropping to Dalton's lifeless body. "He's my friend. Well, *was* my friend. He was the one who negotiated on behalf of our group—the story I told you about earlier. The one who tried to convince me to give everything up to the Reavers. He disappeared soon after we discovered this place."

Izzy shook her head, a cold realization dawning on her. Dalton had betrayed Chris and his group. "He was working with the Reavers," she told him. "He's the one who attacked our camp with a group of them."

Chris stood up and shook his head. "No. No, that's not possible. He was my friend. He wouldn't do that."

"I'm sorry," Izzy said. "He was working with them. He was close with Hawk too."

Chris looked at Matt, who nodded in support of Izzy's claim. "It's true," he told him.

Chris fell silent, processing it all. Betrayal, deceit, and death. It was a lot to take in. They were in deeper than they had thought, and Izzy couldn't help but wonder what else could possibly go wrong.

"That son of a bitch!" Chris exclaimed. "How could he do that to me? After everything I did for him!" He drove his fists into Dalton's lifeless body, each punch punctuating his seething fury with a loud thud. Water splashed up each time he connected with the dead man's chest. "Asshole!" He continued his onslaught, his voice growing hoarser with each word. "All because of you!"

Matt stepped forward to hold Chris back. "He's dead," he said.

Chris shook off Matt's grip. "I know. Just... letting out some frustration."

The three of them remained there in the pouring rain, the silence only broken by the steady rain and occasional thunder. They all seemed to be waiting for someone else to make the first move.

"Just give me a minute," Chris said. "You can go inside. I'll meet you there."

With that, Matt and Izzy left Chris alone with Dalton's corpse.

"You think he'll be okay?" Matt asked.

"Yeah," Izzy said. "If he knew Dalton from before, maybe he just..." Izzy trailed off. A chilling realization washed over her. "Shit."

"What?" Matt asked.

"Chris!" she called out, as she rushed back over to him. "We need to leave, now!"

"Why?" he asked.

"The infected, they're like a homing device for these creatures," Izzy said. "They'll show up at some point. It's what happened to us. Someone we knew got infected somehow and showed back up at our camp doing the same thing as Dalton."

Izzy was taken aback when Chris didn't react. Izzy was taken aback. She had just told him that his shelter was about to be invaded by deadly creatures, and he seemed unfazed. What was wrong with him?

"Did you hear me?" she asked again.

"Yeah, I heard you," Chris replied calmly.

Izzy couldn't believe his nonchalance. "Are you not concerned? The Drifters are on their way! We have to leave."

"Why?" he asked, his tone casual. "Let's just kill it."

Izzy's heart stopped. Kill it? Did he honestly mean that? Until a few hours ago, she hadn't even known these creatures could be injured, let alone killed.

"I'm sorry, you said 'kill it'. How? Have you killed these things before?" Izzy asked.

"Actually, I've killed two," Chris said casually, as if he was discussing the weather instead of killing monstrous creatures.

"Two?" Matt and Izzy repeated in unison, their shock mirrored on each other's faces.

"How?" Matt demanded. "And if they can be killed, how come we've never seen a dead one before?"

Chris simply replied, "I guess you'll soon see why."

With that, he got up and walked back towards the entrance of the building, leaving Izzy and Matt standing in the pouring rain. They stood there, staring at each other. Izzy was speechless. Kill a Drifter? What was Chris not telling them?

"You guys coming, or what?" Chris said, pausing at the entrance, looking back at them. "We have a Drifter attack to prepare for."

| **25** |

Izzy and Matt followed Chris back down the stairs to the basement and into the bunker. The dampness of her clothes made Izzy shiver.

"Let me get you guys a towel. Wait right here," Chris said, and then wandered off.

As Izzy looked around the bunker, she noticed the guy who was injured by Dalton's attack. He sat on a bed with three others around him. One of them was crying hysterically. Izzy could faintly hear her say the name Courtney. Another woman had her arms wrapped around her, attempting to comfort her.

Chris walked back and handed each of them a towel.

Izzy gestured to the woman crying. "What's going on over there?"

Chris glanced over and then back at Izzy. "Sean is injured, so they're patching him up. He'll be fine."

"I meant the woman," Izzy said.

"Oh, her? That's Jessica. Her friend Courtney was the one Dalton shot and killed. She's taking it just as hard as I'd expect anyone who lost a good friend. It's such a tragedy losing people like this." Chris continued, "Come to think of it, Courtney is the first person we've lost since we got here. We've been so good about keeping a low profile."

"I'm sorry for your loss," Matt said.

"Thank you," Chris said. "You kind of just get numb to all the death. We always just need to keep moving forward."

Izzy looked at the bed next to Sean's and saw Sarah sleeping. Shadow was cuddled up at the foot of the bed, keeping her company. It was comforting knowing Shadow could be there for Sarah, when she herself couldn't be.

"Follow me. We need to prepare," Chris said. He made his way through the crowd to the other side of the shelter, calling people's names and waving for them to follow him. It was as if he was just plucking people out of the crowd.

He approached a large door. Izzy's eyes widened as he slid it open to reveal a closet filled with weapons. Even more guns, knives, and explosives sat on a display table in front of them—it was an arsenal fit for an army. She heard Matt, Jason, and Griggs all let out gasps. She had never seen such a stockpile of weapons.

"We have a reason to believe a Drifter is on its way here to attack us," Chris told the crowd of people he had brought with him. There were some grumbles, but Chris put up his hands to silence them. "Guys, we've been in this situation before. Have you all forgotten? We've taken out two of these things already. We've got this."

"How do you kill them?" Jason asked.

"With this," Chris pulled out a trunk tucked under the display table. He unlocked it and opened it up, revealing four giant red canisters. He handed them out one by one.

"What is this?" Jason asked after receiving a canister.

"Gasoline," Chris replied. He reached back into the chest to pull out two thick, wound-up tubes, and passed them to two other people.

Izzy narrowed in on Chris and watched him closely. He clearly had a plan and had killed these creatures before. She was excited to learn how. "Is there anything I can help you with?"

Chris turned to her. "Sure." He reached into the trunk and pulled out a duffel bag, handing it to her. "Find people who are willing to help."

Izzy nodded. She opened the bag, then blinked in surprise at its contents. Was this some kind of joke? "Super soakers?" she asked, pulling out a large, brightly colored water gun.

Beside her, Griggs snorted. "I thought you said we needed to kill the Drifter, not have a water fight with it," he said.

Chris took the gun from Izzy's grip, then popped the top off of it. "You fill it with gasoline. Trust me, this thing won't find anything fun about what we're going to be doing."

"What's with the tubes?" Matt asked.

"It's a makeshift sprinkler system, filled with gasoline," Chris said. He took one of the hoses from someone standing next to him, then pointed along the hose. "There are holes spaced out every foot or so. The hose stretches from our roof to the roof across the street. When the Drifter gets underneath of it, we douse it with gasoline. The people with water guns will be positioned in different windows, shooting gasoline at it too. Then," he picked up a flare gun from the shelf and tucked it into his belt, "we light it up." He smiled and nodded to Izzy before saying, "Alright everyone, let's go. You all remember your positions from last time?"

Each member of the group nodded and voiced their affirmations.

"Good," Chris said, his eyes scanning the group. "Into positions in five minutes. Izzy—bring your friends onto the roof."

"Okay," she said.

With that, the group dispersed, leaving Izzy alone with Matt, Jason, and Griggs. The silence hung in the air, broken only by the occasional drip of water from their still-soaked clothes.

Griggs was the first to speak up. "Did anyone else feel completely lost in that pep talk?"

"For once, I actually agree with Griggs," Jason said. "He didn't explain how we would get the Drifter doused in gasoline. I mean, yes, with the water guns and his hoses, but it's not going to just stand still for us while we do that."

"Yeah, Izzy. I'm not looking to get myself killed in this expedition," Griggs said.

"Let's just see this through," she told them. "He seems to know what he's doing, so let's just go along with it. He says he's killed two of them before. His group seems to be backing him, so let's just see what happens." She tossed a super soaker to Griggs, who promptly tossed it back.

"Don't give me that shit. You know damn well that stupid water pistol is not going to do anything against that ten-foot-tall creature," Griggs said.

Matt chimed in. "Those *water pistols* have some power and distance to them." All eyes turned to him. He shrugged. "What? I used to play with them as a kid."

Griggs shook his head, his expression a mixture of disbelief and annoyance. "I can't believe I'm working with a bunch of nerds. I'm going to die here."

"Shut up, Griggs," Matt said. "We're all in this together. You said you wanted to help—then help." He took the water gun from Izzy, then shoved it into Griggs's chest. "Take the water gun and help us out. Okay?"

As Izzy watched the exchange, she felt the tension crackling between them like an electric current. Griggs stared down at Matt. "I don't take orders from you. I didn't make a deal with you." He turned towards Izzy. "Is this your play?"

Izzy nodded. Her throat was dry. She didn't want any part in this power struggle. All she wanted to do was survive, to fight back against the Drifter that would soon arrive.

Griggs's lips twisted into a bitter smile. "Then I guess we're going to the roof," he said, turning on his heel and stalking off. His footsteps echoed as he disappeared into the tunnel.

"I'll go make sure he does nothing stupid," Jason said. He nodded at Izzy and Matt before following Griggs, leaving them alone.

"You really think this is the right move here?" Matt asked.

Izzy honestly didn't know. She wasn't the decision maker—Jason was. Why was he taking a back seat in this whole situation? Why did it feel like she was in charge now?

"I don't know, Matt," she replied. "I think Chris is going to do this whether we help him or not, and I feel like we owe it to him to help him out, considering he did allow us to stay with him and his group. And he helped us out before."

Matt nodded. "Yeah, I guess you're right, Izzy."

Izzy smiled. "Thanks, Matt."

"For what?" he asked.

She reached out and took his hand. "For being here. For having my back. It means a lot."

"You know I always have your back," Matt said.

She let go of his hand and put her arms around him, giving him a hug. After a moment, she pulled away. "I'm going to go let Sarah know what's going on and then I'll meet you on the roof, okay?"

Matt nodded. "Sure. I'll see you soon." Then they went their separate ways.

* * *

Sarah's bed was tucked away in a quiet corner of the bunker. Shadow perked up as Izzy approached, his tail thumping against the bedsheets. Izzy felt a small smile tug at her lips as she ruffled his fur, then pressed a gentle kiss to his snout.

"How are you feeling, Sarah?" Izzy asked.

Sarah attempted a weak smile, but her pale face was a stark contrast to the dark circles under her eyes.

"I'm okay," she said. "The doctor has been giving me painkillers, which is definitely helping." She paused. Her eyes were slightly glazed. "It also makes me feel a little drunk."

Izzy couldn't help but laugh. She sat on the edge of the bed, her hand resting comfortingly on Sarah's leg. "I'm glad it's helping." Izzy prepared herself for the next part. She looked down at her hands as she was fidgeting with the blanket underneath her. She looked back up at Sarah. "Hey, look. I just wanted to let you know I'm about to go do something pretty dangerous."

Sarah giggled. "Dangerous? When do you *not* do something dangerous?"

Izzy thought back to all the risks she had taken, all the close calls, especially over the last few days. "Yeah, I guess you're right. I guess I do a lot of dangerous things. But this one is big. Chris said he knows how to kill the Drifters."

Sarah tried to sit up. A gasp escaped her lips as pain shot through her body. "Wait, seriously?" she managed to choke out.

Izzy quickly pushed against her, urging her to lie back down. "Stop. Lay down, Sarah. Just rest."

Defeated, Sarah leaned back, but her eyes didn't leave Izzy's. "Fine. But you still better tell me what's happening."

Izzy relayed Chris's plan to her, explaining how he had killed two Drifters before. Sarah listened attentively, a spark of hope flickering in her eyes.

"So you know how to kill them now?" Sarah asked.

Izzy shrugged. "I guess we'll see."

"I wish I could join you guys," Sarah said.

"I know. Me too." Izzy leaned in and gave Sarah a kiss on her forehead. "I have to get going. Take care of Shadow for me." At the mention of his name, Shadow lifted his head and barked once. Izzy gave him one last hug, promising to see them again shortly.

"We'll be fine," Sarah said. "Go kill that Drifter for me."

| **26** |

The rain was beginning to slow to a drizzle when Izzy finally made it onto the roof. Chris was in the middle of the chaos, barking orders as everyone scrambled to complete their tasks.

"What's going on?" Izzy asked Matt, who was standing off to the side.

"Chris had these cords that everyone is pulling on to bring the hoses from the ground up to the roof," Matt explained, his eyes focused on the scene before them.

Before Izzy could ask anything else, Chris joined them. "What we're doing is having these hoses go from one roof to the other," Chris began, pointing towards the hoses that were slowly being pulled up. "Once the Drifters gets underneath it, we dump all the gasoline into the hoses, which then spray out onto it. And then when it's covered, I'll shoot it with the flare gun and that thing will light up like a gigantic fireball."

"Are you sure this is going to work?" Izzy asked.

"It's worked twice before. Have some faith, Izzy," Chris said, his voice reassuring.

Jason chimed in next with his question. "So, you explained how you drop the gasoline on the Drifter, but how do you get it in the right position? Do you lure it there? How do you get it to stay where you want it to?"

"There's a giant net on the street," Chris explained. "Once we lure that thing into position, we'll trap it in the net. It'll piss it off, so we'll only have a few seconds at that point to do what we have to do."

Griggs raised his hand. "I have a question. How do we lure it into position?"

"We pull straws," Chris said.

"What the hell does that mean?" Griggs asked, his eyes wide.

"We pull straws to see who will lure the Drifter into the trap," Chris clarified.

Griggs looked horrified. "Oh, hell no. You mean be bait?"

Chris nodded. "Don't worry, you're not alone when you're down there. It'll be two of you."

"Well whoopty freakin' doo. That surely must make it more comforting, right? Just be faster than the slowest guy running from the Drifter," Griggs said.

"It's not like that. You're way ahead of it. You're there more to get it to head in this direction rather than that direction—that kind of thing," Chris said.

Griggs threw his hands up and turned away. "I'm out. You know damn well I'll be picking that short straw and be down there. There ain't no way I'm being bait for that thing."

"Griggs!" Izzy shouted. "We had a deal. Get back here and do your part to help."

Griggs stopped. He turned and stared at Izzy. Finally, he walked back to the group and stood up close to her. "If I end up with the short straw, your ass is going down there with me."

Izzy knew in order to continue to get Griggs's assistance, she'd have to give in to him. She didn't want his help, but they needed everyone helping on this. A Drifter was coming to attack and they had to prepare. She needed Griggs to comply.

She stuck out her hand. "Deal."

Griggs looked down at it and took it, shaking on the deal.

A loud *snap* caught everyone's attention. Everyone turned towards the source of the sound. Chris had moved to the ledge, grabbed one of the hoses, and locked it into place with another *snap*.

"Hoses are in place," he announced, standing up and brushing off his hands. He scanned the group, and his gaze landed on Izzy. "Now to attach the funnels to unload the gasoline quickly, and then we're all set."

Izzy felt a knot forming in her stomach. It was all becoming real now, the danger of their plan settling in. She looked around, constantly second guessing Chris's plan. Had he *really* killed a Drifter before? Was this plan going to work?

"Izzy," Chris said, "start filling those super soakers from one of the red canisters, and then hand them out to others. Then we'll pull straws to see who'll be on the ground for this."

Matt stood to her left, already holding one of the canisters. "Wanna get started?"

"Sure," Izzy said. They walked off to the side and emptied the duffel bag of six large super soakers. Matt immediately picked one of them up.

"Aww, cool. I used to have this one," he said.

"You're such a dork," Izzy said.

"Oh, see, that hurts. You're starting to sound like Griggs now," Matt said sarcastically.

Izzy punched him in the arm. "You take that back!"

Matt rubbed his arm. "Ouch. You got me right on the joint."

"And I'll do it again," Izzy said, though a smile was beginning to undermine her tough-girl attitude.

Matt smiled. For a moment, the two of them were both all smiles and in good spirits. Then Matt broke eye contact and looked around the roof. The smile slowly faded from his face.

"Do you think whoever ends up being the bait will be okay?" Matt asked. "Seems like a pretty risky job."

Izzy shrugged. "I mean, Chris seems confident, so I'm hoping the confidence pays off."

The two of them continued to discuss the plan while they each took turns filling up the super soakers with gasoline. Once they were done, they started handing them out to other people.

Chris's voice rang out as he called everyone together on the roof. "We all know what to do, right?" he asked, his gaze sweeping over the assembled group. Izzy nodded along with the others. "Good," Chris said. He reached down to grab a handful of twigs from the roof, snapped them into even pieces, then broke two smaller than the rest. "Alright guys, start picking," he instructed, holding out his hand.

One by one, each person reached into Chris's hand as they picked a twig. They all compared sizes, determining who would be the bait.

"Shit," one of Chris's guys muttered, holding up his twig. It was one of the shorter ones. "Looks like I'm one of them."

"Son of a bitch," a familiar voice cursed, drawing Izzy's attention. She saw Griggs throw his twig on the ground, his face a mask of disbelief. "I told you I'd be the one to do this," he grumbled. "Lucky you," he said, pointing at Izzy. "You get to join me. You made a deal."

Fear pierced Izzy like a cold blade. She hadn't expected it to come to this. The odds had been in her favor, or so she had thought. But now, she was facing the reality of being bait for this Drifter. "A deal's a deal," she said, accepting her fate.

"No!" Matt yelled, his voice carrying around the roof. "He chose fair and square, just like the rest of us."

Izzy reached out to put her hand on Matt's arm. She could see the worry all over on his face. "I'll be alright, Matt," she assured him, forcing a smile. "It's only fair. I made this deal with Griggs."

She turned to Chris. "And I trust you'll keep me alive." She felt a giant knot in her stomach. Just a few hours ago, she'd already had the closest call she'd ever had with one of these creatures. She didn't want to chance her luck by getting that close again.

"I won't lie to you—it's going to be dangerous, Izzy," Chris warned her. "But I promise you, I'll have your back. My group and I will protect you and your friend."

Griggs snickered, leaning towards Izzy. "He called me your friend," he whispered.

Izzy ignored the comment.

Jason put a hand on Matt's shoulder, making him flinch. "She'll be alright," Jason said. He looked at Izzy. "Are you sure you want to do this?"

Izzy nodded. "It's the right thing to do. I made a deal with Griggs. I'm sure you don't want to deal with that backlash if I decided to not follow through on that."

"Hey!" Griggs said.

"You wouldn't have given me shit and put up an argument if I didn't follow through on my word?" Izzy said.

Griggs shrugged. "I guess you have a point there."

"Look, if Chris said this is the best way to take out the Drifter, let's just get this over with," Izzy said.

"Good," Chris said. "You and your friend will be in the intersection over there," he pointed to the right. "Once it knows you're there, it'll come your way. Lead it where we're standing and we'll handle the rest. Once that net gets it, we will have to act fast. It won't hold it for long. It'll only confuse it for a moment."

"What about the other guy who pulled the other straw?" Griggs asked.

"We don't need three people down there," Chris said. "Two will be enough, so he's off the hook since Izzy is joining you."

"Lucky..." Griggs said, rolling his eyes.

The plan was risky, bordering on reckless. How long would the Drifter be held in place? Would it be long enough to make sure the plan worked? What happened if she didn't make it there in time? She would be on the ground with a Drifter who would rip her apart in the blink of an eye.

Suddenly, a chilling howl echoed through the night. Everyone turned in the direction it came from.

Chris quickly ordered everyone into position. "It's coming."

| 27 |

Izzy's hands began to sweat as she made her way to the intersection. She wiped them on her pants, trying to dry them off. Her damp clothes sent a chill through her every time the wind blew, but it was the memory of the Drifter that scared her, the terror she had felt just hours ago when she had barely escaped with her life. She loathed the thought of facing another one again. Of being so close to danger, to death.

At least she had Griggs with her. Despite his gruff exterior, he was capable and resourceful. And he had saved her life more times than she had cared to admit. If she had to face this nightmare, there were few people she'd prefer to have by her side.

A part of her felt relieved knowing that Matt was safe rather than being down here with her. Matt, who had been there for her throughout this whole adventure. Who had looked out for her, and cared for her. He would only have put himself in danger trying to protect her if he were here. The more Izzy faced these dangers, the more she realized just how much he meant to her.

And then there was Sarah, safe and secure in the bunker. Izzy drew a sigh of relief at the thought of her friend, glad that she wouldn't have to face the same horrors they were about to confront.

Izzy and Griggs reached the middle of the intersection. The silence of the city seemed to press down on her. She glanced up at the rooftop to see the heads of her friends and Chris's group peeking over the edge. She wondered what they were talking about. Were they just as afraid as she was? Were they praying for them to return safely?

A sudden touch on Izzy's shoulder made her jump. "Dammit, Griggs," she hissed. "You scared the hell out of me."

"Sorry," he replied. "You seemed focused on something else. I'd kind of like to have you present for this."

Before she could respond, another howl carried across the darkened city streets—it came from somewhere much closer this time. Izzy's breath got caught in her throat as a wave of fear flowed through her.

"You ready for this?" Izzy asked.

"Do I have a choice?" Griggs said.

They turned in all directions, looking for any sight of the creature. Darkness consumed three of the four streets. Flashlights and lanterns lit the path to safety and, hopefully, the creature's soon-to-be graveyard.

Another howl.

Closer this time.

"Where is it coming from?" Griggs asked, searching frantically.

Izzy's gaze quickly moved from street to street. She couldn't see anything. "I don't know," she said.

"Watch out!" a voice yelled faintly from the rooftops.

Izzy saw a projectile coming in the air towards them. She squinted to try and focus on what it was.

A sudden force sent Izzy sprawling. The push was so forceful that she stumbled, the rough asphalt scraping her palms as she tried to catch herself. But it was no use. She lost her balance and fell hard onto the ground. She looked up just in time to see a car hurtling towards where she and Griggs had been standing only seconds ago. It bounced twice before rolling over in a cacophony of screeching metal and shattering glass.

"Griggs?" Izzy whispered.

He had vanished into the swirling dust and debris. Fear overwhelmed her. Where did he go? Had the car hit him? Had he sacrificed himself to save her?

A blood-curdling howl echoed through the streets, coming from the same direction the car had been thrown from. The Drifter was there, lurking in the shadows. Slowly, her eyes adjusted to the darkness. Then she saw a monstrous form emerging from the shadows. The sight of its long, slithering tentacles sent a rush of adrenaline through her, propelling her onto her feet.

Acting on pure instinct, Izzy bolted in the opposite direction, the plan completely forgotten in the moment. The car blocked her path, and survival was all that mattered now. She could hear distant shouts, and her name carried on the wind, but they were quickly drowned out by the thunderous roar of the creature. It slammed its tentacles onto the ground, vibrating the ground beneath her feet. It charged into the intersection, a hulking mass of black, slimy terror. With a casual flick of a tentacle, it brushed the car aside as if it was nothing more than an inconvenience.

Izzy bolted through the first door she came across. She found herself in an abandoned restaurant, the air heavy with dust. Without wasting a second, she weaved her way through the maze of tables and chairs, heading for the kitchen.

Just as she pushed through the swinging kitchen doors, the Drifter crashed through the front entrance, sending shards of glass and splintered wood flying in all directions. A tentacle whipped out, reaching for her, but she was already in the kitchen, beyond its grasp. Izzy sprinted through it, knocking pots and pans onto the floor in her wake, hoping the clutter would slow the creature down. She burst through the back door and into a narrow alley.

She didn't stop, didn't dare to look back as she ran towards the main street.

Izzy could hear the sounds of the wall being ripped apart behind her as she turned the corner, pressing herself against the cool and damp brick wall. She was panting heavily. She wished things would have just gone to plan. Why did things always have to get so complicated?

She risked a glance behind her, only to see the creature tearing through the building across the alley. How was she supposed to survive this? She had already beaten death with one of these monsters earlier. Could she do it again? She wished the thought of surviving another Drifter attack wasn't at the top of her mind.

The plan.

She needed to get back to the main street and lead the Drifter into the trap. But how?

Suddenly, Izzy realized the howling had stopped, the crashing ceased. She hadn't noticed until now. How long ago had it stopped? Cautiously, she peeked around the corner. The alley was empty. The creature was gone. But where?

The memory of the plan surged back with a clarity that cut through her fear.

Chris's trap—that was her destination.

With a final backwards glance down the deserted alley, Izzy pushed herself away from the wall. Each step she took was cautious, careful and quiet, and she kept close to the buildings as she navigated back towards the intersection.

The overturned vehicle still lay motionless in the middle of the street.

Griggs.

The possibility of him being hit by that car was a thought she didn't dare entertain. Forcing herself to approach the vehicle, she called out softly, "Griggs?" She looked into the wreckage, bracing herself for the worst. "Griggs?" she whispered again. But there was nothing—no body, no blood, and no sign of Griggs. Where had he disappeared to?

The Drifter's resounding howl sent a jolt of terror through Izzy's body. Its grotesque form burst from the alleyway and into the street. Its gaze met hers and it opened its mouth, letting out a monstrous roar.

She had to stick to the plan.

Izzy turned on her heel and bolted towards the trap. Panic took over. Was she far enough ahead of the Drifter? Would she make it in time? Would it catch her before she made it to the trap? She quickly suppressed these questions. She couldn't afford any doubt right now.

"I'll make it," she muttered under her breath. She forced herself to believe it as she ran as fast as she could.

The sound of the creature rushing through the street echoed in Izzy's ears, growing louder and more terrifying with each second. She could see the others up ahead, their arms flailing wildly as they urged her on. She thought they were yelling at her, but their shouts were drowned out by the deafening roar of the Drifter and the sounds of destruction it left in its wake.

Almost there, she thought. She could see the spot she needed to lead the Drifter to. But just as hope began to bloom within her, a tentacle brushed against her, sending her tumbling onto the street. As she rolled over, she came face to face with the creature looming over her.

Suddenly, a giant net sprung from the side of the building, ensnaring the Drifter in its grip. Its mouth dropped open wide, screaming in frustration and anger. Its tentacles were thrashing violently in an attempt to free itself.

"Izzy, move!" a voice yelled from above—but she was trapped. Her foot was entangled in the net.

"I can't! I'm stuck!" she yelled back in a panic. She tried wiggling her way out of the net, but as the creature thrashed, pulling Izzy with it.

Izzy pulled out the knife that had saved her before and started hacking at the net with all her might.

"Izzy!" Chris yelled. "Get out of the way!"

Ignoring Chris and the fear pulsating inside of her, she focused on cutting herself free. Being pulled from side to side made things more difficult, but Izzy continued slicing the net back and forth. She looked up briefly and saw that Chris had his flare gun aimed in her direction.

"Izzy!" he yelled once more. She ignored him and continued cutting.

Finally, with one last desperate slash, she severed the last threads of the net and pulled her foot free.

"Go!" she screamed, stumbling backwards as liquids began pouring onto the Drifter from the hoses above, and squirted from the windows on both sides of the streets. The pungent smell of gasoline assaulted Izzy's nostrils, making her cover her nose and mouth with her hands.

The Drifter whipped one of its tentacles right against the building Chris was standing by, making him lose his balance as he shot the flare gun. His shot went wide, the flare missing its mark and landing a few yards behind Izzy.

It exploded with a deafening boom, scattering embers like rain of fire—unfortunately, too far away to connect with the creature. The flare burned, casting an ominous glow over the Drifter, illuminating its dark, gooey skin and giving it an eerie orange color. It continued to whip its tentacles around and thrash its body as it tried to free itself from the net.

Izzy looked up to see everyone on the rooftops scrambling to get situated. She glanced back at the Drifter, which had begun to tear apart the net it was trapped within. Strand by strand, the net dripped off and crumbled to the ground like wet paper.

The creature tilted its head and looked directly at Izzy. It opened its mouth wide and let out a thunderous roar.

A crackle of gunfire distracted the Drifter. It swung around to face the new threat, momentarily forgetting about Izzy.

A rough and gravelly voice rang out, "Get away from her, you ugly son of a bitch!"

"Griggs?" Izzy murmured. Four more shots rang out in rapid succession before she heard the distinct *click* of an empty gun.

"Anytime now," Griggs yelled.

Suddenly, an object whistled through the air towards the creature. It connected with a resonating *thud* and exploded into a fiery inferno. The Drifter was instantly engulfed in flames, its piercing screams of agony making Izzy cover her ears. The monstrous beast thrashed wildly for a few seconds before slowing down. Its tentacles dropped to the ground, lifeless. Finally, it collapsed as the fire continued to burn and consume it.

A hand suddenly appeared at Izzy's side. "Need some help?" Griggs offered.

Izzy took his hand, allowing him to pull her to her feet.

"Everyone okay down there?" Chris yelled from the rooftop.

Griggs gave a thumbs up in response, before turning back to Izzy. "You okay?"

Anger surged within her, and she punched him in the chest, knocking him back a step.

"What the hell, Izzy?" he exclaimed in surprise.

"Where the hell did you go?" she demanded.

"After I pushed you out of the way from certain death—you're welcome, by the way—I jumped in the other direction away from the vehicle barreling down on us," Griggs said. "Then I headed into the closest building I could find to get away from that beast."

"Oh, I'm so glad you could get away from *that beast*, because *that beast* came after me," Izzy said.

"I know. I saw," Griggs said.

"You saw?" she repeated. "And you did nothing to help?"

"I helped. I got it away from you, didn't I?"

Izzy rolled her eyes at his self-assured response. "Nothing like waiting until the last possible second, huh?" She couldn't help the sarcasm that crept into her voice. But despite the anger and adrenaline still coursing through her veins, she was alive and safe, thanks to Griggs's timely distraction.

"Izzy!"

Matt's voice was like a beacon of hope. She spun around to see him sprinting towards her, his arms opened wide. She ran into them without hesitation, her own arms wrapping around him in a tight embrace.

"I'm so relieved you're okay," he breathed into her hair.

Izzy pulled away, her hands still gripping his arms as she looked up at him. "Me too. You have no idea…" She trailed off, overwhelmed by the enormity of what she had just survived. The tidal wave of her emotions left her feeling dizzy.

Chris emerged from the building. He pointed towards the creature, still engulfed in flames. "See?" he called out.

The Drifter was melting, its form disintegrating into a pool of black liquid that spread across the street. She stepped backwards instinctively, not wanting to be anywhere near the goo spreading towards her.

"When these things die, they basically turn to liquid," Chris explained, walking up to stand beside her. "There's just no trace of them once they've died."

Izzy couldn't comprehend it, couldn't wrap her mind around what she was seeing. The creature's gooey, black skin was just melting off like hot candle wax in the face of a roaring flame. The sight was horrifying, yet mesmerizing. It was as if the creature was dissolving into the shadows from which it had sprung, leaving behind nothing but the chilling memory of its existence.

"So they just turn into this black goo?" Izzy asked.

Chris simply nodded, his gaze still fixed on the melting remains of the Drifter. "Hence why you don't see any dead ones."

"I guess this makes it three for you," Jason said, stepping onto the street.

"Sure does," Chris replied with a hint of pride. "Looking to continue to add to that number too."

"Yeah, well, it was a little close, don't you think?" Griggs interjected.

"It's always a risk," Chris said. "I told you guys that before we started."

"But you almost got us both killed down here," Griggs said in frustration.

"Hey," Izzy interjected. "The Drifter is dead. We won. We beat it. Let's just leave it at that."

Griggs rolled his eyes and muttered a dismissive, "Whatever." He went to turn but stopped. "I'm not doing this again. And what if another one shows up?"

"Then we'll be ready," Chris said.

Griggs shook his head and walked off. Everyone watched as he approached the vehicle at the intersection and wandered around it.

"Thank you for your help," Chris said. "You were essential in taking this Drifter out. I don't think anyone in my group would have been able to do what you did and survive the mess you found yourself in. Your quick thinking saved your life."

"You did an amazing job," Jason chimed in, surprising Izzy. "I don't think I would have been able to handle what you did."

She blinked, taken aback by Jason's surprising praise. She had never expected to hear such words from him. It was surreal, but it sparked newfound confidence in her. Jason had always been against her judgment and ideas. The man who had always been skeptical of her abilities was finally praising her. It was a strange feeling. Had she finally proved herself to him? Did he finally see what she was capable of?

Jason placed a hand on her shoulder, offering a rare smile. "You did good," he said. He gave her shoulder a friendly squeeze before turning away and walking towards Griggs.

The experience had been terrifying, but she had made it through again. She had faced another monster and survived—this time killing it.

One by one, the members of the group began to thank Izzy. Their words filled her with a sense of accomplishment she hadn't felt before. She had killed a Drifter—at least, she had *helped* kill one. She had made a difference. She had saved lives.

Chris was one of the last to leave. "I guess that makes us even then," he said.

"What do you mean?" Izzy asked.

"I allowed your group to stay here, and you and your friends helped us take out a Drifter," Chris explained.

Izzy considered his words. She didn't want to use her favor on that. She had another favor to ask, a bigger one this time. She hated having to ask Chris for more, but she knew they needed his help. "So—I kind of have another favor to ask…" She trailing off.

Chris chuckled, a wry smile on his lips. "How did I know…" he said, his tone light despite the seriousness of the situation.

"I'm sorry," Izzy said. "I… we… just need help."

"With what?" Chris asked.

Taking a deep breath, Izzy gathered her thoughts. This was it. "We need our friend back—Audrey. The Reavers are still holding her hostage. We want to take out Hawk. He's at the root of *every-thing* that has gone wrong—the kidnapping of Audrey, the deaths of Pete and James, and countless others when he sent his group to attack our camp. He needs to pay for all of it," she confessed. She paused, her gaze meeting Chris's. "I know it's asking a lot—"

Chris cut her off.

"I'm in… we're in," he said.

Izzy blinked, taken aback by his sudden agreement. "You are?" she asked, unable to hide her surprise.

"Yes. They need to pay for stealing Dalton from us and allowing one of our own to be murdered by him. His betrayal has already led to numerous deaths—which is also because of Hawk. Plus, Hawk was the one who ran us out of our previous camp. If he's in charge of the Reavers now, I would enjoy some payback too."

She couldn't believe it. She had help—real, tangible help. With Chris's group on their side, they stood a chance against Hawk and the Reavers.

"Think of this one as a freebie," Chris said, smiling. "We both want the same thing, and I believe we can help each other."

For the first time in a long while, Izzy felt a glimmer of hope. Her group was no longer alone in this fight. They had allies, power in numbers. And with that came the possibility of success.

| 28 |

Izzy and Chris made their way back inside, with Matt, Jason, and Griggs not far behind. Chris's face was set in a determined expression, his brows furrowed, creating deep lines on his forehead, as he parted from Izzy and headed over to speak with his group.

"Where's he off to in such a rush?" Griggs asked.

With the news of their newfound alliance fresh in her mind, Izzy turned to her own team.

"When we were outside, I asked Chris to help us get Audrey back and go after Hawk," she said. "And he agreed to help us. He's getting a group together to join us."

"That's great. The more the better," Jason said.

Before any further discussion could take place, Chris called them all over. He led them into a room that looked like it had been once used for meetings. A long table stretched out across the room, surrounded by chairs that had seen better days. Chris stood in front of a giant whiteboard, clean and ready to use. The room was lit by a string of lights strung haphazardly around the ceiling and walls.

Matt took a seat and pulled out the chair beside him for Izzy. She sat down on the cold, hard surface, and the chair creaked as she leaned back. Across from them, Griggs slid into the last remaining chair, leaving Jason to lean against the wall alongside a few others who chose to stand.

Once everyone was settled, Chris picked up a marker and approached the whiteboard. The room fell silent as he started drawing a square, surrounded by another set of lines. "This is the Reavers' camp," he began, pointing to the square, then the outer lines. "There's a fence that surrounds the entirety of the camp. Is that correct, Griggs?" he asked, turning his gaze towards Griggs.

"Yup," Griggs confirmed.

Chris waved his arms for Griggs to continue. "And?"

Griggs glanced around the room. Everyone's eyes were on him. He shrugged. "And what?"

"Care to elaborate?" Chris held the marker out for Griggs to take.

A loud sigh left Griggs before he stood up and moved to the whiteboard. He took the marker from Chris with a smirk. "I didn't know I was going to be the one giving the speech today," he said sarcastically.

He studied the outlines Chris had drawn. His expression hardened, and without a word, he used his hand to wipe the board clean. He began to redraw the outline of the Reavers' camp, followed by another outline showing the fence surrounding the property.

"So the fence basically surrounds the entire property. But there are some damaged spots." He paused and turned to look at Izzy. "Some more recent than others."

Griggs then drew three X's on the map: one by the front gate, one at the right side of the building, and another towards the back of the property. He tapped the one at the rear. "This one. This is where we will enter. This isn't far from the back door, which rarely has supervision. We may be able to enter completely undetected, as long as no one is watching the back."

"What if someone *is* there?" Jason asked.

Griggs shrugged nonchalantly. "You can either wait for them to disappear, or you can *make* them disappear."

"You mean kill them," Jason corrected.

Griggs nodded, unfazed. "Yes. Kill them."

"I thought the plan was to only go after Hawk?" Izzy asked.

Griggs turned to look at her. "I told you, these people won't hesitate to kill you and take everything from you. If you want to survive, you need to get it through your head that you're going to have to kill these people."

But Izzy couldn't imagine just walking into a place and killing people. Sure, they had attacked her camp, her own group, and had killed some of them. But what Griggs was talking about was murder. She couldn't do that. She wasn't built for that.

"If you were still there, that would mean I'd have to kill you too. Would you have been okay with that?" Izzy asked.

"If I was still there, I wouldn't have thought twice about killing you the moment I saw you in my camp." Griggs's response was blunt, devoid of any emotion. "These people are not your friends. They are your enemy."

Izzy looked at Jason. "You can't be serious. We're not just going to go in there and murder everyone," she said, teetering on the edge of panic.

Jason held up his hands in a calming gesture. "Hold on. No one's going to go murdering people here."

Griggs rolled his eyes. "Your funeral, then."

"Griggs, knock it off," Jason said. He faced Izzy. "We're not going in guns blazing and we're certainly not going to *murder* everyone."

Izzy went to say something, but Jason cut her off. "But we will absolutely defend ourselves if we have to. Our primary objectives are to get Audrey back and to take out Hawk."

Across the room, Griggs stood by the front of the table, shaking his head in apparent disbelief. Jason's gaze flicked to him. "You've got something more to say on the topic?"

Griggs held up his hands in surrender. "Nope. You all will see what I mean when you get there. I've said my piece."

"Good. Now please continue," Jason told him.

"Yes, sir," Griggs replied, saluting Jason mockingly. He turned back to the whiteboard, marker in hand. "Assuming you all make it inside *alive*," he said smugly, turning to smirk at the people gathered around the table, "you'll get to the end of the hallway. If you go any further forward, you'll be heading to the front door. You'll know what I mean when you get there. You'll want to go left. Down the hall is where you were before," he said, nodding at Izzy. "Follow that around the bend and you'll find the prison. Audrey will be in there."

"Are you sure?" Izzy asked, excitement building inside her at the thought of finally getting Audrey back.

Griggs shrugged. "Once Hawk killed your other friend, we moved her into his cell. Unless they killed her already, or have come up with something else to do with her since I've been gone, that's where you'll find her."

"And what about Hawk?" Jason asked.

Griggs turned back to the whiteboard. "Back where you first enter," he began, pointing to a spot on the diagram, "there's going to be a set of stairs on the right. If you take them up to the second floor, you'll walk down a short hallway with a few rooms on either side. It's the room at the end of the hall—that'll be Hawk's room. He uses it as both his office and bedroom."

Jason nodded. "Sounds good. Then that's where we'll go to get him."

"Wait. Hold on," Griggs interjected. "Just because that's his room, doesn't mean he'll be there waiting for you. He could be anywhere inside that building. And not only that, if he knows you guys are there, he won't be just sitting in his room. He'll be out hunting you guys, especially if he knows you're there, Izzy. He'll come after you especially."

"It doesn't matter," Jason said. "We'll get to him before any of that even happens."

"What makes you so sure?" Griggs asked.

Jason paused for a moment before he spoke.

"Because we have no other choice but to succeed."

Izzy felt a sense of pride at Jason's comment. She knew they had to succeed. They didn't have another choice. But it was Griggs's words that stuck with her.

He'll come after you especially...

She could see Hawk in her mind. His cold, calculating eyes that seemed to pierce through her. His cruel smirk as he toyed with their lives like they were nothing more than pieces on a chessboard. She remembered his unfazed look when he murdered Pete right in front of them. The man was a monster, a predator, and she was his prey.

He'll come after you especially...

She was terrified of Hawk, but she also knew deep down that she was stronger than he was. Not in a physical sense—Hawk was a beast of a man, towering over her. But she had something that mattered more, something that Hawk would never have—courage, determination, and a will to fight that stemmed not from a desire for power or control, but from love for her friends and for the people she cared about. For the members of her camp and Chris's camp. For Audrey.

Izzy clenched her fists, feeling the burning hatred of the man flow through her. She knew she'd have to face Hawk, to look into the eyes of a monster and not back down. She knew she could, having done so before.

But this time around, it would be different. This time, it would be to end things, once and for all.

| 29 |

The room was filled with the clatter of weapons being picked out from Chris's arsenal. Izzy watched as her friends armed themselves with guns and ammo. She could see the fear in their eyes, but it was overshadowed by the resolve that lied ahead.

Izzy threw the bow over her back, then filled her quiver with arrows and slung it on her shoulder, the leather of it bouncing against her back. She didn't want to have to use these arrows, but she knew it was an unavoidable battle. She knew there were people there loyal to Hawk who would defend their home, just as she and her friends had defended theirs. But Izzy held onto the belief that not everyone in Hawk's camp was there by choice. There had to be people who were trapped, imprisoned, or manipulated into being there. Griggs might have disagreed with her, but she was certain she was right.

Of course, she also knew Griggs had a point. There would be those who would fight back, those who thrived under Hawk's reign of power. Izzy and her friends were ready for them. She had come this far. She had faced danger multiple times and survived. She knew she could do it again.

Matt came up and wrapped his arms around her. His embrace was warm and solid, grounding her before the mission.

"You ready for this?" he whispered.

"As ready as I'll ever be," she replied. He released her, and she stepped back, meeting his gaze. "Hawk needs to pay for what he's done."

"I couldn't agree more. He absolutely deserves what's coming to him," Matt said.

Gratitude welled up within her for Matt. He'd been her rock, her constant in the whirlwind of chaos. From the moment they had left camp together a few days ago and walked into that building where the Reavers had taken Audrey from them, he had been by her side. His strength, his support, had kept her going when she had been at her lowest. As they prepared to take on Hawk and the rest of the Reavers, she knew she could count on him.

"Look, Izzy..." Matt had started to say. "If we don't make it through this—"

She put her hand over his lips. "Stop." Izzy knew what was coming next, but she couldn't bear to hear it. She didn't want to hear about what would happen if he didn't make it. She had to believe he *would* make it. He had made it this far with her. What was one more fight?

"Whatever you want to say to me, you can tell me after we get Hawk," Izzy told him.

"But—"

Izzy interrupted him. "No. We can have that conversation later. We need to focus on Hawk."

Matt's eyes were filled with concern. She knew he was worried about her. And she also knew he wanted to tell her how he felt about her. She wanted to hear what he wanted to say. She *really* wanted to hear it. Unfortunately, now wasn't the time for emotional distractions. There was a task at hand, an important one. She couldn't afford to worry about Matt's safety more than she already did. She needed to make sure she was focused on Hawk.

"Trust me, I want to have that conversation too," she told him. "But I need to believe you'll be there when the smoke clears, okay? We'll talk after we save Audrey and defeat Hawk." She leaned in, pressing a quick kiss to his cheek.

Matt tried to suppress a smile. "I look forward to it."

Their brief moment was interrupted by Chris. "Ready to go?" he asked, his gaze flickered between the two of them.

"Yeah, we're ready," Izzy replied. "I want to get my dog first."

"That's fine. We're all heading out for a final headcount and a review of the plan," Chris said. "I'll meet you guys outside." He turned and left.

Izzy turned to Matt, his gaze still fixed on her. He reached for her hand, his fingers entwining with hers. The warmth of his touch brought a sense of calmness, a reassurance that they were in this together.

"Let's go get your dog," he said.

| 30 |

Izzy moved with purpose, her shoes crunching on the debris of the abandoned city. Shadow walked steadily at one side, Matt at her other. Behind them, Jason, Griggs, Chris, and about forty of their camp members followed. Their mission was not going to be easy. Izzy knew it. Hawk was unpredictable and always plotting something. The memory of his last assault on their camp was still fresh, a reminder of his ruthlessness. None of his members had survived and returned from that attack, and he must have known by now that Griggs had left. Hawk must know something was wrong.

As they left the city's boundaries and entered open country, Izzy felt her anxiety tightening its grip within her. She tried to suppress it, to keep her mind focused. This was what she'd been waiting for—a chance to rescue Audrey, and to put an end to Hawk's reign of terror. She had the right people on her side. She had the numbers this time. Success was within reach. But the uncertainty of what waited for them at Hawk's camp was nerve-wracking.

Griggs's warning about the Reavers had made her second guess herself. She knew there must be people inside Hawk's camp that didn't want to be there. She knew there had to be people who didn't want to fight and live in fear. But how many of them were there? Was Griggs ultimately right and she was underestimating the amount of people loyal to Hawk?

She knew she would regain her confidence and composure once she was inside Hawk's camp. The familiarity of danger, the adrenaline rush, would help her focus and keep her senses sharp. For now, she just needed to keep moving and stay motivated.

The distant silhouette of the prison loomed ahead. The group kept their distance as they made their way around it, towards the rear and the broken fence. The group was silent and careful, each step measured to avoid unnecessary noise.

Ahead, Griggs raised a hand in a signal to halt as they neared the prison's rear. They took cover among the trees. Izzy's gaze roamed over the looming structure as she contemplated multiple strategies and backup plans.

Griggs stood tall and confident, his voice steady as he laid out the plan. "I'm going to take Izzy, Jason, and a small group of your people in first," he said, his gaze drifting over to Chris. "It's close quarters in there so we can't be all over the place and catch friendly fire. We're going to get their friend out first, okay?"

His words were met with nods from the group.

"Once we get their friend out safely, we'll go after Hawk. He'll most likely be with others, so that's when things will probably get loud."

Griggs's eyes swept over the group. Izzy had to admit she was impressed by his composure. Griggs was calm and collected, a stark difference to her own internal state. But despite his steady demeanor, Izzy couldn't shake the nagging doubts that stuck with her. Griggs had betrayed them before. But his recent actions had seemed genuine. He had saved her life more than once. He had even helped Chris and his group kill one of the Drifters. He had given them insider information about Hawk's camp and where to find Audrey. She hoped he had been honest about it all. She hoped it wasn't just another betrayal, but she couldn't help feeling an inkling of suspicion. As they prepared to infiltrate Hawk's camp, she'd have to keep a close eye on Griggs.

"Ready?" Griggs asked, pulling Izzy from her thoughts. She nodded, her grip tightening on the bow in her hand.

"Let's go," she responded. She turned and exchanged looks with Matt before giving Shadow a quick pat and following Griggs.

The team moved slowly, Griggs leading the way with Izzy, Shadow, Jason and three of Chris's men close behind. They kept low and close to the ground as they passed through the broken fence and moved up the small hill leading to the back door of the prison.

Jason's fingers curled around the door handle. He pulled, but the door remained closed. He tried again, his muscles straining with exertion. "Griggs, the door is locked," he said.

A look of disbelief crossed Grigg's face as he made his way to the door. He jiggled the handle, then pulled on it. The door refused to budge. His teeth grinning as his frustration was evident. "This door is always unlocked. People come out to smoke all the time and they purposely leave it unlocked so they don't have to walk all the way around to the front of the building," he explained, his voice laced with annoyance.

Izzy watched as he stood by the locked door, looking as if he was pondering his next move. Was this the play all along? Did he know the door would be locked? Was this a trap?

"Everybody, over here," Griggs said, quickly rearranging their positions, directing everyone to the side where the door would swing open. Then he released a deep breath and raised his hand to knock on the solid door.

"What the hell are you doing?" Izzy said.

"Shut up and follow my lead," Griggs responded, without looking away from the door.

Izzy clenched her jaw, her mind buzzing with unease. They were already off to a rocky start, and she could only hope that things wouldn't spiral further out of control.

Izzy could hear the muffled sounds from behind the door grew louder. The door creaked open slightly, and a voice rang out, "Griggs?" She held her breath, her body pressed against the wall behind her, hidden from view. She kept a hand on Shadow's head, hoping he'd remain quiet too.

Griggs's voice was calm. "Hey man, sorry. I locked myself out. I was hoping someone was here to let me in." Izzy could hear the forced casualness in his voice. The door creaked opened wider, revealing a man in typical scavenger attire, ripped jeans, a faded and ripped sweatshirt, and a chain that hung from his pocket to his belt buckle.

From her concealed spot, Izzy watched as the man's hand slipped under his sweatshirt, revealing a glimpse of a gun tucked into his waistband. Griggs must have seen it too. She hoped he had.

"Oh, yeah?" The Reavers' voice was laced with suspicion. "Locked out, huh?"

"Yeah," Griggs replied, maintaining his facade of confusion. "I went for a quick walk and the door was locked. When did we start locking the door, anyway?"

The man closed the door behind him. "We started taking precautions when you went missing," he said, his hand hovering near his gun.

"When I went missing?" Griggs said. "I can't even go for a walk without someone being suspicious?"

Izzy watched the scene play out, feeling as if she was watching a ticking time bomb about to explode. Shadow let out a growl.

The man's head snapped towards the sound, his hand darting to his gun.

"Hey!"

The man's protest was cut short as Griggs's arm wrapped around his neck. He struggled, his hand reaching for his gun. The moment he got a grip on his weapon, Shadow sank his teeth into the man's hand, forcing him to drop it.

Gradually, his struggles grew weaker and weaker, his movements slowing until they finally ceased. Griggs gently lowered him to the ground and released him. He picked up the fallen gun, ejecting the magazine and examining it before sliding it back into place. Izzy watched in amazement. His movements were so casual, only moments after killing a man with such ease.

"What?" Griggs asked, catching her gaze. "I told you, many of these people are loyal to Hawk. They'll kill you at first sight. You need to be ready."

In that moment, her doubts about Griggs evaporated. His actions had proved which side he was on. He had shown his willingness to fight against Hawk.

Griggs rifled through the Reavers' pockets and pulled out a set of keys. He unlocked the door, his gun leading the way as he cautiously peered inside. Satisfied, he turned back to the group. "Let's go."

Izzy nodded. This was it. The moment she had been preparing for. As she followed Griggs into the prison, she knew there was no turning back.

| 31 |

Stepping into the prison was like stepping into another world. The dim light filtering in from the outside world was swallowed by the darkness of the prison's interior. Izzy paused, allowing her eyes to adjust. The musty smell of damp and decay filled her nostrils, a reminder of her experience roaming these halls with James.

Griggs waved them on. They moved quickly and quietly, their footsteps echoing softly in the eerie silence. Izzy's senses were on high alert. Every shadow, every flicker of movement, made her jump with anticipation.

As they rounded a corner, a figure emerged from the shadows—a member of the Reavers. Izzy's breath stopped as everyone froze, caught in an uneasy standoff. The man, dressed in a tee-shirt, jeans, and with a backwards baseball cap, looked just as surprised to see them, his eyes wide.

Izzy saw Griggs raise his gun, the metallic gleam barely visible in the dark hallway. She saw the man do the same. She quickly intervened. "No," she said. She swiftly reached for an arrow, her fingers finding it with ease. Time seemed to slow down as she took aim, her heartbeat pounding in her ears. With a quick release, the arrow soared through the air, hitting the man's chest with deadly precision. The man dropped to his knees, his weapon sliding across the ground. He clutched at his chest before falling to the floor. The sound echoed in the empty hallway.

Before they could react, another member of the Reavers appeared. This time, Izzy didn't hesitate. Her fingers were already reaching for another arrow as he reached for his weapon. Her aim was steady as she released the arrow. It struck him in the shoulder, the force making him drop his gun. Izzy quickly readied another arrow, her eyes never leaving her target. The arrow flew, hitting the man in the chest. He crumpled to the floor. Izzy grabbed another arrow and readied her bow, awaiting anymore threats.

The hallway remained silent, the only sound coming from her ragged breath. Izzy slowly lowered her bow.

"Stealth," she said. "We need to be quiet." She pointed to Griggs's gun. "That'll draw too much attention to us right now. I'll handle the Reavers. You lead the way."

Griggs bent over and pulled out the two arrows from the dead man and handed them back to Izzy. She accepted them and placed them back in her quiver.

"Point taken," he said.

Izzy felt relieved at his acceptance. She knew guns were more effective, but in their current situation, stealth was more crucial.

Griggs motioned for the group to follow, whispering, "This way." He disappeared around a corner, leading them deeper into the labyrinth of corridors. Izzy, Shadow, and the rest of the group followed.

As they moved further away from the entrance, Izzy couldn't help but worry about Matt. Was he okay? Had he and the rest of the group found their way inside after Griggs had attacked one of the Reavers outside? The thought of Matt injured or worse gnawed at her insides, but she had to push through it. She had to focus on the mission at hand.

They turned another corner, and suddenly Izzy found herself in familiar territory. The narrow corridor opened up into a large two-story prison cell block, just like Griggs had said it would.

A lone guard sat outside one of the cells, his attention focused on something other than the group entering the prison cells. He looked up as they entered, scrambling scrambled to his feet and reaching for the rifle propped up next to him.

But Izzy was faster. She swiftly nocked an arrow, pulling back on the string with all her might. The arrow flew across the room, embedding itself in the guard's leg. He dropped to a knee, his pained cry echoing in the vast space.

Before the guard could do anything else, Griggs was on him. He kicked the rifle out of reach and delivered a powerful punch to the guard's face. The guard crumpled onto the floor, unconscious.

"Stop!' Izzy yelled.

Griggs froze with his fist midair, a silent question in his eyes. He slowly raised his hands, stepping away from the unconscious man.

"Which one is Audrey's cell?" Izzy asked. Suddenly, a voice rang out from above.

"Izzy?"

The familiar voice sent a jolt of excitement through her. She whipped her head around and raced towards the stairs.

"Audrey?" she called back.

"Oh my God, Izzy! Get me out of here!" Audrey exclaimed.

"Audrey? Where are you?" Izzy called out.

"Up here!"

Izzy followed her voice, her heart pounding as she hurried along the corridor and up the stairs, Shadow running by her side. Then she saw her. Audrey was standing there, wearing the same clothes as when they had last seen her. As their eyes met, all the memories came flooding back to her. Hawk dragging Audrey out to the courtyard. The death of Pete. Izzy's eyes filled with tears, just as Audrey's did.

"Get me out of here," Audrey pleaded. Izzy pulled on the cell door, but it didn't bulge. She remembered Pete mentioning a control panel on the first floor that controlled all the cell doors.

"Hold on, Audrey," Izzy said. She quickly made her way to the balcony overlooking the first floor. "Open cell door eighteen," she called out to Griggs, who stood by the control panel below. She held her breath as he worked, the seconds ticking by agonizingly slowly.

With a loud clank, Audrey's cell door swung open. Both Izzy and Audrey broke into wide grins. They rushed towards each other, their arms wrapping around each other in a tight hug. They had made it. They had found and rescued Audrey. Griggs's plan had worked. For the first time since they had started this mission, Izzy allowed herself to believe they might actually be successful in both parts of their mission.

They had rescued Audrey. The next step was taking out Hawk.

For now, Izzy allowed herself to be in the moment. She held her arms around Audrey and didn't let go.

"Thank you for not giving up on me," Audrey whispered.

"We'd never give up on you," Izzy said, tears dripping from her eyes. "I'm so sorry." She squeezed tighter. "I'm so sorry about Pete."

Audrey held Izzy close, sobbing in her arms. "Me too," she said.

Once Audrey was able to compose herself, she pulled away from Izzy. Shadow took his turn greeting Audrey, hopping on his hind legs and planting his front paws on her chest.

A smile appeared on Audrey's face as Shadow tried to lick her. "I'm glad to see you too," she told him, before pushing him down.

Then Audrey placed a hand on her belly, looking down at it and then at Izzy. "Pete and I were going to have a baby together."

"I know," Izzy said. "Pete told us. He was so determined to get you back."

Audrey's eyes began to water again. "I miss him."

Izzy's nostrils flared as anger flowed through her. She couldn't imagine Audrey raising this child without Pete. Hawk had ruined so many lives in such a short amount of time.

"We'll make Hawk pay for what he took from us," Izzy said.

Jason made his way up the stairs and met Audrey outside the cell. He wrapped his arms around her in a tight embrace. "I'm so glad you're okay," he murmured. He pulled back, his hands on her shoulders as he looked her over. "We need to get you out of here."

Audrey wiped the tears from her cheeks. "You don't have to convince me of that. I've been itching to leave since I got here," she said.

"Then let's go," Jason said, starting down the stairs.

Audrey reached out, her fingers intertwining with Izzy's. Her grip was tight, desperate. "Thank you," she whispered. "I thought I was going to die in here."

Izzy squeezed her hand reassuringly. "We weren't going to let that happen. The entire plan was—" She was cut off as Audrey abruptly pulled her hand away, her eyes wide with fear.

"No! No! Not him!" Audrey yelled, pointing at Griggs and backing away. Izzy didn't catch on immediately but then she realized the problem. Audrey recognized Griggs as one of Hawk's men—the one that took her.

"He's with them!" Audrey said, her voice echoing from the walls of the prison.

Jason tried to calm her down. "Can you lower your voice a little? We don't want to draw any unwanted attention right now."

"What's he doing here?" Audrey demanded. She took another step back, her eyes locked on Griggs.

Izzy waved her hands, trying to get Audrey's attention. "Hey, Audrey, over here. It's me, Izzy." When Audrey finally looked at her, she continued. "His name is Griggs. He *was* working with them, but now he's working with us. He wants revenge on Hawk just like we do. He's a good guy now."

"I am?" Griggs asked.

Izzy shot him a glare. "Not helping."

"Guys, I hear people coming," Jason warned. "We have to leave. *Now.*"

Audrey, however, was still rooted to her spot, her gaze fixed on Griggs. "I'm not going with him. He's the one who put me in here."

Izzy took a step towards Audrey, reaching for her. "He won't hurt you. I promise. He's working with us. Trust me," she pleaded. She was putting a lot of faith in Griggs right now. She hoped he wouldn't do something stupid to jeopardize this. And that was asking a lot.

She glanced down the stairs and saw the impatience in Jason's eyes. They were running out of time, and Izzy knew they couldn't afford any delays right now. As much as she understood Audrey's fears and hesitations, they needed to get out of there. And fast.

Audrey continued to hesitate between taking her hand and taking another step backwards, her gaze flicking between Izzy and Griggs. Izzy knew she was asking a lot of Audrey. She was asking her to trust the person who took her hostage, who kidnapped her in front of her friends. She couldn't begin to understand the emotions flowing through Audrey's mind at the moment.

Finally, after what felt like an eternity, Audrey reached out to take Izzy's hand. She followed Izzy down the stairs. They were moving in the right direction again. They descended the stairs and moved towards the exit.

Two men immediately came through the doorway. They already had their guns raised, aimed at the group. Izzy felt Audrey's hand tighten around hers. Shadow growled at the threat before them, and Izzy put a hand on his head to calm him and prevent him from making any sudden movements. She glanced at Griggs, whose expression was unreadable, his eyes locked on the Reavers who entered the room.

Suddenly, Griggs's demeanor changed, and he made his move. He straightened up, his face hardening into the familiar mask of who he used to be—one of the Reavers.

"What the hell took you guys so long?" he said, walking towards the other men. "They had me at gunpoint and made me release the hostage."

"You're safe now," one of them said. "What should we do with them?"

"Beats me," Griggs said. "Where's Hawk? Let's ask him."

"He's holding a meeting in his office," the other one said. "Want me to go get him?"

"No, stay here and watch them," Griggs said. "I'll go get him."

What the hell, Izzy thought. Had Griggs betrayed them? She had trusted him again, but had he now led them into a trap? She had got Jason and Audrey to trust her that she had a handle on Griggs. She couldn't believe he would do this to them, after everything he'd been through with them.

"You want me—" the man started to say before Griggs, in a single swift motion, pulled out his gun and shot him. The second man turned to see what had happened, but before he could react, Griggs aimed the gun at him and shot him too. The gunshots were followed by the thuds of bodies hitting the floor.

Izzy could hardly believe what had just happened. "What's your problem?" she demanded. "I thought you betrayed us."

"Isn't that the point—to be believable?" Griggs replied.

Jason moved past Griggs. "If they didn't know we were here already, they do now."

Griggs shrugged, holstering his gun. "They were going to find out eventually."

As the group moved past the fallen men, Izzy glanced at Audrey, whose eyes were fixated on the dead bodies. Izzy gave her hand a reassuring squeeze, hoping to offer some comfort, knowing exactly what she must be thinking about—Pete.

Jason peeked down the corridor in the direction they'd come, then addressed the group. "We're going to run into some resistance getting out of here. I need everyone to watch their corners and be ready for anything." He glanced down the hallway again before waving everyone to follow him.

The prison was eerily silent. Their soft footsteps were the only sound as they passed along the hallways. They moved as a unit, taking each step carefully to avoid making too much noise. Despite the silence, Izzy couldn't shake a feeling of unease. She strained her ears, listening for any telltale signs of the Reavers. Voices, footsteps, anything. But all she could hear was the sound of her own breathing and the occasional rustle of clothing from the group.

Abruptly, Jason held up his hand, signaling for them to stop. The hallway fell silent, everyone holding their breath. Then Izzy heard a faint murmur of voices and the distant sound of boots against concrete.

They were coming.

Jason cautiously edged towards the corner, peering around it to get a better look before continuing forward. Without warning, a gunshot bounced off the wall, making him instinctively retreat. "Shit," he muttered under his breath.

Before anyone else could react, a familiar voice called out, sending chills through Izzy. It was a voice she wished she could silence once and for all.

"Oh, Izzy... I know you're back there. Why don't you and the rest of your friends put their weapons down and come out and say hi?"

Izzy felt a knot form in her stomach. Hawk knew they were here. He knew *she* was here.

She couldn't just walk out there. Hawk would kill her on the spot. But staying put wasn't an option either. They were probably outnumbered and cornered. Every option seemed fraught with danger. Every decision could lead to disaster.

She glanced around at the members of the group, who stared back at her. Hawk had specifically called her out, and the group was looking to her for answers. Audrey's face was pale with terror. Griggs had a blank stare, as if he didn't care about the dire situation he was in. Izzy finally looked at Jason, who was staring back at her. The man who was always leading was now looking to her for answers. She usually knew what to do. She always had a plan. Now, everyone was counting on her. And for once, she had no idea what to do next.

| **32** |

"I know you're back there, Izzy..." Hawk repeated.

Izzy felt the cold, damp wall against her back, the rough stone pressing hard against her clothes. She quickly tried to come up with a way out of this mess.

"What are we going to do?" someone whispered from behind her. It was one of the members of Chris's group. His voice shook with fear.

Izzy instinctively looked to Jason for answers. But even he seemed lost, his eyes reflecting the same uncertainty that was gnawing at Izzy. Usually, she would have a plan, a way out. Or even be able to act on instinct. But now, her mind was blank, frozen in response to Hawk's icy calls to her.

Hawk had them cornered, trapped like rats in a cage. Stepping out into the open was akin to suicide, but it was starting to look like the only option they had left. The only way to keep everyone else safe.

Izzy looked down at Shadow. She gave him a gentle pat, whispering for him to stay. He sat and stared at her. She wished she could explain more to him, help him understand.

"What are you doing?" Jason asked as Izzy tried to push past him.

"I'm going out there to talk to him," she said.

Jason stiffened and stood his ground, not allowing her to move any further. "He'll kill you the moment you walk out there," he warned.

"Yeah, I'm likely to agree with Jason on this one," Griggs chimed in. "You know he has it in for you."

But Izzy had made up her mind. "I don't care. If it gives you guys the time to figure another way out of here, then I'm doing this. He has us trapped and probably outnumbered. Going out there will buy us some time. Figure something out." With that, she pushed past Jason and peered around the corner.

Hawk's voice bounced around the hallway. "Izzy, is that you?"

Taking a deep breath, Izzy readied herself. "Yes. I'm coming out," she called back.

She stepped into the open, her hands slightly raised, careful not to make any threatening moves that would get her killed immediately. Time seemed to slow down. At the end of the hall, guns were raised, their barrels aimed in her direction. Fear clawed at her, but she pushed it down, forcing herself to be confident and strong.

At first, she didn't see Hawk, only unfamiliar faces. But then he emerged from behind the wall of weapons, his boots thudding against the concrete floor.

"There she is," he said, his voice filled with sickening delight.

Izzy forced herself to meet his stare, refusing to show fear. She was terrified, but she wouldn't give him the satisfaction of knowing that.

"Here I am," Izzy said. "What do you want?"

A cruel smile twisted his lips. "I want you to be gone. Disappear. Vanish." He placed a finger on his chin in a mockery of thought.

"Fade away?" Izzy said.

"No," Hawk said. "Not that."

"Dematerialize?" Izzy said.

Hawk's eyes lit up. "Oh, I like that one. *Dematerialize.*"

"What's your point?"

"Straight to the point, that's right," Hawk said, pointing at her. "Death, Izzy. I want you dead. You annoy the hell out of me." He sighed and rolled his head back before looking at her. "You know, you have a lot of traits I look for in a person, a partner, a friend. In another life, I think I'd really like you."

"Gross," Izzy said.

Hawk let out a haunting laugh. "Humor. Another trait I enjoy. You're always making me laugh, Izzy. I'm going to miss you when you're gone."

"Wait," Izzy said, knowing she was running out of time. "There's no other way to work something out?" She needed to buy more time for someone to make a move before Hawk ended this.

"I'm sorry, Izzy," he said. "You're kind of a giant pain in my ass, and have caused me and my people way too many problems. I mean, I sent a group to destroy your camp and kill you all. And you walked away just fine. I asked someone I once believed to be a close and trusted companion of mine—who is now missing and I assume is with you—to place you in a jail cell so I could come kill you at a later time… and you get away. And speaking of jail cells, I had you in one a few days ago, with that stupid mutt of yours tied up, and you escaped that too. You're like a damn cockroach that just won't die, no matter how many times I try to step on you."

"Sorry to disappoint you," she said.

"Okay, I've had enough," Hawk said and held up his handgun, aiming it at her.

Izzy flinched and took a step back. "Wait!"

"Sorry, Izzy," Hawk said, and took aim.

Izzy squeezed her eyes shut, her body tensing up as the gun went off.

As the pandemonium began to unfold, Izzy opened her eyes in time to see Hawk drop his gun and stumble to one knee. A bewildered expression played across his rugged face as he clutched at his side.

"What the hell...?" he muttered.

The pain Izzy had expected never came. She glanced around in panic, wondering what was happening.

"Run!" someone shouted through the chaos, jolting Izzy from her frozen state.

Matt?

The voice was unmistakably his. A surge of adrenaline coursed through her veins, sweeping away the shock that had momentarily paralyzed her. She seized the moment and bolted for cover behind the wall. Jason's hand closed around her arm, pulling her back just as she found cover. The hallway erupted with gunfire, the deafening roar of bullets reverberating off the concrete walls.

"You okay?" Jason asked.

She fought to regain control over her overwhelming emotions, forcing herself to focus on the immediate danger around her.

"Yeah, I'm okay," she replied.

She turned around and peeked out from behind cover. The Reavers were distracted, their attention drawn in another direction. Hawk was nowhere in sight. Where had he gone? Was he injured?

She spun around to address the group with newfound authority. "Return fire," she ordered. "I believe Matt at the rest of the group are inside and distracting the Reavers out there. Clear them out and watch for friendlies."

For a split moment, there was hesitation. Then Jason's voice repeated her command. "You heard her," he said. "Return fire."

Jason and the three members of Chris's group leaned out from behind the wall, returning fire. Having Jason listen to her and repeat her orders made Izzy feel like a leader. He had trusted her judgment. While surprising, it gave her a newfound confidence. Jason, after all this time, was finally beginning to believe in her.

She turned to Griggs, who was standing next to her, an amused smile across his face.

"What?" she asked.

"Look at you, taking charge like that. Even giving orders to your superior," he teased.

Izzy rolled her eyes. "I want to say thank you, but you're always up to something."

Their banter was interrupted by Jason's announcement. "They're retreating."

Izzy turned the corner and noticed a few of the Reavers' bodies lying down the hallway. How many had they had taken out?

Izzy slowly moved out from cover and readied her bow. "Jason, cover me," she commanded. The two of them moved across to the opposite wall. Izzy stayed low while Jason stood tall. With cautious steps, Izzy and Jason moved along the hallway. Izzy's senses were heightened, ready for any sudden movements.

"Izzy?" Matt's voice called again, this time closer.

"Matt?" she called out.

"I'm coming out," he replied. "Don't shoot."

As Matt emerged from the shadows, Izzy felt relieved. She lowered her bow, her muscles relaxing for the first time since Hawk had called out to her. She ran towards him. Matt's face lit up as he saw her approach. They opened their arms simultaneously, their bodies colliding in a desperate embrace.

After a moment, Izzy pulled back slightly, studying his face. "Did you see where Hawk went?" she asked.

He shrugged. "I lost him in the chaos of it all. There was gunfire all around. I saw him aiming a gun at you and just... reacted." He shook his head, his eyes unfocused as he relived the moment. "I guess it was a right place, right time, kind of thing. I thought I got him, but he must have moved slightly at the last second. I definitely hit him, though."

The thought of Hawk still out there, injured and potentially even more dangerous with the idea of revenge on his mind gave Izzy a sudden stab of terror in her gut.

"We need to find him," she said.

Matt's gaze shifted past her, his eyes widening in surprise. "Audrey!" he exclaimed.

Izzy turned to see Audrey standing behind Jason, her smaller body pressed behind his for protection.

"Hi, Matt," Audrey whispered.

"I hate to break up your little family gathering, but I can guarantee you that you guys all alerted the entire camp with that little shootout," Griggs said. "I suggest we move out of here before they come back."

"I hate admitting when Griggs is right, but Griggs is right. We need to move," Jason said. He looked at Izzy. "What's the next move here?"

Izzy realized all eyes were on her again. But this... this was different. They were looking to her for guidance. They trusted her. And Jason was looking at her with a new respect in his eyes. It was exhilarating, terrifying, and empowering all at once.

Out of the corner of her eye, she saw Matt. He too was waiting, his usual confident demeanor replaced by a patient expectation. It stirred something within her, a deep-seated desire to prove herself, not only to Jason, but to everyone else now, too. She wanted to show them all that she could lead, and that she knew what to do. And then an idea began to form in her mind.

"We split up," she told the group. She pointed to four people from Matt's large group. "You four are with us." She did a quick head count. There were twelve in her group, and Matt had another twenty or so. They had numbers, but they needed to use them wisely.

"Matt, take your group, head back outside, and go to the front of the prison. Take Audrey with you. Have someone stay outside with her. Once you're in position," she went on, turning her attention to Chris, "you take half the group and enter the front of the prison. Start going room by room. There will be people who will not fight back. We're not on a seek and destroy mission here. I know there are people who do not agree with Hawk's leadership, and they will join us. Our mission is to find Hawk. You find him, you know what to do."

Izzy paused, letting her gaze travel over every face in turn. She was leading them now. She was dictating their actions. And it felt... right.

"We're going to take out Hawk and put in a new leadership in this prison," Izzy said. "One that works with others. One that doesn't threaten others. We can develop a community amongst others. A group that others will look to for support, that will fight to eliminate those monsters that threaten our existence on a daily basis. The one man standing in our way... his name is Hawk. And he will put up one hell of a fight, as we all know. He's not afraid to get down and dirty."

She glanced around the room again, making eye contact with everyone. "This is it. We will be successful. Remember what Hawk has taken from you, from all of us. He's taken our homes, our shelters, our friends. He deserves what's coming to him."

Matt's eyes were focused on her. It calmed her a little bit. Knowing he was behind her helped her feel more confident.

"Let's go!" she commanded, and the group began to move.

When she noticed Matt hadn't moved, she asked, "What's wrong?"

Suddenly, he reached out, grabbing her shirt and pulling her towards him in a passionate kiss. The world seems to shrink down to just the two of them. Izzy placed a hand on his cheek as she kissed him back. For a moment, she forgot about the surrounding chaos.

She pulled back and looked into his eyes. Smiles played on their lips. "Make it back, okay?" she whispered.

"Promise," he replied, before turning and leading his group towards the exit.

As she watched him leave, Izzy sensed herself blushing. She pushed away the embarrassment, focusing on the task at hand.

"Let's go," she said.

As she moved on, Griggs walked up beside her, a smirk on his face. "That was adorable," he said.

Izzy punched him in the arm before moving ahead. Her mind was focused, her body was ready. She readied her bow and led her team through the hallways, each step bringing them closer to their final goal—to find Hawk.

| 34 |

Izzy took point, leading the group deeper through the labyrinths of the prison hallways. They were heading to the staircase that led upstairs to Hawk's office. She figured if Hawk was injured, that must be where he was. She assumed that he'd want to be somewhere he felt comfortable, where he felt protected and secure. They'd probably run into more Reavers along the way there, possibly trying to stop them from getting to Hawk. She hoped scattering her group around the prison would pull the Reavers in different directions, weakening Hawk's protection.

They quietly moved through the prison's dark and damp hallways. They were hunting, but also being hunted. Izzy knew Hawk's men, the Reavers, were armed and ready for them. She couldn't afford any mistakes.

The sound of footsteps and muffled voices ahead of them made them freeze. Izzy looked back at Griggs, whose nonchalant shrug did little to help dispel her concerns. Griggs moved past her, his confidence bordering on recklessness. He pulled out a knife from his belt, which gleamed in the faint lighting. He pressed up against the wall and checked his corner.

He signaled to the group with three fingers. Izzy understood—three Reavers were a potential threat that had to be neutralized.

Izzy noticed one of the members of Chris's group raise his gun and aim towards the hallway. Izzy shook her head. "No guns," she whispered. "Stealth." He then lowered his gun but seemed to keep his finger close to the trigger. She hoped he would keep quiet. They couldn't afford to alert more of the Reavers to their location.

Suddenly, Griggs sprung from cover swiftly, his hand yanking the first man by the scruff around his neck. He grunted a muffled sound of surprise, but before he could struggle, Griggs plunged his knife into his chest. It was a horrifying act to watch, and Griggs did it without hesitation. The Reavers' body went limp, a puppet with its strings cut, as Griggs released the blade, dropping him to the ground.

A second later, the second man appeared from around the corner, gun brandished, and charged at them. Izzy readied her bow and released the arrow instantly. The man flicked backwards as the arrow embedded deeply into his chest and slipped onto the floor.

As Izzy reached for another arrow, the third man appeared, his expression of shock and fear. His gun was already raised in a fight-or-flight desperation, the barrel sweeping towards them with deadly intent.

In a blur, Shadow launched himself at the man, acting on primal instinct. His teeth sank into the man's arm and the gun clattered to the ground. The Reavers' scream was strangled, his face contorting in agony as he tried to shake the dog off him.

Izzy tightened her grip on the bow, her aim wavering due to the erratic movements of the man trying to shake Shadow from him. "Shadow, down," she commanded. She didn't want to accidentally hit him when she aimed.

Before Shadow could comply, the man choked and fell silent, his body sagging. Izzy caught Griggs stepping away from the fallen man, his knife dripping with blood.

"Let's go," Griggs said dismissively, as if death were a mere inconvenience.

This man, with his easy violence, unnerved Izzy, but his ruthlessness was an asset she couldn't afford to push away. A part of her recoiled at the brutality of Griggs's methods, but his earlier words still haunted her.

If you want to survive, you need to get it through your head that you're going to have to kill these people.

She followed Griggs as he took charge and began leading the way.

"Hey!" a voice called out from behind them.

Izzy turned. One of the Reavers stood at the far end of the hall in the direction they had come from. His gun was half raised, but just as Izzy realized the gravity of the situation, he must have too because he aimed his gun at her.

Izzy went to aim her bow, but multiple people were in her way and she couldn't get a clear shot.

Gunshots went off.

The man at the far end of the hallway collapsed.

A member of Chris's group slowly lowered his weapon.

"Well, there goes our element of surprise," Griggs said.

"Hey, knock it off," Jason said. "He just saved our lives."

"Saved our lives... killed us... whatever," Griggs said.

"We need to go," Izzy said.

They continued on, but then Izzy heard loud gunshots, followed by voices screaming for help. They didn't sound like they were coming from the hallways of the prison.

"What was that?" Jason asked.

Izzy gestured in the direction of the noises. "Where's the front of the prison?" she asked Griggs urgently.

Griggs's eyes snapped shut for a moment, as if he were mapping the hallways. When he opened them, there was clarity in his gaze.

He pointed decisively towards the noise. "There," he said, confirming Izzy's assumptions.

Izzy smiled in triumph. "It has to be Matt. They made it," she murmured to herself, a spark of hope igniting within her. Matt and Chris's distraction was working. Now it was their chance.

"There's our distraction," she told the group. "Everyone will be heading towards the front of the prison now. It'll give us the space to head to the second floor and find Hawk."

"If he's even there," Griggs said, skeptically.

"Won't people come after us because the gunshots?" Jason asked.

"Maybe," Griggs said, "but most of the Reavers are stationed towards the front of the prison." His words were followed by another set of gunfire that seem to ring out like fireworks on the Fourth of July. "We may still run into a few of them, but with the amount of gunshots we're hearing," he paused, allowing the group to listen to the sounds from outside, "most of them will probably head in that direction."

A direct path to Hawk could be theirs for the taking. The distraction outside was a gift. The plan had come to fruition. The window of opportunity was creaking open.

"Then let's keep moving," Izzy commanded.

She nocked an arrow and aimed her bow into the darkness.

The hallway ahead of her was empty.

She waved for the group to follow her and she pressed on.

"Up ahead, turn right, and we should enter the main corridor," Griggs said. "Then you'll see the stairs."

"Got it," Izzy said, nodding. She continued forward until she made it to the next corner. She slowed and checked her corner. As she leaned forward to scan the hallway, a rough hand shot out, snatching her and yanking her into the darkness.

A startled yelp escaped her lips as she was dragged away. But before she could react further, Shadow leaped into action. The dog's teeth found the Reavers' leg. He growled as he shook his head, pulling at the man's leg. His scream bounced off the hallway.

Freed from the man's grip, Izzy's instincts kicked in. She swung hard, her fist connecting with the side of his face. His balance faltered, and he tumbled to the ground, his gun clattering away from his outstretched hand.

Izzy aimed her bow at the man as he tried to reach for his weapon.

"Shadow, stop," she commanded. Shadow obeyed instantly, letting go and slowly backing away, making a low, threatening growl.

"I wouldn't do that if I were you," Izzy warned the man.

The man's eyes flicked up to hers, and he raised his hands in surrender.

"Pick him up," she said.

Jason sprang into action, circling around her to raise the man to his feet, then stood with his arm around the man. The man lifted his injured leg slightly, attempting to keep the pressure off of it.

"We won't hurt you if you help us," Izzy told him, hoping for a peaceful resolution.

"With what?" the man huffed.

"We need to know exactly where Hawk is," Izzy said. "Is he upstairs?"

He let out a short laugh. "You think I'm going to tell you that? I'm a dead man if I give him up."

"You're a dead man if you don't," Griggs said.

He looked at Griggs and then back to Izzy. He shrugged. "Sorry, I'm not telling you guys shit. You can go f—"

Griggs stepped forward. In a flash, he brandished his knife, placing the cold steel against the man's throat. "I'm sorry—what was that you were about to say?" he said.

Izzy's stomach lurched. She wanted to intervene, to say something—anything to prevent Griggs from escalating the situation. She knew what he was capable of. She hoped his intimidation was nothing more than a bluff.

Griggs continued, "You'll tell us where he is, or there will be no use for you. Then we can just dispose of you."

"You mean kill me," he managed to say.

"You learn quick," Griggs replied.

The standoff seemed to last forever. Izzy desperately hoped the man would give Griggs the information he asked for. She didn't want to see if he'd follow through on his threat.

"Okay, okay," he finally said. "I don't really want to get my throat sliced." He sighed, then continued, "He's upstairs in his office."

"Anyone else with him?" Jason asked.

He nodded. "Maybe half a dozen or so."

"Someone grab his gun," Jason said. "Griggs, he's coming with us."

One of Chris's guys grabbed the man's gun, and the group begun making its way into the main corridor. Izzy stopped at a barred window and wrapped her fingers around the cold metal as she stared through it. She saw her team outside, slowly making their way through the camp and taking out the Reavers one by one. She so desperately wanted to join them, to be with Matt. But this was all part of the plan. She was exactly where she needed to be.

"Come on, Izzy," Jason said. She nodded, tearing her attention from the skirmish outside and followed his lead.

They found their way to the staircase. Griggs, with his hostage in tow, moved to the staircase first. Izzy's mind raced with visions of bursting into Hawk's room, bow and arrow at the ready. But she immediately quietened the reckless impulse. She knew the importance of patience. She had made it this far. She wasn't about to do something that could jeopardize this whole mission.

"Which one is his?" Jason asked.

Griggs nodded to the door at the end of the hall. "That one."

Jason stepped in front of Griggs as they approached the first door on their left. "What are these other rooms?"

"They used to be offices," Griggs said. "But some of the higher ups use them as their own bedrooms."

"You think they're empty?" Jason asked.

Griggs nodded. "Everyone is probably out defending the entrance from your group. That, or they're with Hawk." He nodded towards the end of the hall.

Jason turned his attention to the door on his left and slowly opened it. He peeked inside the dark room, waving his gun in all directions, then pulled back into the hallway, closing the door.

Izzy followed Jason as he approached the second door on their left. He glanced back at Izzy before placing his hand on the handle and slowly opening the door. Jason peeked inside the new room, scanning the darkness before slowly closing the door. He shook his head, giving the go-ahead that it was all clear, then motioned for everyone to move forward to the door at the end of the hall.

Unexpectedly, the hostage in Griggs's grasp shattered the tense silence. "Hawk! Watch out!"

Griggs responded instantly. "You asshole!" he shouted before propelling the man forward with such brute force that he stumbled and slammed against Hawk's door with a loud thud. The impact sent the door swinging wide open, revealing the room beyond.

Time slowed as Izzy raised her bow. Her actions were automatic, and her muscle memory guided her as she prepared to confront whatever, or whoever, awaited them.

The abrupt explosion of gunfire snapped Izzy into motion. One of the Reavers burst forth from the doorway with his gun blazing. Izzy reacted without hesitation, aiming and releasing the bowstring. The arrow found its mark, striking the man in the chest, whose momentum carried him forward before he crumpled. Without missing a beat, Izzy reached for another arrow, nocked it, and drew her bow, ready for the next threat.

The man Griggs had tossed through the door, scrambled to his feet and rushed to safety. Izzy's second shot sang through the air, meeting the flesh on his leg. His cry of pain was muffled as he fell and disappeared from her line of sight.

Another one of the Reavers peeked around the door. Izzy nocked another arrow and immediately released it. It struck the wall next to the door frame, making him retreat behind cover.

"We have to get in there," Izzy said.

When no one responded, she glanced behind her. One of Chris's members was on the ground, a pool of blood around his head. She shook her head to cast aside the anger and mourning that filled within her. Every second she hesitated, the odds turned further against them. They were sitting ducks in this hallway.

Izzy nocked another arrow. "We will all die out here like he did if we don't continue moving," she declared. "Look, according to the guy Griggs held hostage but let go—"

"Let go?" Griggs snapped. "I didn't expect him to go through the door like that. I thought—"

"It doesn't matter now," Izzy interrupted. She didn't have time to dwell on mistakes. "You're going to cover me when we go in there."

"We?" he questioned.

"Yes. We," Izzy told him. Plans formed in her mind faster than the bullets could fly. "You have the gun. You'll fire, giving me cover, and I'll sneak in and get behind that desk in there." She pointed to the desk a few feet from the entrance.

With her strategy in place, she approached the entrance and looked inside. A gunshot rang out and the wall beside her erupted, sprinkling plaster and dust. She quickly retreated back to cover.

"And you want me to take your position?" Griggs said sarcastically.

She ignored his comment. "Return fire. Now," she commanded.

Griggs raised his rifle. Silent nods passed between them. Then the chaos unfolded as Griggs unleashed a barrage of gunfire into the room. Seizing the momentary distraction, Izzy darted through the doorway, staying low and out of sight. She slid behind the desk to remain hidden from view.

"Shoot back!" she heard a voice shout from the far end of the room. It resulted in a surge of movement throughout the room, and Griggs was forced to withdraw as the Reavers returned fire. But it was exactly what Izzy wanted. Their momentary victory was their downfall, as they had exposed themselves.

She readied her bow and listened to the gunfire, waiting for her moment to strike. The rhythm of gunfire began to slow, signifying that they would have to reload. She continued to be patient.

And then she had her opening: the telltale pause and the sound of reloading. In one quick motion, Izzy leaned from behind cover and released her arrow. She quickly moved back behind cover, knowing before it even made contact that the arrow would meet its mark.

The sound of impact was followed by a thud.

"What the hell?" one of the Reavers exclaimed.

Griggs, seizing the moment, burst back into the room, firing his rifle once more. He shot controlled bursts before he turned back to the entrance for cover.

Izzy crawled out from her cover to see one of the Reavers fall backwards after being shot by Griggs. If Griggs's hostage was correct, there would be about four more left in this room. Izzy placed the back of her head against the desk, trying to calm her nerves. She wrapped her fingers around her bow, then reached for another arrow. She pulled back on the bowstring as she peered out from behind her cover, waiting patiently waiting for another one of the Reavers to show themselves.

Suddenly, one of the Reavers looked out from behind the desk he hid behind, exposing himself. Izzy steadied her breathing and aimed in his direction, releasing the arrow. But just as she let go, the man begun to raise his arm to aim at the entrance, and the arrow struck his arm. He whipped his arm around and screamed in pain. Then he turned in her direction, looking for the source of the arrow. Just as Izzy was getting another arrow ready, he found her.

"There's that bitch with the bow and arrow," he yelled and pointed in her direction. "Get her!"

Izzy quickly retreated to cover just as bullets ripped through the air, tearing into the wooden desk she hid behind. Chunks of wood and splinters exploded past her, forcing her to shield her head with her forearms. Amid the chaos, she glanced at Griggs, who was still outside, inching towards the entrance. But the second he tried to assist her, a volley of gunfire pinned him back behind cover.

Moments later, the gunfire ceased. It suddenly became hauntingly silent.

"Drop your weapons," one of the Reavers said from the back of the room, "or we'll kill her."

Me? she thought.

Griggs responded immediately. "What's stopping me from coming in and just killing all of you?"

"Because we have your girl surrounded," the man responded. "That desk she's hiding behind won't take much more damage before she has nowhere else to hide. So, drop your weapons and come out."

Izzy locked eyes with Griggs. He turned away from her and spoke with Jason. She couldn't hear or see what was going on, but she was too far away. She wished she could just tell them to come in, guns blazing. There were only four of them left, and two were injured. Did they even know that?

Griggs spun around to face the entrance, his arms full of the weapons they were using.

What the hell was he doing? Why was he just giving up like this? She wished to be inside his head so badly right now. She wished she knew what the plan was because there was no way Griggs would just give up like this.

"Okay," Griggs said. "We're tossing our weapons in."

Izzy looked at him wide-eyed. He responded with a smirk and a wink.

Griggs tossed the weapons to the floor inside the room.

"Good," the man replied. "Now the girl—drop the bow. Slide it out to us."

Izzy and Griggs exchanged looks. She didn't want to let go of her weapon. She knew this was a bad idea. Giving up all their weapons seemed like the wrong decision to make. But in this moment, she had to trust Griggs had a plan, a plan that would save her.

Griggs nodded, reassuring her. She sighed, not wanting to give up her weapon. She tossed the bow out from the desk towards the Reavers on the far end of the room.

"Now, one by one, come in with your hands raised," the man said. "And stand up, girl. Show us your hands."

Again, Griggs nodded, telling her to obey. "We're coming," he said.

He waved the group in one by one, starting with the members of Chris's group. Izzy raised her hands and slowly stood up. All four of the Reavers had guns trained on her and waved them back and forth between her and the group entering the room. She saw the man Griggs had held hostage, who she had shot in the leg with an arrow. He was in the corner of the room, struggling to stand, his gun directly trained on her unwaveringly, as he stared at her.

The members of Chris's camp entered the room in a line, and Jason followed them inside. Seeing him walk in unarmed sent a ripple of unease through Izzy. She didn't know what was happening, and was becoming more nervous as the seconds ticked by.

A loud smack came from the hallway, and Shadow came sprinting in at full speed, a shadowy blur.

"What the hell is that?" one of the Reavers said. Another opened fire at Shadow, but Shadow moved with such speed that the bullets always seemed to be behind him.

Suddenly, gunfire erupted from the doorway. Griggs had held onto a handgun and had opened fire upon their attackers. As he advanced, he sent a handgun from the pile of weapons sliding across the floor with a swift kick. Izzy reached down to pick up the weapon, and opened fire at the few remaining Reavers.

Chaos erupted as all of the Reavers opened fire. Two were taken out by either Griggs or Izzy, she didn't know, or care to know. Everyone standing in the open ran for cover, but not before another member of Chris's crew crumpled to the ground. Then came the sound of teeth on flesh and a growl Izzy knew all too well. Shadow lunged at the man behind cover and took him to the ground.

Izzy and Griggs pushed forward to the remaining two Reavers. Izzy, arriving first, bore witness to the life-and-death struggle—Shadow's jaws clamped down on the Reavers' abdomen. The man reached for his gun just within his reach and wrapped his hand around the grip, bringing his arm towards Shadow.

"No!" Izzy shouted, and pulled the trigger of her own gun multiple times. The man dropped his gun and grew still. Shadow let go of him and joined Izzy. She rubbed the dog's head, glad to have him by her side.

Izzy looked at the last of the Reavers, who was cowering in the corner, the arrow still embedded in his leg. "Don't kill me," he whimpered. He raised his hands in surrender.

She eyed the man with suspicion as she ordered him to stand. His trembling and vulnerability seemed genuine as he leaned on the wall for support.

"Where's Hawk?" Izzy demanded, her eyes darting around the room, expecting him to suddenly appear from cover somewhere.

"I don't know," he replied. "I thought he was here too."

Izzy scanned the fallen bodies. None of them were Hawk. "You're going to help us find him now," Izzy stated, not allowing for an argument.

"Fine with me," he said. "After all of this, I don't want to be associated with that psycho anymore."

Izzy turned her back to the man and started looking for clues of where he may be. She was immediately startled by the sound of gunfire right beside her. Izzy's reflexes made her duck. Whirling around, she was met with the dull thud of the Reavers' lifeless body hitting the ground.

"What the hell, Griggs?" Izzy exclaimed.

Griggs nodded towards the dead body. The man had his hand still wrapped around a handgun. "He pulled it out from behind his back when you turned."

Izzy couldn't believe it. He had sounded sincere. It had seemed he really had surrendered and wanted to turn on Hawk.

"I told you," Griggs said. "You can't trust these people. They will try and kill you the first chance they get."

Griggs had saved her, yet again. As much damage as he had caused over the last few days, he was finally beginning to show his true colors.

"Thank you," Izzy said.

"I'm going to have to start charging you for my services with the amount of times I've saved your life," Griggs said.

"Where's Hawk?" Jason asked, as he joined them.

Izzy recounted the Reavers' claim to Jason. But could he have lied with his dying breath?

"Could he still be hiding in here?" Jason asked.

The room seemed not to contain many hiding places—no closets, no crevices to crouch within. The bookcase lay victim to the skirmish. The desk was barely a desk anymore. A bed laid in the opposite corner. There was nothing suggesting a suitable hiding spot for a man like Hawk.

"He has to be here. We need to find him," Izzy said, and started trying to move the table.

"Izzy…" Jason said.

"Help me move this," Izzy said.

"Izzy…" Jason repeated. "He's not here."

She let go of the table and looked around the room. "Fine. Then he's somewhere else in this prison. We need to find him." She ran out of the room, followed close behind by Shadow.

"Izzy!" Jason yelled. But it was no use. Izzy was already far down the hallway. She needed to find Hawk. She had to find him.

She started down the stairs and immediately bumped into someone. She took a step back and raised her weapon. Another gun barrel was staring back at her.

"Izzy?"

It took a moment to see with the lack of light in the hallway. But a second later, the barrel of the rifle lowered, and she finally recognized the person standing in front of her.

"Matt!" she said. She lowered her gun and wrapped her arms around him. "I'm so happy you're okay."

His arms fit perfectly around her. "I'm glad you're okay too."

She broke the embrace and pushed him back. "Wait. Did you see Hawk out there?"

"No," Matt said. "Did you find him in here?"

She explained the run-in she had with him earlier, but that when she looked for him in his office, he was gone. "I swore he should have been there. Everything led to him being there. We have to find him."

Matt nodded. "We will. I promise."

Izzy noticed him hesitate. Was he hiding something?

"What?" she asked him.

"Follow me. We found something you need to see," he told her.

As he led her through the hallways, Izzy wondered where he was taking her. What had he found? If it wasn't Hawk, what could possibly be so important? She followed him in the opposite direction she had taken earlier. She wondered where the rest of his group was. Was he all that was left? Were they waiting for him to return with her?

Matt reached an open door. "This way," he said.

It led to a basement. She didn't know this place had a basement. As she followed Matt down the stairs, she wondered what was waiting for her. Was it a trap? Why wouldn't Matt tell her anything?

The staircase wrapped around the walls in a circular fashion. Once they made their way to the bottom, she saw Matt's team, plus Chris and his group.

The other thing she saw completely blew her mind. As much as Griggs had been right about Hawk's loyal companions, she had been right about everything else.

"Oh my God," Izzy said, placing a hand on her mouth. There must have been fifty people down here. Some of them had children with them. They looked dirty, sick, and hungry. These were people Hawk and the Reavers had held captive.

"I know," Matt said. "They need food, medicine. The Reavers kept it from them. Made these people work for them."

"How do you know?" Izzy asked.

Matt waved off in the distance. Izzy saw two people approaching, a man and a woman. As they got closer, Matt introduced them.

"This is Corey and Jessica," Matt said. "They got married just before they were taken by the Reavers."

Izzy extended a hand. "I'm Izzy," she said, shaking each of their hands. "It's nice to meet you."

"We're so glad you guys have come," Jessica said.

"Thank you for rescuing us," Corey said.

"What a cute dog," Jessica said.

Izzy looked down and smiled at her loyal companion. "His name is Shadow," Izzy told her.

"May I pet him?" she asked.

Izzy nodded. "Of course."

Izzy was still trying to make sense of it all. She narrowed in on the questions she needed to ask.

"How did you guys get here?" Izzy asked.

"Hawk told us he would work with us, become a partner in trade," Corey explained. "One day, his group just came in and took everything from us. Killed many of the people in our group and took the rest back here."

"What did you guys do here?" she asked.

"We had to keep the land just as he wanted," Jessica said. "He made the woman cook for everyone."

"He'd send us on scouting missions. Basically hunting and gathering so he could stay here and do nothing," Corey added.

"Why didn't you just leave when he sent you out to get things for him?" Izzy asked.

"We had family here," Corey said. "Friends. Plus, many times, he'd send one of his guys with us to watch over us."

"What do you want to do?" Matt asked Izzy.

Izzy thought for a moment. These people needed their freedom. They had been locked away, working for a psychopath and his group of minions. But that was no more. They were in charge now. They were in control of the prison. This was their place now.

"You guys are free to go," Izzy told them. "But I don't know if Matt here told you what we've done. We took out the Reavers. Hawk is still missing, but this prison is now under our control. We plan to turn things around here. No one will be a prisoner here. We won't ask you to stay if you don't want to. But the larger our group is, the more of a threat we become. No one will want to mess with us. We'll find room for everyone who wants to stay."

"I... I don't know what to say," Corey said.

"You took them all out?" Jessica asked suspiciously.

"We did," Matt said. "We're a team here. We all work together. We're not like them."

The husband and wife faced each other silently before turning back to face Izzy and Matt. "Considering we don't really have anywhere else to go at the moment, we'll stay under your watch," Corey said. "I'll go let everyone else know what's going on."

"Please let them know that if they want to leave, we will not stop them," Izzy said. "They are free to decide if they'd like to stay or go."

Jessica smiled. "Thank you. Seriously. Thank you. This means so much to us."

Izzy returned the smile, then watched as Corey and Jessica returned to their own group. These people had all been prisoners under Hawk's leadership. She had known there would be people who had been held against their will, she just hadn't believed it would be this many. Her heart was full of pride, knowing she had just rescued so many people. But something else still dug at her—where had Hawk gone?

"Hey, you okay?" Matt said, fulling her away from her thoughts.

Izzy nodded. "I just can't figure out where Hawk went. He was right there. I was certain of it."

Matt placed an arm around her. She put her head on his shoulder, finally feeling comfort after everything that had happened.

"We'll find him," he said. "I promise."

Izzy and Matt stood there, watching as the prisoner's eyes begun to light up at the news of their freedom. One by one, they started cheering. They all had smiles on their faces.

For once, something was going their way. And Izzy was going to take a moment to enjoy it.

| **35** |

Hawk's office was permeated with the smell of stale air and burnt wood. Jason stood across from Izzy, his stance relaxed but his eyes piercing. She assumed this meeting was bad news for her somehow. Meetings with Jason were always bad news for her.

"I'm sorry," he said bluntly.

Izzy cocked her head to the side, her eyebrows lifting in confusion. "Why?"

"Since I've known you, you've been this kind of *do whatever you want* kind of girl. You always disobeyed my rules."

"You did have some shitty rules," Izzy joked, trying to break the tension.

Jason smiled.

"You just always did whatever you wanted, regardless of the consequences. Sometimes that led to failures and sometimes successes. This... this was a *huge* success, Izzy. None of this would have been possible without you."

Her heart slowed its frantic pace as Jason continued to paint her in shades of courage and resourcefulness. It wasn't just acknowledgment she heard in his voice, it was respect.

Jason continued, "It was your determination that led us to find Audrey. It was your leadership that got us through this ordeal. You knew where to go for help when our camp was attacked. Somehow, you got Griggs to trust you and be on our side."

His recognition of her success was a relief, and her pride helped Izzy overlook all of his past doubts. She absorbed his praise, allowing herself the rare luxury of basking in the warmth of his words. Izzy had never craved acceptance, yet his affirmation felt great.

"You sound like you're giving up your leadership," Izzy said.

"Oh, no," Jason laughed. "Don't mistake this for letting you take control. There's still a lot for you to learn. But you've earned a seat on the leadership team. I'm making you second in command."

Immediately, Izzy wanted to shout her triumph to the ceiling above. But she tempered the impulse, forcing herself to respond with composed gratitude instead.

"Thank you," she told Jason. "This means a lot to me."

Their conversation drifted into a discussion of strategy and a future that involved Chris and his group in the bunker.

"He wants to remain a part of our team," Jason said. "Well, let me clarify. He wants to remain a part of our team as long as *you're* a part of it."

"What do you mean?" Izzy asked.

"I mean, Chris and his group are staying because of you. Chris said after seeing what you did taking out the Drifter with Griggs, and now leading the takeover of this prison, this is the group he wants to remain close with," Jason said.

Izzy realized she was at the epicenter of a new reality. She stood surrounded by individuals who didn't just depend on her—they believed in her. She savored the feeling. She had proven herself not just as a survivor, but as a leader. She couldn't wait to tell Sarah.

"I... I don't know what to say," Izzy said, stumbling over her words.

"You don't have to say anything. Just keep doing what you're doing," Jason said. "And not to change the subject, but you need to talk to those prisoners downstairs."

"Why? Have you spoken with them?" Izzy asked.

"I have," Jason said. "Most of them are staying. But they really only want to talk to you and Matt. They kind of didn't want anything to do with me. They think you saved them all."

"I'll talk to them," she stated, with a newfound resolve due to the role she had taken on.

"Good. You have a way with people. Just keep up the good work," Jason said. He patted her on the shoulder as he headed for the door.

"Where are you going?" Izzy asked.

He turned and paused in the doorway. "The person who runs the prison has to have the biggest room, right?"

Her mind reeled, thoughts scattering like leaves in the wind. "What do you mean? This is my room?"

"Izzy, you're second in command of our entire group. But you're going to be running this prison. These people look to you, not me. They trust you. They want you." He smiled. "And leaders get the big room." He nodded at her, and then disappeared from sight. "Good luck!" he shouted from the hallway.

A chuckle escaped her lips, half in disbelief and half in awe of the path her life had taken. Izzy, the lone wolf, had become Izzy the leader. She couldn't believe Jason was giving her total control of the prison and everyone here. She couldn't, and wouldn't, let him down. She wouldn't let her group down. Or herself. Failure wasn't an option. She had come too far for everything to unravel now.

A knock at the door jolted her back to the present. There in the doorway stood Matt. "I saw Jason come downstairs. I figured it was safe to come up and see you."

"Come up and see me?" she repeated. Her eyes narrowed on his. "Do you know?"

Matt's smile was all the answer she needed. "Chris told me. You're running the prison and Jason is going back home to rebuild. He said he's overseeing both places."

Izzy smiled. "News certainly travels fast," she said, not that she was surprised.

"Are you excited?" he asked.

The question elicited an instant reaction from her—a smile so broad it felt like it could light up the darkest corners of the room. "Hell yeah, I am," she admitted.

Matt reached out and hugged her.

As they pulled away slightly, their gazes locked. Then Matt leaned in to kiss her. A wave of emotions shot through Izzy. Time stood still and the world outside faded into obscurity.

Eventually, Izzy broke away. She gazed into Matt's eyes. "Does the door lock?" she asked.

Matt went to the door, closed it, and flicked the lock. He tried the handle, then confirmed, "Yup, it's locked," as he turned to face her.

"Good," Izzy said. She moved towards the bed deliberately. Matt joined her without hesitation, their kisses continuing with renewed passion as they wrapped themselves around each other.

* * *

Izzy's eyes fluttered open. The thought of being snuggled in Matt's arms flashed in her mind. But when she looked for him, she saw that the space next to her was empty. Her thoughts were foggy with sleep. How could he just leave without saying any-thing? Where did he go?

She sat up and noticed Shadow lying peacefully and snoring at the foot of the bed. He hadn't been there when Matt locked the door to her room. She glanced at the door and noticed it was open.

Izzy slipped from beneath the sheets, her hands groping on the floor for her scattered clothing. Once clothed, she stepped into the hallway, taking a moment to get used to the dark again.

"Matt?" she said, her voice more of a whisper than a call. She took a few steps into the hallway. "Matt?" she called out again. But again, there was nothing but silence.

She made her way to the stairs at the end of the hallway. At the bottom, one of Chris's men stood guard.

"Excuse me," Izzy said, attracting the man's attention. "Have you seen Matt?"

The man shook his head. "No, sorry. No one has come down here."

"How long have you been there?" she asked, her mind trying to weave together a timeline.

"I was down here talking to Matt when Jason came down, and then Matt went upstairs to talk to you. I haven't seen him since," he replied.

She tried to put the pieces together, but they didn't make sense. Where had Matt gone? Why hadn't anyone seen him? He couldn't have just disappeared into thin air. Panic had begun to overwhelm her when she saw Griggs stroll past the staircase.

"Griggs!" She hadn't meant to shout, but her urgency had overpowered her. His startled reaction was almost comical, but Izzy had no room for humor now.

"Oh, hey, Izzy. What's up?" he asked, recovering from his surprise.

"Can you come up here? I need you," she said.

"Look, Izzy. I appreciate the offer and all, but I don't think that would be a good idea," Griggs replied.

"Eww, no," she said in embarrassment and irritation. "Not that. Just please come up here. I need to talk to you."

Griggs moved past the guard to ascend the stairs.

"Matt is missing," Izzy told him.

Griggs shrugged. "Okay. And?"

"We…" Izzy paused. The personal nature of her last interaction with Matt made the words stick in her throat.

Griggs's smirk deepened because of her discomfort. "Yeah, yeah. I get it. You two slept together and he left afterwards. So what?" His causal dismissal felt like a slap in the face.

"The guard down there said he hadn't seen Matt," Izzy told him. "He said he's been there since Matt came up here. Where did he go?"

"He probably went to get a drink or something," Griggs said. "Just relax."

"Relax?" Izzy said. "Relax?"

"Okay, okay. Wrong choice of words. How about I help you look for him?"

"Thank you," Izzy said.

They walked back into Izzy's room. Shadow was snoring loudly at the foot of the bed.

"So, tell me what happened," Griggs said. "In detail." He winked at her. She punched him in the arm. "Ouch, okay. Just tell me what happened. I'm here to help."

"I woke up a few minutes ago and he was gone," Izzy explained.

"He didn't tell you he was leaving or give you an idea of where he went?" Griggs asked.

"If he did, I wouldn't be asking you for your help," Izzy said.

"Touché," Griggs said. He looked back into the hallway. "Have you checked the other rooms up here?"

How could she have been so stupid? The other rooms. She mentally smacked her head.

"I'll take that as a no, given the blank stare you're giving me," Griggs said. "Come on, let's go check the other two rooms out."

He led her into the hallway and opened the first door on their right. He pulled out a flashlight from his utility belt and shined it throughout the room.

"Where'd you get that?" she asked.

"There's a lot of stuff here," he told her. "Maybe being the leader and all, you should take a look instead of—"

"Okay, stop," she said. "I will handle my duties. I'm allowed to have a moment to myself after everything that's happened."

Griggs shrugged. "Just sayin'..."

They searched the room from top to bottom. No one was hiding in here and nothing seemed to be out of place. Griggs opened the door of the next room and shined the flashlight around.

"There's nothing here either," Griggs said. He turned and begun walking back into the hallway, leaving Izzy in the dark. Suddenly, Izzy tripped over something. She fell hard onto the floor. Griggs turned and shined the flashlight back on Izzy, who was lying on the floor. "Come on, Izzy. Stop playing around."

She sat up and started feeling around by her feet, looking for the source of what she had tripped over. She rubbed her hand over a raised piece of the floor. "Griggs, shine the light over here," she ordered.

He took a few steps towards her and shined the light over her hands. "What do you see?"

"It's not what I see," she said. "It's what I *feel*." She moved her hands down the crease in the floor until she found a small hook that she could grab onto. She pulled on it and could lift the floor up slightly. "Holy shit, a trapdoor."

"There were rumors about this place having a hidden passage," Griggs said.

Izzy looked at him, anger piercing through her. "You knew about this and didn't say anything?"

"Whoa there, girl. Calm yourself. I said I heard rumors about it. I didn't know if it was true," Griggs said.

"Still would have been good to know." Izzy's fingers curled around the floor and pulled. She watched in disbelief as it pulled aside, revealing a dark abyss beneath them. "What the hell is this?"

"I don't know," Griggs muttered.

They approached the hole. A battered ladder clung to the side, its metal rungs disappearing into the darkness.

"Ladies first," Griggs offered.

"Nice try. You have the light. You're first," she said.

Griggs tossed her the flashlight. "You have the light. Plus, he's your boyfriend. You go find him."

Izzy wasn't having any of his joking around. "I'm the boss around here now. And I'm ordering you to go first," she said, and tossed the flashlight back to him.

Griggs let out a disgruntled noise. "Fine. But you better be following close behind me."

With that, he swung his leg over the edge and began his descent. Izzy drew in a steady breath, her palms damp as she watched him lower himself into the hole.

Could this be the same path Matt had taken? If so, why hadn't he told her about it? And then there was Hawk—was this his secret escape route, a passage unknown to even his closest allies?

Izzy placed her foot on the top rung of the ladder and started her descent.

36

When Izzy jumped off the last rung of the ladder, her shoes splashed into a shallow pool of water—at least, she hoped that was what it was. The unmistakable scent of decay and moisture invaded her nostrils.

"Are we in the sewer?" she managed to ask, her nose wrinkling in response to the rancid air.

"Sure seems like it," Griggs said, his voice echoing. His flashlight beam danced around them, making the slick, damp walls glow.

Izzy's brow furrowed as she scanned her surroundings. Why would Matt come down here? *Had* he even come down here? She tried to piece together his potential motivations, but none made any sense. Did he stumble upon the hidden hole and enter due to his curiosity? Was he after something? She shook her head. That wasn't Matt. He wouldn't just leave her without saying a word.

After a few minutes of walking, Griggs asked, "Do you think Matt's down here?"

"I have no idea where he could be," Izzy said. "But if he *is* down here, he'd better have a good explanation for it."

"Sounds like trouble in paradise to me," Griggs said.

Izzy ignored him and continued looking around, but all she saw was water and damp walls.

The moonlight shined in through the grates as they moved under the street. It reflected in the small puddles throughout the sewer, giving them a little more light than Griggs's flashlight provided. As they pressed on through, Izzy vowed to herself that she wouldn't leave without answers. She was determined to know why Matt had vanished and where this sewer led.

"Can I ask you a question?" Izzy said.

"Shoot," Griggs replied.

"Why did you help us back at the prison?" she asked.

"What do you mean?"

"When you took everyone's guns. When you saved my life."

"Again."

"Yes, again," she said, rolling her eyes. "You could have tricked us all into turning ourselves over to the Reavers. You could have given me to Hawk multiple times. But you didn't. Why?"

Griggs snickered. "Because... I don't know. The guy betrayed me. I have a thing about trusting people and them betraying me."

"Hawk didn't really betray you though, right? He just gave your position to Dalton," Izzy told him.

"He used me. He told me I was his go-to man. The one he could count on," Griggs said. "He lied to me. I don't like liars. I don't like people who manipulate me or use me the way he did. And he threw me away for that little prick, Dalton." Griggs spat on the ground. "I'm glad that asshole is dead. Did he suffer?"

"Dalton?" Izzy asked.

Griggs nodded.

"It sure seemed like it," Izzy replied, remembering that creature wrapping its tentacle around him and opening up on his face. She shook as she visualized it again.

"Good," Griggs said. "He deserved every—"

"Shhhh," Izzy said, holding a finger up to her mouth. "Turn the light off," she whispered.

Griggs flipped the switch, leaving them in darkness.

"What's—" Griggs started to say before Izzy shushed him again.

Then she heard it again. A distant howl from a Drifter, from somewhere nearby.

"No way," Griggs whispers. "I ain't doing this again."

"We're underground. We should be fine," Izzy whispered back.

Something blocked the light streaming through the grate overhead, casting a brief shadow and dousing the moon's glow. It was right above them. Izzy held her breath. She only hoped that being underground made her safe.

The howl started again, but this time seemed further away. She released her breath. It was moving away from them.

"Let's go," she whispered. Griggs turned the flashlight back on and they started walking again.

Instantly, Griggs shined his flashlight at a hole in the wall and said, "What's that?"

"I don't know," Izzy said, approaching it. She stuck her hand out, silently asking for the flashlight. Griggs handed it to her and she shined it into the hole. "Looks like it leads upwards. Ready to start climbing?"

Griggs shrugged. "Do I have a choice?"

"Nope." Izzy climbed into the man-made dirt hole and started crawling upward. After a few feet, she could see a light ahead of her. "I think I see something." She continued to push ahead until she hit the end of the tunnel. She put the flashlight down and pushed on the wall, blocking her path. It was heavy and sounded like it was sliding across a floor. She pushed harder and crawled through the opening. She stood up and turned to look at the bookcase she had been pushing aside. As she glanced around, she realized where she was.

Griggs climbed through the hole behind her and made his way to his feet, looking around. "Where are we?" he asked.

She couldn't believe it. She knew why she was here. And she knew who else was here—probably waiting for her.

"Izzy?" Griggs asked. "Do you know where we are?"

Finally, Izzy nodded. "I do," she said. She then pointed to a door ahead of them. "We're going to go through that door. We will then make a right, which will lead us into a much larger room, something like a cafeteria. There will be a cage in there. And that's where we'll find Matt."

"How do you know this?" Griggs asked.

"Because Hawk kept me in that same cage."

37

"He kept you in a cage?" Griggs whispered, his features contorting with disbelief and horror.

Izzy nodded. "Get your gun ready," she instructed him. Griggs held his gun by his side as he moved behind Izzy.

She reached the entrance of the room and inched forward, looking in both directions. With a quick wave, she made her way to the right. Just ahead, she saw a flickering light within the cafeteria she had spoken of. As she entered, she noticed two lanterns, one immediately to her left and another at the far end of the room.

In the center of the room was the cage she knew she'd find. Matt was lying inside it, curled up.

"Matt?" Izzy whispered.

His head snapped up, eyes wide with recognition. "Izzy," he said.

She ran to his cage and got down on her knees. She reached between the bars, their fingers interlocking. "I'm so glad you're okay," Izzy told him. "I had no idea what happened to you."

"I'm okay," Matt said. "How did you find me?"

"We found this trap door—"

"In the room at the top of the stairs," Matt said, interrupting her. "Hawk must have hidden there the whole time."

"Hey, lovebirds," Griggs said. "Little less chatting and let's maybe get out of here."

Izzy moved her fingers around the cage, feeling for the lock. Her hand rubbed over the bent metal she'd broken during her previous escape. It had clearly been repaired. Hawk must have been busy.

A shadow stretched across the cafeteria wall, morphing as it approached. Izzy turned and saw the shadowy figure approaching Griggs.

"Griggs, look out!" she screamed, but it was too late. The shadow solidified into Hawk, wielding a bat. A sickening thud resonated as Griggs tumbled to the ground.

Adrenaline surged through her as Izzy lunged for the gun, only for Hawk to place his boot on top of it. "Nice try, Izzy," he sneered, bending over to snatch up the gun. Within moments, its barrel was trained on her. He dropped the bat and placed both hands on the gun.

Izzy rose slowly, refusing to let her gaze waver from Hawk's. "Now what? You going to shoot me now?"

"Don't be so quick to give me ideas," he taunted. "You may not like it when I follow through on them." He shook his head in frustration. "I should have done this earlier when I had the chance. I won't make the same mistake twice."

Suddenly, Griggs kicked out Hawk's leg, tripping him and messing with his aim. The gun fired, missing Izzy but striking the chain of fluorescent bulbs overhead. The light shattered and glass cascaded like rain over Izzy, who shielded her head, then shook it to rid herself of the pieces of glass.

Hawk regained his balance and aimed his gun down at Griggs. Griggs quickly grabbed the bat and swung it at Hawk, connecting with his hands. The gun clattered away from his grasp, skidding across the grimy floor. Griggs swung the bat again, but Hawk's reflexes were quicker. He caught the bat mid-swing, leveraging it downward, the force driving the butt of the bat into Griggs's chest.

Izzy couldn't let Hawk prevail. Without a second thought, she picked up a large piece of jagged glass from the fluorescent lights and charged into battle.

She ran towards Hawk, stabbing him in the side at the spot where Matt had wounded him before. Hawk screamed in pain and rage. But he was far from defeated. He spun around, elbowing Izzy in the face, sending her sprawling backwards.

Her vision was blurry as she propped herself up on her elbows, shaking her head in an attempt to clear the fog. She watched as Hawk withdrew the glass from his flesh with another scream of pain. He turned to Griggs, who was trying to climb back to his feet and get away. Hawk struck Griggs, embedding the shard deep into his leg. Griggs let out an agonizing scream.

Hawk then turned to Izzy and limped towards her, blood dripping from his reopened wound.

"I'm going to kill you all," Hawk said as he approached.

Izzy climbed to her feet but Hawk was suddenly on top of her, pushing her back to the ground. He climbed on top of her, using his body weight to pin her down. Her fist met his face once, but his smirk only grew wider. She went to strike again, but his fingers closed around her wrist in a vice-like grip. He slammed her hand to the ground and used his other hand to wrap his fingers around her throat, squeezing the life from her. She tugged at his arm, her nails scraping his skin, her body bucking, her legs kicking out—but nothing seemed to weaken his determined hold on her.

"Izzy!" she heard Matt yell.

Izzy's lungs were empty and craving air. Each attempt to breathe was like inhaling through a crushed straw. Pain overwhelmed her body. Her lungs burned. Her free hand flailed and her legs kicked, but Hawk was immovable.

"Izzy!" Matt cried out again. But with every passing second, his voice grew fainter, as if Izzy was being pulled away on a current.

The pain in her chest grew more intense as her body waged a losing battle against suffocation. She fought to keep her consciousness, her body becoming weaker and weaker. As her physical strength weakened, so did her awareness. Everything was becoming darker.

"Die, Izzy. Die!" Hawk said. She saw his lips moving, but the words sounded very distant.

Suddenly, Izzy was able to grasp a breath.

Hawk's heavy body rolled off of her. Her mind was spinning, her neck throbbing beneath the ghost of Hawk's grip. But she clung to consciousness, coughing and breathing in precious air.

Griggs stood above her, clutching the baseball bat. "Let's see how *you* like a bat to the head, asshole," he said, staring at Hawk's slow-moving body. He put one end of the bat on the ground and leaned on it for support, looking at Izzy. "I'd offer you a hand, but at this point, I'm sick of doing everything for you."

She had no energy to make a retort. She propped herself up on her elbows to examine Hawk's body. He laid face down, breathing slowly, and moaning into the floor.

She climbed to her feet and reached out for the bat. "I need that, please," she told Griggs. He offered the bat, but his grip faltered as she took it from his outstretched hand. He hopped over to the counter and used it for support while Izzy made her way to Matt's cage.

Then, from the corridor outside, came a haunting howl. The three of them all exchanged glances. Izzy expected the Drifter to come barging in at any moment, given how close it sounded.

"We need to get out of here," Izzy said.

"You don't have to tell me twice," Griggs said.

"Matt, back up," Izzy said. She focused all her remaining strength on the weakened hinge of the cage. As each swing connected with the metal, her hands vibrated with shock.

Another howl came from the hallway, closer this time.

Izzy continued the assault on the cage, not giving up after each strike. She had to act fast. If she didn't get Matt out of there soon, they'd all be dead.

"Izzy, come on," Griggs pleaded.

"Almost there," she gasped, more for her own encouragement than anyone else's.

Finally, with a gratifying screech, the metal snapped. The cage door was free. She dropped the bat and pulled the cage door open. Relief surged through her when Matt crawled out and reached for her hand.

"Thank you. Now let's get out of here," he said.

They made their way to Griggs and assisted him as they left the cafeteria. But a crack of gunfire halted their escape. A chipped piece of the wall exploded next to Izzy. She turned to lock eyes with Hawk. His face was a twisted mask of pain and malice and dripped with blood. The blood from the wound on the side of his abdomen had soaked through his shirt and dripped on the floor where he knelt. He aimed his gun at them.

"No one is leaving here," Hawk taunted.

"I don't think you have too much of a chance either," Izzy told him. "You don't look too good yourself."

"Don't start with me," Hawk said, and pulled the trigger. Izzy flinched as the bullet missed her, striking the wall next to her.

Hawk shook his head slightly, attempting to regain his vision. He wiped the blood above his eye with his sleeve. "Let's try this again."

But before he pulled the trigger, a loud and haunting howl stopped Hawk. He looked around, trying to pinpoint the source of the noise. Izzy did the same thing. It didn't sound like it was coming from the hallway anymore. It sounded like—

A sudden, deafening blast shook the room as the wall behind Hawk erupted in a shower of dust and debris. A Drifter hovered in the hole that used to be a wall. A primal roar filled the air. It opened it's mouth wide as blackish goo dripped from its sharp teeth.

Panic clawed at Izzy's mind but was swiftly kicked aside by Griggs's command to run. Her survival instincts surged to the forefront. Dodging chunks of rubble, she and Matt helped Griggs limp out of the cafeteria.

Gunshots echoed from behind them. Izzy didn't let it slow her down. They had to keep moving. They had to get to get back to safety.

She saw the familiar outline of the bookcase that concealed the hole in the wall. They made their way around it and she and Matt assisted Griggs as he made his way down.

"Go," Matt told her.

Izzy nodded. As she went to crouch behind the bookcase, a gunshot sounded behind her, too close for her liking. A bullet struck wood, inches from her face, sending splinters flying. Her ears rang. She glanced in the direction from which the bullet had come.

"Izzy!" Hawk screamed from the entrance of the room.

Just as he stumbled through the doorway, a dark, gooey tentacle whipped around the corner, knocking him over. It wrapped around his leg, tugging him back into the dark hallway. Hawk's fingers found the door frame, clasping it for support.

"Help me!" he bellowed, his voice filled with terror, something Izzy never heard from him before. She watched the pleading expression of the same man who had been moments away from ending her life, now begging her for help.

Before Izzy could do or say anything, Hawk's grip failed and he was yanked from sight, screaming as he was pulled away. Within seconds, his screams stopped abruptly.

Izzy stood frozen. She couldn't believe he was finally gone.

"Goodbye, Hawk," she whispered.

Then she slipped through the opening and back into the sewer.

| **38** |

O ne week later.

The meeting operated differently than in the past. Jason would have sat at his desk, scolding Izzy after she had done something he disagreed with. This time, Izzy stood behind a desk of her own, and Jason was addressing her.

"How's David's team working through the farming in the front yard?" Jason asked.

"He and his team were able to gather some seeds we think we can use," Izzy began. "Green beans, corn, tomatoes, lettuce—and he thinks he may be able to plant an apple tree. We should be able to produce some of our own food rather than constantly having to risk our lives to search for it."

"Sounds good," Jason said. "And Matt? How are his scouting efforts?"

"Really good. He found a small group a few miles south of us that can create bullets," Izzy told him. "He's been negotiating with them for three days now. He's using our strength in numbers and our newfound agricultural efforts as leverage. I think he'll figure it out soon."

"That's good to hear," Jason said. He turned his attention to Sarah, sitting on the bed, Shadow lying by her side. "And how are you feeling?"

Sarah smiled. "I feel good. Everyday is better than the last. I don't have much pain anymore."

"Keep taking it easy," Jason said. "And keep making sure this one stays out of trouble."

"Hilarious," Izzy said, sarcastically. Changing the subject, she asked, "How's Chris doing with the new changes?"

"I just spent the last few days at the bunker with him," Jason said. "He's looking to put together a kind of system or trap that will take out the Drifters automatically, without everything that you and Griggs went through last time."

Izzy rolled her eyes. "Yeah, let's try to avoid that again."

"He is. Once he can figure it out over there, he wants to do the same thing for you here," Jason said.

"Good," Izzy said.

Awkward silence fell upon them until Jason broke it with a question that had been weighing heavily on Izzy. "I have to ask, what's Griggs going to do? Is he staying?"

Izzy shook her head. She hated losing such an ally and protector as Griggs. He had truly proven his worth. "He's very adamant about leaving. He got what he wanted—Hawk dead. Now he just wants to be on his way."

Jason's disappointment mirrored her own, yet she knew no words would sway Griggs. The man had made up his mind and no one would be able to change it.

Jason got ready to leave. His promise to return was a brief but comforting contract between them. As they shook hands, Izzy's grip was firm with the solidarity of their shared struggle with everything they've been through.

"I'll see you soon," he told her. "Be careful."

"You too," she said, before he turned and walked out the door.

"How do you feel about being the one in charge now?" Sarah asked.

That question was like a grenade, and Sarah had unwittingly pulled the pin. How did she feel? Was there a word for the turmoil that rolled inside her? Grief, anger, excitement. If it meant going through everything she had to again, losing everyone she had to, going through the near-death experiences over and over, she would not repeat it. James. Pete. Audrey being kidnapped. The Reavers. Hawk. The battles had left a scar on her heart.

"Izzy?" Sarah's voice pulled her back from her thoughts.

"It feels good," Izzy told her, simply not wanting to pick at that scar. They all relied on her now. She needed to be strong for them all.

"You're going to do great!" Sarah said excitedly.

* * *

Izzy stood at the entrance gate of the prison with Shadow next to her. The sun was beginning to crest the horizon, casting long shadows across the yard, and painting the sky in hues of orange and pink.

"I can't convince you to stay?" Izzy asked.

Griggs leaned on his makeshift crutch, his injuries still healing after their recent battle.

He shook his head firmly. "There's nothing here for me. No offense, but I can't do this group thing anymore. Too much betrayal and manipulation. I'm tired of it and can't be a part of another one."

"That won't be the case here, I promise. It'll be different," Izzy said.

"I'm sorry, Izzy. Your personal bodyguard has to be on his way," Griggs said.

"But you're still injured," Izzy said. "Wouldn't you feel more comfortable staying here until you're feeling more like yourself?"

"I'll be fine," he said. "You don't have to worry about me. Maybe I'll come back and check in on you guys." The faintest smile touched the corners of his lips.

It brought a sense of happiness at the thought of seeing Griggs again. Izzy smiled. "I'd like that. You're welcome here anytime."

Griggs offered his hand, and Izzy took it firmly. "Good luck out there," she said.

Shadow let out a quick bark at Griggs. "Yeah, yeah, I'll miss you too," he said.

With a slight nod, he turned and limped past the entrance, becoming a solitary figure that receded into the sprawling fields that stretched into the distance.

A familiar voice called from behind Izzy. "Hey, there."

Turning, Izzy's saw Matt and reached out to hug him. "I missed you," she confessed.

"I missed you too," Matt replied. "Guess what?"

"What?" she asked.

"We managed to snag some venison on our way back," Matt said. "Are you hungry?"

Izzy's stomach responded with hopeful growls. "Oh, I'm starving," she said, her mind already savoring the meal ahead.

Hand in hand, they strolled back towards the prison, now a symbol of their perseverance rather than captivity. The walls that had once echoed with cries of despair now resonated with sounds of laughter and conversation—the beginnings of a community.

As the doors closed behind them, sealing away the harshness of the outside world, Izzy felt an unprecedented sense of peace settle over her. They had weathered the storm, and here, within these walls, they were finally home.

The End

About The Author

Justin Richman is a graduate from Temple University with a degree in Risk Management, Insurance, and Actuarial Science. When he's not immersed in his professional world of insurance, he's exploring the realms of science fiction – a fascination he's had since childhood. His office is a treasure trove of science fiction and superhero memorabilia from both the DC & Marvel Universe, which provides a daily source of inspiration for his writing.

Justin resides in the suburbs outside Philadelphia with his wife, Madeline, and his two sons, Aiden and Declan.

Follow Justin on social media and sign up for his newsletter at www.justinrichman.com to stay up to date on what Justin's working on.

www.ingramcontent.com/pod-product-compliance
Lightning Source LLC
Chambersburg PA
CBHW032012310726
48972CB00002B/379